# sweet bye-bye

# sweet bye-bye

## Denise Michelle Harris

Walk Worthy Press

West Bloomfield, Michigan

WARNER BOOKS

NEW YORK    BOSTON

Published by Warner Books with Walk Worthy Press™

Warner Books

Time Warner Book Group
1271 Avenue of the Americas, New York, NY 10020

Walk Worthy Press
33290 West Fourteen Mile Road, #482, West Bloomfield, MI 48322

Visit our Web sites at www.twbookmark.com and www.walkworthypress.net.

Printed in the United States of America

First Printing: September 2004

10  9  8  7  6  5  4  3  2  1

Library of Congress Cataloging-in-Publication Data

Harris, Denise Michelle.
    Sweet bye-bye / Denise Michelle Harris.
        p. cm.
    ISBN 0-446-50008-9
  1. Parent and adult child—Fiction. 2. Fathers and daughters—Fiction. 3. Conduct of
life—Fiction. 4. Single women—Fiction. I. Title.
    PS3608.A7825S94 2004
    813'.6—dc22                                        2004005249

*This book is dedicated to my son, Jerry.*
*Keep Him close and follow your dreams.*
*Love,*
Mom

# Acknowledgments

I'd first like to take this opportunity to say thank you to my Lord and Savior, Jesus Christ. I can do everything with you and nothing without you.

And I would like to give a huge hug and thank-you to my family for enduring with me through this incredible experience. To my parents, Overton Harris Sr. and Evelyn Harris, thank you for always supporting me. To my grandmother Delthine Tolbert and my grandparents who've passed on: Odia Tolbert Sr., Maggie Lee Glover, Joe Riley Harris, and Olar Glover.

To my brothers Michael O'Neal Sr., Thomas Harris, Overton Harris Jr., Otis Harris, and to my son, Jerry Gaines Jr., my sister-in-laws, nieces, and nephews—Terry O'Neal, Tasha Harris, Latoya O'Neal, Leah Harris, Tenisha Harris, Tevin Harris, Michael O'Neal Jr., Cameron O'Neal, Jordan O'Neal, Elijah Harris, Josiah Harris, Mya Harris, Tarrel Harris.

To Jerry Gaines Sr., Charlene, Tommy, Pam, Tammy, Charles, Myresha, and the entire Gaines family. To Aunt Shirley, Professor George "Uncle Sonny" Jones and family, Aunt Louise Courtney, Aunt Henny Courtney and the Courtney families in Barstow, California, Aunt Grace and Uncle Sam Archer, Aunt Lula Mae Dixon, Odia "Brother" Tolbert Jr., James Glaze and family, Linda and Kenny Logan, Nancy Harris, Priscilla Tolbert, Karen Tolbert, Norene

"Angel" Dixon, Marlene "Molly" Dixon, Rosemary "Rosy" Dixon, Lawanna Tolbert, Marcelus Anthony Davis and family, Tanae Lastar Bowens, Atara Tolbert, Daniel Brown and family, Montrel Williams, Marcel Antonio Williams, Dijon Boswell and family, the Perkins family—Ronald Jr., Patrice Perkins, Susanna, RJ, Ronnie, Frankie-Dijon and Irene, Lisa Tolbert, Tanya Logan, Lisa Prince, and Deanna Gaston. To the Hatchett family, the Tolbert family, Aunt Sis and the Meadors family, Katie Calloway and family, Dorothy Clemmons and family, the Glover family, Ray Dillingham Jr., Jennifer Dillingham, Kamisha Dillingham, Cecilia Dillingham and the whole Dillingham family, the Cummings family, Latreva Cooke, Ryan Cooke Jr., Hanna Cooke, Haley Boucher, Lavisha, Tiffany Pigg, Obed Pigg, and Damion Brown, Tanisha Hopkins, Porsche, Shay Shay, Fabian Vickers Jr., Shaprice Chan, Andrew Chan, Kristen Quarrels, Ashley Quarrels, Shavondria Davis, Treyvon and Peto, Justice Roxbury, Patrice Watkins, Zack Deed Jr., Gloria and Teray, Betty "Moma Betty" Duncan, Sandra "Mama Sandy" Webster, Anita "Mama Nita" Edwards, Karen Williams-Edmond, John D., and Georgia Williams and family, Barbara Willis, Shelly Willis, Florence Danae Willis, Mandisa and Brian.

To Delisia Lemmons, John and Felicia Waldon, Makesha Smith, Wendell and April Ferguson, Roy and Franchesta Hammond, Angela Webster, Kimberlay Williams, John and Sandra Scott, Lashone Williams, Solomon and Jennifer Cason, Jengea Phillips, Jeanette Bell and family, Danny Williams, Kim Tingoncieng and Kevin Farley, Abdul Mahid Kargbo and the Kargbo family, Susanna, Alen, and Lark James, Darryl Mills, Conley Gaston, Savonda Blaylock and family, Maurica Taylor and family, Nakia Epperson, Adrian Duncan, Miss Duncan, Zim Miller, Eric Bell and family, Porter Deese, Alton Pearce III, Letha Harris, Charlene Adams, Brenda Curry and family, Daphne Williams. Peter Atherton, Terry Brown, Cheryl Morris, Layra Jackson and family, Frances Larkins, Beverly Larkins, Betty Sloan, Linda Lavow, Juanita Newell, Mary Kelly, Kayla Lemmons, Sydney and Hunter Waldon, Ania Ferguson, Micah Butler, Rodney, Ryan, Jasmine, Rhakim and Rolan Edmonds, Brian Kyrie, Breanna Phillips, Andre Phillips Jr., Cameo Phillips, Dkhari

Phillips, Jordan Davis, Mia MaKenna Farley, Marcus Hammond, and Naomi Hammond.

To all of my writer friends, teachers, colleagues, and role models who are taking this journey with me, thank you for all of the love, encouragement, words of wisdom, and support. Renee Swindle, Eric Jerome Dickey, Lolita Files, E. Lynne Harris, Terry McMillian, Junot Diaz, Tbone, Elmaz Albinader, Diem Jones, Jackie Luckett, Kira Allen, Leslie Easdale, Kamal Ravikant, Jante Spencer, Phillip Whilhite, Jay Laplante, Victoria Leon Gurerro, Willy Wilkinson, Erika Martinez, The San Francisco Writers Group—Wil Lutwick, Jean Washington, Marita Valdmanis, Ruta LaFranco, Andy Moore, Marc Cohen. To Juevenal Acosta, Edie Meidav, Sarah Stone, Eric Martin, Carolyn Cooke, Calla Devin, Melinda Misuraca, David Dzurick, Denise Bostrom, Alia Curtis, Kristina Del Pino, Dawn Gernhardt, Paul Stukowski, Anna Rosenblat, Anika Hamilton.

To the Sorors of Alpha Kappa Alpha Soroity Inc., and Xi Gamma Omega chapter in Oakland, Danii Taylor @ Studio 36 Hair Creations by Danii salon in Hayward, California, Vona-Voices Writers Workshops in San Francisco, Maui Writers Conference, to Paula Aloi, Brandon, Kelley Konnof, Master June Yoon at Sky Martial Arts, Gregory Ben and Pankaj Mohan over at Microsoft.

To my angel network: Mike Lynch, Betty Weibe, Hal Pearson, Charles Buettner, Richard Moore, and Donna Jackson. Thank you!

To my pastor, Bishop Ernestine Cleveland-Reems, and my church, the Center of Hope Church in Oakland, California. What an awesome praying place!

To my publisher, Denise Stinson, and the Walk Worthy Press family. My words can't thank you enough. But I will try—you believed in me and my work from day one, thank you. But also, thank you for the title, and your artist for the great cover! They rock. I love them. Thanks!

To my editors, Frances Jalet-Miller, Mari C. Okuda, Karen Kosztolnyik, Roland Ottewell, and the folks over at Warner Books. You guys are fantastic-al! Thank you!

To the readers, thank you for supporting me and this project.

I hope you have a great time reading the story of Chantell Meyers (and all the drama and issues and love that she brings to the table!).

Well, I'm going to go get started on another book, so I'm signing off. Feel free to visit my Web site at denisemichelleharris.com, and drop me a line or two; I'd love to hear from you. Until the next time, God bless.

Take care and keep Him close,
Denise Michelle Harris

# Contents

# sweet bye-bye

# 1

## a new beginning

It was a Tuesday afternoon, I'd say about 12:45, and my next appointment was near my parents' home. I had a little over an hour to kill, and a serious craving for a fruit salad. My stepmother, Charlotte, who I'd known was in Portland visiting her sister, had a knack for picking the sweetest fruit in the market.

I remember a rich Sarah Vaughan–sounding voice flowing through my speakers as I pulled into my parents' driveway. I closed my eyes and listened as the old sounds merged with the new over a smooth melodic rhythm. When I turned off the engine, I was still trying to figure out who was singing. I took my Dior sunglasses from my eyes and placed them atop my shoulder-length mane just so. I walked up the driveway with a click-click sound coming from the heels of my shoes.

The lawn's long blades of vibrant green grass swayed lightly with the breeze. I chuckled because I couldn't believe that my Home Depot–loving, do-it-yourself father had let it grow so long. Daddy was serious about his lawn, but I'd caught him sleeping on the job. I was going to tease him about it too, as soon as I got in the house. I smoothed out my white linen pants with my hands and passed through the garage.

I opened the door and yelled from the kitchen, "Dad!" My mouth started to water as I wondered if there were any mangoes in the fruit bowl. "Dad, it's me, Chantell, your most favorite daughter. You home?"

I walked into the living room, past the pictures on the glass shelf. The picture of me and my boyfriend, Eric, stood out, probably because we were cheesing from ear to ear in front of Caesar's Palace. Eric was holding me over his head, me lying sideways like a lovely assistant in a Siegfried and Roy magic show.

"Daddy, where you at?"

I went upstairs and heard the television on in my parents' room. The bedroom door was cracked, and I pushed it open. "Dad."

Golf was on the TV, but I didn't see him. I walked in a few paces, and immediately felt faint when I saw his brown legs on the floor sticking out between the bed and the wall.

"Daddy!" His feet were still in his house slippers.

It felt like a dream. I ran over to the big almond-colored man in his late fifties. I knelt down and shook him, all six feet and 250 pounds of him, but he didn't respond. "Daddy! Daddy, get up!" My heart beat faster as the reality of that moment set in. "Come on, Daddy, don't do this. Wake up!"

His head was cold, and panic raced through me. "Daddy, please don't die. God, please!" I flashed back to my mother. Her funeral. I remembered sitting down in the front row with Grandma Hattie, some relatives, and my dad. Everyone was wailing, and I sat there looking up at the roof and ignoring the light teal casket with my mom in it. "Oh God no. Not again."

I wiped my dad's forehead. My mind went to the last time my grandmother took me to church before *she* got sick and passed away. She'd bought me a new green dress and I wore it proudly as I sat next to her on Sunday.

First my mother, then my grandmother, then my best friend Keith . . . Then I broke down. "No! Noo! Nooo!" My voice was choking me, and I fought to speak. "What to do! What to do?" I felt under his jaw line for a pulse. There was a slight one.

"Daddy, listen to me," I said. "You can't leave me, okay? Okay?" He had dark circles around his eyes and he looked like he'd lost twenty pounds since I'd seen him a couple of days ago. I reached in my purse, found my phone, and dialed 911. With my father's head resting on my lap, I sat there calling his name until the ambulance arrived.

The prognosis wasn't good. Daddy had had a massive heart attack that required a triple bypass, *and* they'd found prostate cancer. Apparently, when he fell he hit his head, and he'd been unconscious for over an hour when I found him. As soon as we arrived at the hospital, the doctors rushed him into surgery and tried to clear the valves that led to his heart. A rush of uncertainty, instability, and loneliness came flowing back to me. I'd called Eric several times, but he wasn't picking up.

I asked the doctor what they were going to do about the cancer, and he said that they had to do things one at a time. Once they got Daddy's heart working, they'd get him started on chemotherapy. I was a complete mess, and that didn't make me feel any better.

My father, my compadre, lay unconscious as I sat by his bed. Tubes were sticking out of everywhere, and machines were beeping. I didn't know what to do. I'd called my stepmother, Charlotte, and she said she'd be on the next plane back to California. But why had she left him in the first place if he was sick?

Signs were plastered all over the walls, saying, "No Cellular Phone Use." I picked up the tan phone from the bedside table and pulled it over to the window.

"Eric, it's me, Chantell, again. I wish you would answer the phone. I'm really going through it, Daddy just got out of surgery and he is on a breathing machine." My words felt again like they were choking me. "They have operated on his heart, and he has cancer." I broke down. "Eric, call me, okay? I'm at Summit Medical Center, the second floor, room 231, okay? Bye." I hung up.

The physician attending to my father walked into the room in green scrubs and Reeboks. I asked him what was going to happen next for my dad. When he looked at me and suggested I call my relatives, I just blocked him out. When he hinted that they weren't even sure if Daddy would wake up, I told him off good. Then I marched straight down to the nurses' ward.

"Who is the chief of staff?"

"That would be Dr. Lambert," said a nurse with a smile.

"Well, get him. I'd like to speak to him," I said.

"Ma'am, I'm sorry, that is not possible."

"All things are possible!" I screamed through my tears. "Now go get him! Go get him right now!" My arms were outstretched and moving all around limply. "I will *not* call my relatives! I will not call anyone!" The nurse ran from around the station and put her arms around me.

"Ma'am! Ma'am?"

I cried out, "And I, I, I'm not going to! So you just— So—"

"Ma'am! Dr. Lambert's in Atlanta."

In my father's hospital room, I rested my head on his bed, and thought back. He'd done a good job of raising me. I'd blocked out a lot of my really early years, but I remembered how miserable my father was after my mother died. He was trying to raise me, take care of the bills, the house, and the garage. Folks said he gave me too much, and that I was spoiled. But my grandmother said I wasn't spoiled. She said I just had the gift of gab, like her. My dad would say we were having meatloaf and mashed potatoes for dinner, and I'd talk him into pepperoni pizza and jawbreakers for dessert.

I laid my head on my dad's bed and smiled. I remembered Grandma also used to say that she thought I'd end up marrying Keith Talbit, an ashy little boy from church. She said we matched like hot and cold. She said that when you put us together, we could surely warm a room. I didn't know about all of that, but we were best friends up until junior high. Then, just like Mom and Grandma, Keith left me too.

Anyway, just about four months after my mother died, my father met Charlotte. They married almost a year later. Charlotte and I got along pretty well. She treated me decent, and I liked that my dad seemed to be getting back to his old self. The three of us, we had our ups and downs, but we made it.

I looked at my daddy in his coma-like state, and it broke my heart. I looked up at the machine that monitored his heart. His life. And that was when it hit me. That's when I remembered. "All things are possible." My grandmother Hattie Brumwick's words came back to me like the north star returning to its place in the sky. When her words registered, I grabbed hold of them. My grandmother used to say, "When all else fails, call on God. He'll never leave you and He'll never forsake you."

I knelt down beside my dad's bed. "God, please. I hope you hear me. Spare my dad. Please. He's all that I have. He's a good guy, God, he loves everybody." I hadn't prayed in years. And I didn't know if I was praying right.

"You won't be sorry if you heal him, Lord. I know you can do it. Because you can do all things." I hoped that God was listening.

"Through you everything is possible. And, God, forgive me for my attitude, and everything that I've done wrong. If you do this for me, and let him live, God, I will work hard to be a better person. I promise you I will. I promise."

Through the tears, I prayed harder, as I'd seen my grandmother do probably a hundred times. "Please, Lord, thank you for your intervention. Thank you, Jesus. Thank you, Jesus . . ."

Then I sort of zoned out, and I was on this consciously unconscious level. And I kept praying my grandmother's words. "Nothing is too hard for you, God. Through you everything is possible. You can do all things, God. Thank you, Jesus . . ."

And I'll be darned if when I opened my eyes Daddy didn't turn his head toward me and whisper, "Hey, pumpkin. Whatcha know good?"

## 2

# my mind's eye

Eric and I arrived at the Sushi Boat in downtown Fremont before Ron and Tia did. We sat at a little table for four and held their places and talked.

"Eric?"

"What?"

"You know that I do love you."

"Then why am I being punished?"

"You're not. It's uncomfortable for me too. I miss you too, I just feel—no, I know—that we're doing the right thing."

Eric was silent. He looked so sad.

"Baby," I said, "I'm trying."

I felt sorry for him, but I wanted him to understand me clearly. It felt good connecting with God. God woke up my dad, He did it right there with me in the room. And He was helping me to be a better person too. I mean, I knew that I could probably be a little high-maintenance, maybe a little high-strung, but I was starting to feel more peace, and I was really trying to be right.

"So the solution is to sacrifice my needs for your promise," said Eric.

"Well, babe, it's not like we're going to go without sex forever. It's just until we make that next level of commitment."

I thought maybe he'd catch a hint and ask me something, but he didn't. Then he blew out such a sigh that I thought his glass of water would tip over. He spoke very carefully. "Chantell. We've already been through this. I know that you made a promise to God, and that's a good thing. I am not knocking that, but you are going to have to chill out on the pressuring me thing. I mean, we've already been having sex. Why can't we keep doing what we've been doing?"

"Eric, we're supposed to be more connected."

"After two years I think that we are about as connected as we're going to be."

"We can be more connected, Eric—"

"Chantell," he interrupted, "just stop, aiiright?"

On the one hand, I thought Eric was being selfish; on the other hand, I understood. He missed me and he wanted me. I looked up. "Okay. Shh! Here they come. Let's finish this later . . . Tia! Ron! Over here."

"Hi, you guys!" Tia strode over in a powder and navy blue pantsuit that had been tailored to fit her little waistline. Ron was right behind her.

"Hi!" I said and gave them both a big hug.

"Hey, how is it going?" said Eric, standing and shaking Ron's hand and hugging Tia before he sat back down.

We ordered our drinks.

"Chantell, how is your father?" That was Ron.

"Dad is hanging in there. He's a trouper. On Friday they let him go home, and he was talking about ordering more redwood for the deck out back that he was building but we told him to slow his row."

Everyone chuckled.

"Thanks for the flowers, you guys."

"You're welcome," said Tia.

At that table, we all wore something that I think we were particularly proud of that day. Tia's husband, Ron, a forty-two-year-old real estate developer originally from Naw'leans, wore his traditional smile. You heard it when he spoke, almost more than his drawl. And Eric, my handsome, six-foot-two-inch, twenty-seven-year-old boyfriend, wore a new tattoo that resembled a thick bolt of lightning going all the way around his big biceps. I, Chantell Meyers, a twenty-eight-year-old newspaper executive, wore a black wraparound dress that accented my small waist and ample hips. My best friend Tia, a thirty-one-year-old sistah friend, wore a look of admiration, and love, that showed up whenever Ron was anywhere in her sight.

Love. As a naive teenager, I used to say that I'd rather meet my soul mate in my dreams than give my heart to anyone else. But by the time I finished college, I'd determined that my prince had pulled a no-show. I decided that soul mates were relative to your situation. For example, if you were a big L.A. Lakers fan and you went to a game and were attracted to another avid L.A. Lakers fan, and the two of you decided that you were going to be together and spend all of your free time going to games and buying Lakers paraphernalia, then, voilà!—you were soul mates.

That's why I kept my eyes open whenever I frequented places like the Stoneridge Mall in Pleasanton. I didn't meet Eric at Stoneridge Mall, though. Nope, I met him at the outlets in Vacaville. He came up to me with those Eddie Bauer bags in hand and told me that I reminded him of a beautiful, exotic butterfly. He said I moved with a grace that was only matched by my beauty. I knew that it was love. I didn't have to look anymore.

"Ay, Chantell, tell them. Tell them how looong I, I mean we, had to wait before we could get in to see the movie the other day."

"Huh? It wasn't that long, only maybe fifteen or twenty minutes," I said.

"Sure it was. I had to wait, and wait, and wait." Eric fixed me with a stare, and continued sarcastically, "The line ahead of us was so long, I just knew that the ticket sales were going to just suddenly get *cut off.*"

I eyed Eric and he beamed with this ridiculous smile. "It was okay," I said. "We finally got to see it." I looked at Eric and bit the side of my lip.

"Yeah, I guess," said Eric. "I just think it's wrong to make somebody wait, then cut them off." He looked across the table and added, "Ron, man, I bet Tia never cut you off—"

"Stop it, Eric. We saw the freakin' *movie!* Okay?"

Eric's lips went into a bit of a smirk but his eyes looked so serious.

Tia tried to save our lunchtime bonding session before it turned sour. "Chantell, gurl, did I tell you? I am lovin' that dress on you!"

She was such a peacemaker. I smiled. "Why thank you, darling," I teased with a deep, sexy tone. "You too look quite lovely, as usual."

"So true. So true," she teased back.

We laughed like schoolgirls.

The guys just shook their heads at our silliness.

"So, let me tell you how my father woke up," I said.

Ron and Tia sat next to each other and shared one cup of water while I talked.

"So then I was crying and I was calling out to God and asking Him to help. It was strange because in some kind of way, while I was crying, I knew Daddy was going to wake up."

"Wow." Tia nodded.

"God does do things like that," Ron said.

"Yep, and maybe God woke him up because He needed to stop you from disturbing the other patients," said Eric with a smirk.

"Wrong. Whatever, Eric, you're not funny."

I looked at Ron and Tia, who sat close together comfortably. I was always amazed because I didn't think that they even consciously decided to share the cup of water. They just automatically sipped from one glass. I was still trying to figure out what "it" was that Ron and Tia had in common when the waitress came over and took our order.

When the lady asked what we would like, it was Ron's turn to get silly. "Um, yes, I'll have the avocado and shrimp sushi roll, and the salmon lunch special . . . And my wife here will have the eel—the *unagi.*"

Tia, who was taking a sip of hot tea, suddenly put her hand up and tried to swallow her drink quickly. "Um, no, stop! Please excuse my husband. He knows I don't eat eel."

Ron laughed. "Aw, baby, I thought you were going to live dangerously today."

"Stop it, Ronnie. I'm not foolin' with no eels and you know it," she said while leaning over and pecking him on the lips. Then she looked at the waitress and said, "May I please have the chicken teriyaki lunch instead?"

Ron just smiled. He was so funny. I teased her often about Ron being her sugah daddy, but they had something great. I scooted over and got a little closer to Eric. We had been together for over two years and were headed into the village of soul mates ourselves. He always made sure he looked nice, as did I, so we shopped a lot, and traveled a lot, and had lots of fun together.

We ate our food and chatted as tiny fishing boats rode past the front counter, circling the kitchen and chefs' area in a tiny metal pond displaying varieties of sushi. Orange ones, yellow ones, sushi with crab legs sticking out, sushi wrapped in seaweed, and sushi covered with rice.

Yep, I'd adapted my recipe for happiness a couple times over the last five or ten years. The latest version was a lot simpler, and it didn't really involve a soul mate per se. It basically said, there were three things that you should always keep. Keep your man by your side, keep your game face on, and if at all possible, keep a Coach bag in your hand. If you were a person who could manage all three of those things, then I'd bet that you were somewhere having a nice life.

Yeah, Eric and I had some good times. He was funny, and he had this really deep, sexy voice. We usually took advantage of all that the Bay Area had to offer. Salsa dancing, Rollerblading, festivals, concerts. We'd do whatever sounded good. He liked to project a bit of a bad-boy image, but basically he was a pussycat. He liked excitement. And although I was happy when we began dating, I sometimes still found myself feeling a little lonely. Sometimes I questioned us. When I found myself doing that, I'd remind myself to stop being silly and look at what I had. I mean, Eric was Boris Kodjoe fine. Eric was make-you-wanna-haul-off-and-slap-somebody fine! He had a six-pack that a lot of models on television would envy, and he was always dressed to the nines.

People always said that I was beautiful too. I don't think that I ever completely bought into it, though. I didn't necessarily think that I was bad-looking; I got hit on often. I was five feet eight inches, curvy, and 140 pounds. I had brown skin, the color of caramel, and blunt-cut shoulder-length hair that Tia normally took great care of for me. I was experimenting with it then, though, and had taken to washing and conditioning and just letting the air lock in the body and natural texture. I had curious eyes that slanted, and pouty lips, and a little mole above my right brow that every boyfriend that I ever had found irresistible.

However, of all the people in my lifetime that had said to me, "Wow, that's a great mole," or "I wish I had a little mole on my face," I never forgot a comment from my childhood, made by the little boy next door. Little Timmy said it looked "jus' like a booger on yo head." Oh, I laugh now, and I punched him in the stomach then, but that's the kind of thing that one doesn't easily forget.

So it wasn't so much that I thought I was unattractive. No, no, I used what people saw when they looked at me, when I needed to. It was just that, well, I had a good mind. And I worked hard to show people that I was smart. But lots of times folks weren't interested in that.

My mole, my eyes, my looks, they came from my real mother. I didn't know her, though, because she died when I was five years old. She had sickle-cell, and she lost so much weight that I thought she was melting. A strange thing about that, however, is that when she died, I started to cry, and Dad told me not to. He'd hug me and say, "Don't cry, princess, everything will be okay." So I'd wipe my eyes and try to smile. Every time the tears started to fill my eyes, Dad would get really anxious, and he'd try to tell me jokes or take me to a movie, and he'd tell me to "just try not to think about it." I didn't like to see my dad act so strange, so I learned to stop crying. It had been twenty-three years, and I'd never cried another day over my mother.

I suppose I got my theories on soul-mate-ism from my parents. I remember once, my dad told me that he married my real mother because from the moment they first conversed, she tugged at his soul. I wasn't sure what tugging at your soul felt like, but I'd guess that Eric and I did that, sometimes. Tia herself said that we looked like black models from a Gap commercial. And that's important. You should look happy and vibrant. People treat you better when they think you have money, or are beautiful. They want to be your friend.

Besides that, if you keep up the front, then people never really know how bad you feel.

Dad always said I was a princess, and I believed him . . . In a way I still did. A princess was attractive, and single, and she had beautiful clothes. Yeah, I tried to fill the bill, but I didn't like it when people called me snooty or stuck-up. I just wanted to put my best foot forward so people saw me in a positive light. Just because you want to look presentable, that didn't make you "a piece of work." Just because you didn't go around showing everybody your pain, that didn't mean that you don't have any. People should know that. But hey, if they couldn't understand that, too bad. I wasn't going to go around with my hair undone, waving a white flag and looking like I had trials in my life, cuz it wasn't nobody's business. With me, everyone got the same story: The life of Chantell Meyers is fantastic!

"So, are you guys going to the big game this year?" That was Ron.

"For sho," said Eric. "I went down to the Berkeley ticket office last Friday. You guys?"

"Definitely. Ron's client brought him over some great Stanford seats," said Tia.

I knew that my real mother went to Stanford. That perhaps should have been something that I was proud of, but it was deep in my past. After you've ignored something for so long, the desire to speak about it just subsides. I kept eating in silence.

I'd always been private that way. I had my share of bills, and despite the way things may have appeared, they were hard to juggle by myself. I was getting older and my biological clock was ticking. But I figured, once Eric and I got married, things would fall into place.

I took another sip from my glass and looked over at my beau. The water was refreshing. Eric had let his goatee grow a little thicker than normal. He was talking to Ron about the junker car that he was restoring.

". . . And I'm going to get two racing stripes painted on the doors before I take it down to the track." The ice hit the bottom of my empty cup as I set it back on the table.

"Oh, yeah. That's going to be nice!" said Ron.

"Yeah, it should be. I named her Margarita." He looked over at me.

"Chantell's jealous. She doesn't like me spending all of my spare time going to wrecking yards looking for parts for Margarita. But trust me, when she's all finished and looking beautiful"—he pointed at me— "she'll want a key." He chuckled.

I laughed too, because I probably would want a key. Not because I was into race cars or anything, but because he was ready to share with me. I really liked him, though he sometimes was a little inconsiderate, like when he turned off his phone and my dad was sick. He was out at the Pick and Pull under the hood of a car with his phone off at the time. I was so mad at him, but, hey, it was just happenstance, and I was trying to be about peace. I smiled at him while he talked. Eric Summit was a keeper, and I was in it for the long haul.

The back of my throat was a little dry and the waitress hadn't been back around yet, so I picked up Eric's glass and put it to my mouth. But before the water could roll down and reach my lips, Eric said, "Hey! What are you doing? That's not your cup."

# 3

# workin' 9 to 5

It had been three weeks since my father's collapse, and he was still improving. Yesterday he had even tried to go for a walk, but both Charlotte and I weren't having any of that. We sent him right back to bed.

So I was back to work still trying to make good on the promises that I'd made to God at the hospital. I adjusted the earpiece to my phone and walked toward my building.

I stood out on the sidewalk for a moment and took my cell phone out of my purse. The bright San Francisco sun towered above. I needed to remind Eric about our plans for tomorrow night before I started what I knew was going to be a hectic day at the office. I looked around the haze-free sky and saw that the San Franciscans were loving it. Everyone had sunglasses on. A couple of ladies had tied their suit jackets around their waists and were power-walking. I dialed the number and Eric's phone rang. Around me, the tone of businessmen's mellow laughs appeared to have picked up an octave. People went on about their lives just a bit more animated.

"Hey, babe, it's me. I just wanted to leave you a quick note to remind you about tomorrow night. The boat leaves at eight, so let's meet at . . . say, seven o'clock? Okay, that's it. I'll talk to you later. Bye." I hung up and rushed inside to catch an elevator already filled up with people.

It didn't feel like my life had changed all that much. I mean, with me now being close to God and all. As soon as I got to my cubicle, my desk phone rang. "Hello. Yes, Mr. Felton . . . Sure, no problem!" I said in a bright and chipper voice.

It was my new client, Kauffman's Sporting Goods. John Felton, the small chain's marketing manager, was getting jittery about the success of their half-yearly sale that was fast approaching that weekend.

He was nervous about the headline that he had chosen for the ad. "Do you think it sounds okay?" He was nervous about the number of readers who would see the ads. "How many people did you say read the paper?"

There was quite a bit of stress in my life, and to be honest, I'm not sure how conscious I was of it. I was busy reassuring him that we could help him get his company's message around the Bay Area when I overheard two of my coworkers talking.

Mina, a woman whom I had unfortunately worked with for four years, was whispering to Gary, the new account manager in the office. Even at a whisper, her high-pitched voice came right over to my side of the thin cubicle.

"Shhh! Don't even worry about it. It's new business," she said.

I tried to ignore her. She was the kind of coworker that the rest of us could do without. Gary definitely didn't need *her* training him.

I jotted down a few follow-up notes and wrapped up the call. "Sure. Your ad will run in the Monday Business edition for three of the six months . . . Nope, I have everything I need." I closed the file and put my new Kate Spade bag in the bottom drawer of my desk. "Sure. And, Mr. Felton, please call me if you have any more concerns or questions. That is what I am here for. You too, bye-bye."

I hung up the phone and tried to ignore the woman on the other side of the cubicle. To be fair, it's not that we hated each other, it was just that we kept butting heads. I couldn't count the number of times in the past that the newspaper had held contests and Mina and I had fought tooth and nail to win the trip to Palm Springs or the $500 gift certificate to Nordstrom. She was as money-motivated as I was, so yeah, it got personal.

And, yeah, I know that I said that I was trying to live right, but I was not exactly ready to say "God bless you" when she'd just rolled her eyes or scrunched up her lips at me.

I ignored the two and called to check on Daddy. "So how's he doing this morning?"

"He's sleepin' now, but he's doing okay."

"Oh, that's good." I silently thanked the Lord, my new best friend again.

Charlotte went on to say, "I made a big pot of chicken noodle soup last night. He ate some of that this mornin'."

After we hung up, I sent an e-mail to the sales assistant, asking her if she could help me in getting some changes quickly made to another client's ad before tomorrow's press run.

It was a few minutes later that I heard Mina come back over to Gary's cube, and this time I had reason to be concerned. It was muffled, but I was sure she said to him either ". . . support Skyway Modems" or ". . . separate from Skyway Modems." Either way, Skyway was my account, and nobody at the newspaper should have been dealing with them except for upper management or myself. I'd found them last year and had grown the account from a tiny, one-time, business-card-sized advertisement into an account worth over a million dollars. I made as little noise as possible and strained my ears to hear . . .

"It's a spin-off, so it's new business," Mina boldly encouraged.

My account, Skyway Modems was launching a new service in the fall, and I guessed that was what Mina was encouraging him to go after. Gary was new to the *San Francisco Daily News* and just a tadpole in the pond of account managers, but Mina was determined to turn him into a snake. I got up and walked around the thin carpeted divider and over toward his desk to see just what was going on.

Sure enough, they were looking in an *Adweek* magazine at Skyway's blue-and-white logo at the bottom of a black page. Mina was standing over Gary while he made notes in a crisp, new manila folder.

I started to walk up to them, wanting to say, "Excuse you! You're busted! That's my account, you account thieves!" But a sistah had to be more professional than that. My mind raced with options as I neared Gary's desk. I could have approached them and acted surprised and said, "Is that something for *my* account, Skyway Modems, that you're working on for me? Thank you!"

I chose a different tactic. "Hi, guys, I see that you are checking out Skyway's new product line. It doesn't launch until September. Are you writing that up for me?" I said with a smile.

"No. Well, uh, this is new business, and actually it's going to be separate from what you're doing with them," said Gary, who then looked at Mina like he expected her to give him a thumbs-up.

Mina pushed her glasses up closer to her face with her index finger. With her fiery red hair twisted up into her trademark bun, she just gave him a subtle approving nod. I looked at the new employee, then back to Mina. Was she so desperate to be the lone big dog in the yard that she would resort to setups and account stealing? Why was she encouraging this kind of shenanigan (shenanigan—a word I picked up from my grandmother)?

"Nothing about Skyway is new," I said confidently. "They have been with me all year, Gary. In fact, I'm very aware of the new division that they are planning to launch." This was getting ridiculous. "Thank you, Gary, but I've got Skyway Modems covered. Really I do." I was smiling but I was getting a little irritated. I folded my arms and said with certainty, "So, are you writing up that paperwork for practice, or are you starting that file for me?"

Gary shook his head no. "I'm sorry, Chantell, it's new business. It hasn't run in our paper before, so I found it."

Mina smiled and shrugged her shoulders. Then her cell phone rang. "Hey, I'll let you guys work this out. Excuse me," she said and walked away.

"You can't do that. It's clearly a part of my account."

"I can respect your opinion, but I've already put in the request to management."

Apparently, Gary wasn't a tadpole in the pond after all. Nope, homeboy was a piranha. A piranha who wanted to play hardball, so I grabbed the bat and stepped up to the plate.

I did what any top-producing sales rep in good standing would do. I stormed into Canun Ramsey's office and acted a plum fool! With my arms outstretched, I told Canun that I was shocked at what was going on on the sales floor! With my hands at my hips, I said I'd been with the paper far too long to have to deal with that kind of tom-foolery! I held my shoulders back and spoke with authority. "This is outrageous! We are supposed to be a team. Where is the teamwork in self-thievery?" When I walked out of Canun's office, my Skyway Modem account was fully intact. I breezed back to my desk cool and calm. Oh yeah! Shoot, I may have even switched a little when I walked. And that Mina Everett, I didn't see her face for the rest of the day. One point for the home team, zero for the visitors. I put on a fresh coat of lipstick and thought, Go team!

If I only had known. The game was just getting started.

# 4

## sail on

I pulled into the pier's parking lot. The networking event was being put on by a company called mymail.com, aboard a dining cruise. The e-mail said that the event would last from 8 p.m. until 11 p.m. It was still pretty early, so there I sat in the parking lot, one of the first people to arrive.

Except for location changes, the monthly networking events were pretty much the same, month in and month out. Folks would start out ultraconservative: "Oh, hi there! It's Sarah, right? Ben, dear, look, it's Sarah. You remember Sarah, don't you? We met her at the Society of Online Marketing's event last month? Sarah, you were working for bigheadhuntingmonsters.com, right?"

Then at the end of the evening, after the speeches and the announcements, and after Grand Marnier and tequila shots, it was: "Whooohoo! Ceelll-a-brate Good Tiiimes, Come On!"

I knew the routine and was pretty used to it. I looked in my rearview mirror and put on my lipstick.

The night quickly moved in and I still didn't see Eric. I decided to wait for him in the lobby on the ship. I walked up the ramp that led to the ship and felt my new pink-and-red dress's jagged edges dangle at my knees each time I took a step.

These networking events were pretty mundane, but this looked like a lovely ship, so maybe it would be a good night. Either way, my objective was clear. I was there for one reason and one reason only. I wanted to meet and get the business cards of the people who controlled the advertising budgets for mymail.com. If I could make a strong connection with the VP of advertising or the marketing director, I was in. Just one good joke, or maybe a flip of my hair if it was a guy, or a name-drop of a company he admired, and the person would remember me when I called him from my desk tomorrow. And I'd exceed my goal for the year with just one account. Again. Yep, I was feeling real good about myself that night.

The five-leveled ship wasn't set to sail for almost an hour. I walked over to the bar area and surveyed the place. There were maybe only fifteen people dressed in party clothes wandering around. A bartender was wiping down the glossy tan counters and hanging beautiful wineglasses upside down in brass slats above his head. I checked the time again and walked over and sat at a stool. I felt silly sitting there by myself. I took out my phone and called Eric. His voice mail picked up. I hung up.

A handsome and nicely dressed white guy in his early forties with piercing seawater green eyes that shone through his designer black wire-frame glasses walked over to me and sat down.

"Hello."

"Hi."

"My name is J. R. Mitchell," he said, extending his hand.

"Chantell Meyers." I gave him a firm shake.

He had pretty white teeth, and I could smell a hint of alcohol on his breath. "So what company are you with?" I asked.

He said he was a vice president of business development for Yahoo. We exchanged business cards and made small talk. He promised to connect me with his brother, who was a senior media buyer for Wolfe Advertising, and I promised that tomorrow morning I would get his press release to the business reporter who handled Silicon Valley.

The conversation was a nice mix of business and pleasure. "I haven't been to that blues festival since they moved it to the amphitheater," I said.

"Oh, it is a nice one. What would you like to drink?" asked my handsome new friend with Courvoisier on his breath. He reminded me of the actor who played Magnum PI, only thinner.

"Oh, nothing, thank you," I said. "I am fine."

"Are you sure?"

"Yes," I said with a smile.

He ordered himself another one. I thought of Eric and got worried. I hoped the ship didn't set sail without him. I excused myself, and J. R. Mitchell watched me as I headed toward the other side of the room. My shoulder-length hair was pinned up, but stray wisps fell about my face and tickled my neck as I walked. Okay, I was flirting. It was sort of nice when people noticed you. I looked in the big mirror along the wall, and homeboy was still looking. But now his wife or girlfriend, whom I hadn't even noticed, was nearby and had noticed him noticing me. She didn't look pleased either. In fact, she looked at me with an expression of disgust.

Which brings me to an important issue about who I was. I didn't have many women friends, and that was just fine by me. I mean, I had Tia, and there were a few girlfriends that I did stuff with from time to time. But in general, I didn't go around looking for women friends because sooner or later there was bound to be a catfight. They always thought you wanted their boyfriends or something. I was twenty-eight years old, and I'd never gone after anybody's man. Okay, well, maybe I did a couple of times in college, but I was young, and that is not what I was about! I was almost thirty years old. I was about prospering, building my new relationship with God, doing the marriage thing, and stuff like that.

I was not interested in him. So she could just stop with the piercing-dagger-look thing that she was trying to do, and check herself.

I needed to find Eric. I checked my watch and gave the couple a last good-riddance glance, and about fell over when I saw that the woman who was giving me the ugly looks was Mina Everett!

Mina had taken off her glasses and let loose her long, curly red hair. She wore a low-cut red-striped shirt that accentuated her fake D cups, with matching bright red capri pants and high heels. She was talking angrily and quickly in her friend's ear. This let me know there might be trouble on the boat. I hoped that everyone could swim.

"Forget her," I said aloud. I was there to meet some key players who controlled advertising dollars. "I'm sticking to my plan," I told myself. Some people just loved to try to win at everything. Drama queens were full of negativity. Divas. Some people fed on chaos and confusion. It's who we were.

I turned and looked around for my guy. When I passed by again, Mina's date took another swig from his glass and smacked his lips at me. I shook my head. Drama kings existed too. When Mina put her arm in his and they walked in the other direction, I wanted to yell through the crowd, "Buh-bye!" And just where was Eric? What was the point of being in a relationship if I was still out dealing with that type of drama?

I went up to the third level. The host for the evening announced that mymail.com was celebrating receiving $50 million, their second round of venture capital funding that year. He welcomed us and said that we would be departing shortly on our cruise around the bay. "Here's to revolutionizing the way that we send mail today!" he said and raised his glass. I raised my glass and toasted with everyone else.

A brunette in her early twenties with a cute little pixie haircut was standing to my right. She put her hand out toward me, smiled, and said, "Hi, I'm Heidi Wadore, with pets4u.com. Who are you with?"

I shook her hand and said, "Chantell Meyers. I work for the *San Francisco Daily News.*"

"Oh, the newspaper. Are you a writer?"

"Oh, no, I work advertising," I said.

The ship was moving. I still hadn't found Eric.

I said, "So, tell me about pets4u.com."

"Well, we're going to revolutionize the way people shop for pets. See, when people decide they want a pet, they go to pet stores, or look in the paper, or go to a shelter. Well, what pets4u does is it has a robust database with all of the local breeders. It locates all of the domesticated animals . . ."

Oh Lord! Everyone there had his spiel memorized and could recite it faster than Quick Draw could have his gun in hand. She continued: ". . . area including but not limited to shelters and pet stores.

We then post them so that everyone has access to them on the Web for purchase."

"Oh, interesting," I lied. Too many dotcoms. Too many spiels; some just didn't make sense.

The room was filling up fast. People were chatting and servers were walking around with platters serving hors d'oeuvres. I was so happy when I saw Eric making his way over to me. He was a sight to behold. Gorgeous. Six foot two, smooth Baileys Irish Cream skin. Muscular frame. Hair freshly cut because that is the only way that he would present himself. He had a thin face and curly black hair. His nose came to a semi-point at the end of his bridge. And his lips were thin and held his usual smirk that looked like an upside-down smile. His mustache was thin yet hard to miss. His five-o'clock shadow contrasted against his golden skin. Today he wore a button-down khaki-colored shirt open with a crisp white T-shirt underneath and dark blue J. Crew trousers. Meticulously casual.

"Oh, Heidi, excuse me. There's my fiancé. It was nice meeting you," I said, and walked over toward him and stood by his side.

I was five foot ten with heels on. My lipstick was a stylish brick color. My toes were freshly pedicured, the nails colored a dusty rose. And even with my pink sweater on, my bright pink-and-red Wilma Flintstone dress screamed: "Ladies and gentlemen, I have arrived." Eric and I got nods of approval and glances of envy. Yep, together he and I told a great story.

"What's up? How long have you been here?" Eric asked with what could have passed for a smile on his face.

"I've been here for a little while," I replied with the same contagious half-smile. Eric and I, we were a lot alike. We prided ourselves on being tough. His was muscle. Mine was a mind of steel. So I said nothing to him about Mina and her boyfriend.

"I was afraid you weren't going to make it."

"Oh, I'm sorry, babe. I had to make a run, then I got tied up, and my car wasn't running right. Dang, it's just been a crazy day!" he said, looking up toward the roof.

"Oh," I said, just relieved to see him. I put my arm in his and we started walking around.

The ship was now filled up with people and had set sail. People were playing games and talking. I heard a man in a blue suit say they were forming a conga line below. Eric and I gambled with pretend money at the blackjack and roulette tables for a while. The speaker said dinner was going to be served soon and asked everyone to start heading up to the next level.

"Are you hungry?" I asked Eric.

"Yes, I could eat. You?"

"Yup. Let's go."

We went up to the fourth floor and found a seat at a table in the dining area. The waiter came over and asked us if we were having salmon, chicken, or vegetables. I ordered the chicken, then excused myself and went to the restroom. In the bathroom, I stood in front of the mirror and relined my lips in my new brick-colored liner. Then I applied a light rose-colored gloss that glistened over it.

One lady made her way out the door as two others walked in, laughing, with wineglasses in their hands. They stopped laughing when they saw me. One was a black lady with an unmistakable Australian accent, and the other was Mina. They looked at me from my feet to my head and smirked at each other. Mina set her drink down and went into the stall while the other fixed her makeup. From the stall Mina shouted, "People are always trying to show off, aren't they?"

"Yes, and it is so sickening. I mean, d**n, we see you. Advertising at work is one thing. Advertising yourself, that's prostitution," said the black lady with the accent, who had apparently gotten her boobs done too.

"Thank you!" said Mina, in a voice filled with laughter. I am sure they would have high-fived had they been standing next to each other. Whatever, I thought; who advertised more than they did?

"Some people are just tacky. Trying to steal other people's men, when they really need to worry about their own!" The Australian woman was looking at me, smirking.

I promised God that I would try to live right. For me, that meant avoiding confrontation and turning the other cheek, but they were going too far. Had she been gossiping about me to her friend? They didn't have to worry about Eric and me. We were just fine.

"You two need to mind your own business," I said. I wanted to say more. I wanted to tell Mina that she needed to worry less about Chantell and more about her MCI account at work. I'd overheard Canun talking about it and there were some problems with a recently run ad. I wanted to tell her that her eyebrows were arched crooked. But I'd said too much already. It was a ladies' bathroom, and there should have been at least one lady in it.

And I almost walked right out of there too. But when one of them mumbled that it looked like I had a pen mark on my forehead, my blood boiled. Who did they think they were talking to? My beauty mark came from my mother, and I refused to let them insult me any further. So I smiled in the mirror, like they'd just paid me a compliment. I took the pins out of my hair and freed the soft-wild golden-streaked kinky curls that had been pulled into submission. My lips glistened. Never saying a word, I touched up my Asian-like eyes with a little liner and puckered my rose-colored lips in the mirror. They frowned and pretended like they weren't paying attention. I smirked. Yeah, right. I touched my little mole like I didn't have an insecurity in the world. Then I took off my sweater and stood back and took a good look at myself. The Australian lady rolled her eyes, along with Mina, who was washing her hands. I left the bathroom never saying a word.

I walked back over to Eric and we had our dinner. He didn't say anything about the change to my hair and I didn't say anything about the incident in the bathroom. It was over, after all, as far as I was concerned. They had tried to verbally attack me, and it had backfired. Now I was back at my table enjoying my guy and my meal. It was that simple. A woman holding a black and teal, catlike party mask to her face with a stick came up to our table. The mask's feathers sprouted out all around its eyes. Then she removed the mask and confirmed what we'd heard so many times over the past two years. "I just had to come over and say something. You guys look so great together!" Her hair was brown and big and curled under right at the nape of her neck. Her face was small, and laugh lines etched the out-side of her smile.

"Thank you," we said, almost simultaneously.

Folks liking to be around us was an important thing to me. It was good because I wasn't required to explain a whole bunch of personal stuff. Nope. They liked me for what they saw. I'd learned the hard way that you should never let people know when you're down. Because they'll pretend to empathize and understand, and as soon as you turn your back, they'll get on the phone and call all of their friends. They'll tell everyone in town, "Guurl, that Chantell Meyers is not really all of that. She is perpetrating. I'm telling you that she is as phony as a fifteen-dollar bill. She tries to act like everything is good, but she told me that her boyfriend did this and that . . . ," or they'd say, "I called her on her cell phone on Friday, and don't you know, it was turned off!" No, thank you. Not going out like that.

I looked over at Eric, who picked up his string beans one at a time with his fork and chewed slowly. He was an ex–high school football star who'd grown accustomed to the limelight, and often reminisced about how life used to be. Nowadays he was a manager at Safeway, in the meat department. Now, I know you're probably thinking that Eric and I weren't evenly yoked. But my man was fine, he was straight, and he had a good-paying job. That is a good man. We were as evenly yoked as we needed to be. He'd been there for over ten years, and he was a union member, but I think he got a little bored with his job sometimes.

We enjoyed all of the events that my job afforded us. These Silicon Valley parties were mostly gracious, but they'd been known to get a little wild. It was funny to see a company president sprawled out on a couch or dancing a jig through the dining room. Last year, a dotcom flew us to Aspen, Colorado, for a weekend to celebrate. Lavish was the only way to describe it. Eric was in heaven, and so was I. Hot tubs, golfing, massages, expensive red wines—we did it all. Now we were planning a little vacation of our own. Next month, right about this time, we'd be in Cabo San Lucas.

"They've posted the schedule for next month already," Eric said with a raised eyebrow.

"Oh, great. Did they schedule you off for our trip?"

"For the most part. They have me scheduled to work on the Friday that we are supposed to leave," he said.

"Oh no. Did you tell them about it?"

"Nobody was around in the office so I left a note on the desk." He said, "Don't sweat it, though. I'll get it all squared away on Monday."

I nodded and took a sip of my iced tea.

We did a lot for each other, Eric and I. He craved attention and adventure, and I helped him get it. Having Eric on my arm helped me to tell the world the story that I felt I needed to tell—that I was complete, that I was happy in every way. We were good for each other.

Being together also helped us in other ways. It took us out of the singles hustle and bustle, which was great for me. It was wild out there, and a magazine article that I'd just finished reading agreed. It said the single-black-female to single-black-male ratio had been as high as sixteen to one in some places in the country. So I counted my blessings and was glad that we were committed to being together.

Eric stabbed a bite of salmon and put it in his mouth. He looked at the menu and said, "They have crème brulée on the menu for dessert. Are you having it?"

"Oh yes, I—"

I looked up, and Mina and the other woman from the bathroom had made their way over to our table and stopped.

What now! I rolled my eyes and let out a long sigh. I was going to say, "Look, I'm not sure what this is about, Mina, but if it's about the guy, let me say, I do not and did not want your man." But before I could get a word out, the black Australian woman thrust out her chest and said, "Mina, how do I look?"

Mina struggled to contain her laughter. She said, "Oh, quite perky, I think. But get a man's opinion. They know best."

Then her Australian friend turned to us, putting her knee in our booth. She bent over our table. Her boobs almost touched Eric's garlic potatoes. She looked at him and asked in that Australian accent, "Say, how do you think I look?"

Eric didn't say anything, he just smirked that little upside-down smile.

Enough was enough! In the nicest, kindest, voice that I could muster up, I said, "You look okay except for those hard hairy coconuts sticking out of your shirt, and now if you don't mind, get them off *my table!*"

The women walked away giggling, but not before saying I was just a jealous b———. Eric was so full of himself that he didn't even ask me what all of that was about. He just smirked and finished the last of his salmon. But it didn't matter, I didn't feel like talking.

The little incident had taken its toll on me a little more than I wanted to admit, as everything had lately. I smiled calmly, but my insides were in turmoil. To try and calm myself I took slow deep breaths and counted to ten.

"I don't feel so good. I need to get some fresh air," I told Eric.

"Okay, babe, I'll be right here. Take your time."

I smiled, got up from the table, and walked up the stairs, careful not to show any signs of anything being wrong.

Up on the top deck, all was dark. It was nice, with a little breeze every so often. There were a few people up there. A small group stood huddled together smoking cigarettes and talking. A few couples snuggled together, and some people sat and relaxed on big, comfortable-looking couches with their legs up on the tables. I pulled my sweater closed, went over to the rail, and looked out onto the water. Gentle waves rippled about and they seemed to help me to calm down some.

Downstairs, I had been so upset that my eyes burned, but now the coolness on my face helped me to come alive again. I took in the scenery and felt my body temperature returning to normal. I could hear the music of Boney James coming from below. I'd never told a soul, but in moments like this I thought about my mother. Would she have given me skills to better handle catty women like those two below? I just wondered how my life might have been different had she lived. To be perfectly honest, I couldn't really even say that I missed her. I was only five when she died, so I didn't remember too much. Her name was Zarina Meyers, and she was pretty. She was talented too, an artist and a grade school teacher. I remembered a level of comfort and ease when I thought of her. I remembered her smell.

She smelled like White Linen perfume when she wasn't baking with peaches and pears. She liked to dance, and she loved Marvin Gaye, and Frankie Beverly. That's pretty much what I knew. That, and the fact that I sat there dry-eyed at her funeral staring at the lady next to me with a black-and-white dress on and an auburn wig. The lady was crying in a tissue while I sat there pretending nothing was the matter.

The huge ship ran so smoothly that I could hardly tell we were moving. The city of San Francisco lit up the night. Skyscrapers were all around, with unpatterned lights that reflected against the sky. It reminded me of Christmas. I could see another ship like the one we were on. Another dotcom celebration no doubt. Composed again, I headed back down the stairs to the dining room.

I tucked my hair behind my ears, smiled, and nodded hellos on my way back to the table. It was with utter disbelief that I saw Eric, the two ladies, and my drunken admirer all sitting at our table. They were laughing and woofing it up, like two couples that had arrived together at this party. The Australian black lady had one hand on Eric's biceps and was cracking up. Eric was moving his hands like he was in the middle of telling some hysterically funny story.

"Eric, may I talk to you?" I said.

His new friend got up so that he could get out. The ship's table moved and all of their glasses shook slightly. I was steaming. Ugly cow. I thought of tripping her, but I didn't. She and Mina had the audacity to say that I was jealous of them, then helped themselves to my man and my table. I couldn't believe them! This ship was full of people. Go harass somebody else! And as for Eric, where was his loyalty? I felt like taking their drinks and throwing them in their faces.

"What's up?" Eric said, like nothing was the matter.

I put my hands on my hips and said, "What in the world are you doing? That's what's up."

"Hey, I didn't call them over here. They just came and sat down. Anyways, we were just talking."

"You've obviously lost yo mind."

He pointed at me with both hands and said, "You need to calm down."

"Eric, you are being disrespectful!"

"Okay, here you go with that 'disrespectful' crap. You know what? You're going to drive me away with all your new rules!"

I could not believe him! "Eric, how dare you stand here and tell me that you're not being disrespectful, and that I'm going to drive *you* away!" I almost started to cry. But those heifers were looking over at us, and I wouldn't give them the satisfaction. I looked around; we were starting to draw attention. "Come on, Eric. Let's just go somewhere else."

"Nah, Chantell."

"Huh?" I must have heard him wrong.

"You're the one always talking about that connected soul mate crap. We're not connected," he said. He touched his mustache and looked over at the table. Then he said to me, "I'ma holler at you later, alright?"

The room was spinning. I felt like I was going to pass out. I grabbed my purse and went back upstairs on the deck. It hurt so bad. I hurt so bad! I clenched my teeth and closed my eyes to hold back the tears. Then I stood out there alone.

When the cruise was finally over, I headed to my car. I saw Eric talking to Mina, and the woman with the new boob job. He looked at me and threw up the peace sign . . . Peace. That was something I didn't know anything about.

# 5

## sit up

The next day, to cheer myself up, I wore my favorite black work suit and a sheer pair of black pantyhose. I snagged them on my desk at work and got a run that worked its way in both directions from my waistline to my toes.

Relieved to be home at the end of the day, I walked in the door and put my keys on the coffee table. Mina had been in the field all day, so I had managed to see her very little. And that was a good thing because I was certain I would have gone into combat mode had she even snickered in my direction. All the tension in my life had me stressed and eating unnecessarily. Today I'd had a tostada lunch, then someone brought pizza into the office and I had two slices of that.

I touched my stomach and felt the little bulge that had attached itself to me in the last couple of weeks. I had a cruise to get ready for, with or without lying, cheating Eric. This was my vacation, and I was determined not to carry any more baggage than I needed.

I washed my face, then pulled my hair back into a ponytail and gathered it into a scrunchy. I removed my clothes and looked down at my pink toenail polish. Tomorrow I'd get a pedicure, a manicure, and maybe a facial too. I put on a pair of black cotton drawstring shorts and a little white T-shirt with a yellow smiley face on the front.

Sitting with my legs crossed on the floor next to my bed, I stretched my arms out behind me and extended them to the floor. I had not cheated on Eric ever, yet he dissed me at every opportunity. I knew he cared about me. Was sex that big a deal to him? Is that what this was about? I tilted my head back toward the ceiling. If we were married, we wouldn't have any of these issues. Will Smith and Jada Pinkett-Smith always talked about how they were best friends and they communicated to keep it that way. Maybe Eric and I needed to communicate better.

I'd read somewhere that exercise released endorphins that made you feel better, and that meditation helped to clear the mind. So I closed my eyes and tried to clear my head. Eric was a jerk. Mina was trying to steal my accounts and give my boyfriend to her friend. "Hummmmmmmm," I said aloud with my eyes closed. Sure, I probably looked silly, and sure, I had no training in meditation, but hey, I had a ton of stuff on my mind.

I opened one eye and peeked down at the new roll sticking out from my sides. Now my weight was going to end up being a problem too. "Ummmmmmmm," I said.

After a few moments, I opened my eyes and turned around toward the bed. I placed my feet where the embroidered bed skirt almost touched the floor. Putting my hands behind my head, I tilted backward slowly, letting my weight pull me down to the floor. My shoulders led and pushed me upward until I reached my knees. Down and up. Down, and up again.

It burned around my stomach area, but I kept going. Somehow, someway, I was going to do a hundred.

"Thirty-three, thirty-four . . ."

Wait until Eric saw my abs; he'd regret that he acted up. He'd practically beg me to walk by his side. I hit the fifty mark.

"Sixty-one, sixty-two . . . I can do this," I said and kept going.

My phone rang, but I wasn't moved. I closed my eyes and imagined ten pounds just melting away.

It rang again.

"Seventy-four," I said. My toes started to burn too. The phone rang again. My body temperature must have risen five degrees higher than normal. My back was damp, so I took off my shirt and tossed it across the room. I saw that I should have changed into a sports bra before starting this little attempt at discipline. My new black satin bra was getting damp. I kept going.

"Eighty-two."

I kept crunching. The answering machine on top of my chest of drawers clicked on. "Hi," said my recorded voice. "You've got me, now do that thing you do, and I'll get back to you. Bye."

*Beeeep,* went the machine.

"Hello, umm yes, hi. My name is Keith. (*Chuckle*) I don't—" *Click* (another call was coming through on my line) "—is the right number, but I'm looking for Chantell Meyers," said the unfamiliar voice. "If this is the right number, please call me at 617-67—" *Click* "—55. I look forward to hearing from you. Bye-bye."

"Eighty-eight . . . Eiightty nine . . ." I didn't know any Keith, except the guy who worked downstairs who wore shirts with loud Christmas colors all year round. I made a note to myself to get caller ID.

I was almost home free. "Niiiinetyyy-niiiiine, one hundereeed," I exhaled.

I wrapped my arms around my knees and rested. "Whooo!" I'd done it. If I did this every day for the next couple of weeks, who knew, maybe I could have a Janet Jackson six-pack. I was going in the right direction, anyway. I was so proud of myself that I headed right to the kitchen to celebrate with Ben and Jerry.

# 6

## superwoman needs a spa day

Tia was popping her fingers and moving to the song at the end of the Jason's Lyric video we'd just watched.

Girls' Days were becoming something of a rarity for us. Earlier that day, we'd gone shopping at BCBG at the Great Mall in Milpitas. Our personal shoppers had sent us each a certificate that said we'd get $100 off anything in the store if we spent $300. Please! We were all over it.

I tossed a kernel of popcorn her way. It flew over the edge of the coffee table and landed in her lap, where she sat on the floor with her legs stretched out.

"So your trip was good?" I said.

"Yeah, it was good, now stop throwing popcorn in the house," she teased.

"Heifer, this is my house."

"Oh yeah, I forgot." She laughed while putting the kernel in a napkin. "Philly was good, but I am glad to be back home." Then she turned and looked at me. "So, how've you been doing?"

I shared a lot of stuff with Tia, but there were some things that I wasn't telling anybody. Because she knew that I was a private person, Tia also knew when she was treading on thin ice, but that didn't stop her. She'd always try to encourage me or force me to explore roots of pain. She was very into the yin-yang and wholeness and stuff like that.

On my twenty-eighth birthday, I remembered being a little nervous about nearing the big three-oh. To help me be more accepting she'd told me all kinds of things—for example, that being thirty years old would feel great. "It's like breathing deeply after holding your breath for a very long time," she'd said.

I'd told her that she was full of it, but I loved her anyway. We'd been best friends for over five years. We met when she came into the newspaper one day to file some papers for her cosmetology school, Elnora's Beauty Training Center, which had been passed on to her by her mother. I was leaving when she came in. She asked me where the public notice office was, and her hair looked great. I showed her where it was (upstairs), and asked her where she got her hair done. She'd been my best friend ever since.

She stared at me, waiting for me to answer her question.

"I'm alright. I guess. I've been better."

"Chantell, you're like little black Barbie. You have your own house, car, college education, clothes, and credit," she teased, "and you've got bruhman with all them muscles. That is all the stuff that you've said you wanted. What's the matter?"

I laughed dryly. I hadn't told her about the little breakup yet. "I don't know. I think I am just in need of a break."

"Well, you and Eric are still doing Mexico, right?"

"Yes, but that's over a month away, and we're not exactly the happy couple."

"Uh-oh. What's happened?" I had to love her, she knew me so well.

"Nothin'," I said as I swayed my head and pretended to really be into the song. We sat on the couch in the living room, finishing up the last of a greasy bag of microwave popcorn.

"That long silver skirt that you bought is off the hook. Which shirt did you get to go with it?" I said.

"I got the first one I tried on. Remember? The white one with the long sleeves?"

"Oh yeah. That one was cute." I nodded.

I bopped around a little more and put a kernel in my mouth. "Girl, I love me some perfectly microwaved popcorn." It was my weakness, and I'd certainly had my share of it that day.

"Mmm-humph. So, are you going to tell me what's wrong?"

"Nothin', I don't know. Eric is just out there being Eric, and I just don't know if I am happy."

"Well, you have to take care of yourself first. Love yourself, Chantell. Treat yourself good." She pointed to our bags that sat beside me on the couch. "And I am not just talking about clothes and stuff. I mean, spend some time thinking about what you're made of, Chantell, and meditate. That helps me."

"I'm taking care of me, but my relationship isn't making it any easier right now."

"What'd he do?"

"Nothing, Tia. You know Eric, flaunting himself around, like he is all that. Flirting with other women. You know."

"Yes, I know. Chantell, you love beautiful men. You've been through this kind of thing before. You know what happens. You know the pros and cons of that kind of relationship."

Okay, here we go. *"That kind of relationship."* Now Tia, my very holistic friend, was going to remind me of her golden rules that she lived by the whole year that she was single as an adult: Never date a man who thinks he looks better than you do. Don't build your relationship on looks or sex. Always use a condom. Blah blah blah blah blah.

Whatever. Anyways, we did use condoms. Plus, Eric just flirted. He just liked attention. He wouldn't go any further than that. Besides, we didn't have sex anymore anyway. But back when we used to, he and I really did practice safe sex. Most of the time. I mean, there were a couple of slip-ups, but probably 90 percent of the time we were safe.

Actually, this was a sore subject with me, because the thought of diseases scared the daylights out of me. Always had, and truthfully, I hadn't had an HIV test since that one time I'd gotten the nerve to be tested in college. And all of those "Get tested" commercials that they showed on television didn't help me.

I remembered when I took the test. The school's health center gave them out free and anonymously. That was eight years ago. It was negative, of course, but I could never bring myself to go and take another one. So from then on out, I'd just tried to "be careful."

"Look, Chantell, all I'm saying is for you to know yourself and know your man." Then she added, "I like Eric, and I think that you should be with him if you want to. I just want to see you happy. So if you love him, hang in there and work it out. I know that you can get to where you need to be."

I giggled.

"What?" she asked.

"Who do you think you are, Oprah Winfrey?"

"Whatever!" She laughed.

I laughed too, then said, "Tia, it's easy for you to say. You're married. If you tried dating, you'd see."

"No thanks! I'm committed."

I laughed, but in all seriousness, she was always a source of encouragement for me, and I appreciated her and her efforts. She was conservative, but she had a great sense of humor. She had to have one to be married to her husband, who kept everyone laughing all the time.

"Make jokes if you must, but take care of yourself," she said.

"I will. And I'll be just fine. Really," I said with a shrug to let her know I had no worries.

She didn't look totally convinced when she picked up her keys off of the table and put her jacket over her arm. I got up from the couch and followed her toward the door. She added, "And remember, if you need to get away before Mexico, you can always use the cabin in Tahoe. Just say that word, and it's yours."

"Thanks, girlfriend," I said and gave her a hug. "And Tia, we're not going to wait six months before we do this again. Right?"

"Nope, we're not. How about we plan something for next week?"

"Okay, I'll call you on Monday and we'll set it up."

She put her cheek to mine. "Okay, love you."

"Love you too."

I would have felt like a fool telling Tia about the disaster on the boat. I was a walking, talking, breathing robot that always prevailed. I never got hurt. I gave good advice to friends and loved ones. If anyone had a problem, all they needed to do was see me, and I'd help them to get through it. You see, I was an expert. Oh, the friends that I had, I had their backs. Need a makeover? Go see my guy at my health spa. Having legal problems? Go see my friend Jonathan, the attorney. Having relationship problems? Tell Chawnee what was the matter. Just pick up the phone and call me, we'd talk for hours. My difficulties? Now they were another matter altogether. Rarely did anyone see any. Because you see, I was perfect. I was a strong black woman. I was resourceful, and I defended myself at all costs.

I put my feet up on the couch and tried to relax. Actually, I didn't know when I had started acting this way, but I'd played this game for so long that I couldn't shut it off. Humph, I wore more masks than Barry Bonds had hit home runs.

# 7

# tit for tat

Mina and I couldn't stand each other! But we had something of an unspoken truce at the office. We ignored each other above all else. That way, nobody got slapped and we both got to keep our jobs. Mina would have been the one getting slapped, though. I just put the fact that she was the cause of my and Eric's current falling-out in the back of my mind and stored it. Nope, I was sick of her and not about to take another smidgen of that overly competitive little cow.

I played with a pencil on my desk, glancing at the photos sitting on the shelf above my desk as I spoke into the phone. "Yes, Mr. Strautimeyer, I'll swing by your office first thing tomorrow morning to pick up the disk with the artwork . . ." The photo of me and Daddy dressed alike in blue Meyers Automotive coveralls was on the end. ". . . No worries, Mr. Strautimeyer. As long as your agency has the ad designed and we don't have to make any revisions to it, we'll make the press time for this Sunday's paper." The picture was taken a couple of years ago. A day when the guy that worked at the front counter of the shop had called in sick and I used a personal day to go fill in for him. Daddy was so proud I was there with him. "I'll handle it . . . Okay, you too. Have a good evening."

I hung up the phone and made a note in my Palm Pilot that I was to stop by Skyway Modems tomorrow morning to pick up their full-page, full-color ad that they were running in the main section of the paper this weekend. Mr. Strautimeyer had pulled a full week's budget from a radio station and another paper to be able to run this ad. It was a nice upsize compared to the half-page black-and-white ad that they usually ran in Sunday's paper. I knew Mina Everett was probably fuming because several of her smaller accounts' advertisements were being bumped out of the highly sought-after and widely viewed Main News section.

I was glad that my dad was recovering, and I tried to keep that spirit of gratefulness about myself all day every day. But at work, things got so heated, sometimes I just forgot.

I tried not to gloat when I thought about how Mina's new account, Fashion Nails, would likely end up in the Sports section. The account probably wouldn't want to do business with her again. She had to be a little bit upset about that. Served her right! God do not like ugly.

I hadn't seen her up close since she sat at my table with her friends and Eric at that boat party. Now she approached my area in a yellow button-down shirt that barely covered her up, her fiery red hair down again.

"Hi there, Mina," I said with a smile and a voice that dripped with sarcasm.

She squinted her green eyes at me as she walked past and stopped two desks down. She was probably stealing an account from someone who was away. I chuckled a bit and tucked my hair behind my ear.

She looked over in my direction. "Chantell, would you do me a favor and tell Eric that my friend Stephanie said to meet her at their normal place for dinner?"

That did it! I'd vowed that I wasn't taking any more mess from Mina, and that was exactly what I meant. She would say *anything* to try to hurt me!

"Oh, okay, Mina," I said to her. "I'll be sure to do that."

What a liar! Eric didn't have any "normal place for dinner" spot with anyone except for me. Mina Everett was going to find out that I could get just as petty as she could.

# 8

# the test

I was still fuming on the ride home. I left San Francisco and had gotten through the Bay Bridge, but then the traffic came to a standstill. When it started to creep along again, I got off the freeway and took the side streets. I cracked my window and drove down the city streets. I thought about that silly woman at work as I rode past the old church that my grandmother used to take me to.

The beige-and-white two-story building still sat there, its grass looking green, its bushes cut in a long rectangle. The parking lot was filled with cars. I wondered what they were doing in there on a Friday night.

It had started to rain a bit by the time I got to the grocery store. A lady sat outside the store and asked for donations for the Veteran's Relief Fund. As I approached her, she shook her white bucket. I heard change rattling at the bottom. Usually, when I had extra, I gave. I gave to the homeless, I gave to the United Negro College Fund, and I gave to the local women's shelters. But today I was tired and not in the mood.

The lady sat behind a card table, with a nurse's hat pinned in her hair and a badge clipped to her candy striper uniform. She had a cigarette in her mouth, but she'd unknowingly turned it the wrong way. She shook the white bucket at both another man and me as we grabbed carts and headed into the store at the same time. She stared at us and flicked her lighter with her thumb. The fire rose up and she put the flame to the brown filter of the cigarette. The filter melted a bit. I tried to look straight ahead and not notice.

"D**n it!" she said as she threw the cigarette to the ground.

I went into the store, toward the meat and cheese aisle. I grabbed the envelope sticking out of my purse, thinking it was the grocery list that I'd made that morning. It was actually a doctor bill. I looked in my purse and discovered that I'd forgotten the list at home. This was how I ended up exceeding my planned budget every month. I continued down the cheese aisle. I knew that Colby-Jack cheese was on the list. I grabbed a block of cheese and moved farther down the aisle to the turkey breast. A man was pushing a grocery cart containing two little girls whose coal-black hair was tied with green ribbons. They were probably three and four years old and singing Barney songs while bobbing up and down, and making a bunch of unnecessary racket. *"I love you, toot, toot, toot . . ."*

They argued over whose turn it was to sing. "Okay, you go. Okay, now it's my turn! Okay, you go. No, it's my turn!" They were squealing and whining, and their father just walked along pushing the basket, like he didn't hear a thing. The two children, in light blue nylon jackets and pink ski boots, finally got on one chord, and sang, *"Standing outside with my mouth open wide . . ."* and proceeded to make gagging noises. Forget the turkey breast, I needed to change aisles.

I walked fast toward them and got over in the lane to pass. A lady and her husband walked toward me pushing a cart. They were arm in arm, and poking along. They both had handfuls of the fresh pistachios that were sold in bulk in the big white tubs near the fruits and vegetables. They munched and laughed and dropped the shells of the stolen nuts on the floor. They were too close for me to pass. I was trapped, and the kids continued to sing. I tried to wait for them to pass, but it had been a long day.

"Umm, please excuse me," I said. "I'd really like to get by."

The man with the children walked past the couple and made enough room for me to go around them. The couple looked so happy, just grinnin' at each other and poking along. Standing close

to each other and pushing their cart together. I looked at the pista-
chio thieves and rolled my eyes. Then I tisked at the man with his
humming brats as they stomped their little feet on the metal bars
below them like little marching drummer boys. It sounded like a
miniature earthquake to me. I left the aisle glad that I wasn't in either
of those scenarios.

Finally I got to the soap aisle and put a box of dishwashing powder in my basket. I needed to find the pet food area. I looked up at
the signs that hung overhead. Three aisles down, 6B, pet food, pet
collars, kitty litter. I thought about Mina Everett. I couldn't stand her.
I walked down the row and looked for pet cleanup products. The
store had everything for animals. There were baby-powder-scented
cleanup gloves and flea-repellent cat collars with colorful beads in
them. There were special odor-neutralizing sprays and compounds.
For $9.99 I found a poop-scooping gadget that looked like two claws
coming together. I put it in my basket.

My cell phone rang. I answered, "Hello, it's Chantell Meyers."

"Hey, it's me, Eric."

"Eric, what do you want?"

"What are you doing?"

"None of your business. Why don't you go and call your little
friend from the ship." I hung up the phone. Did he really think that
the world was supposed to cater to him? Be at his beck and call
whenever he felt like playing cat and mouse? Put up with him even
when he was blatantly misbehaving? All because he was beautiful.
He thought wrong. If we were going to get back together, then he was
going to have to learn this before we got married. That way I
wouldn't have to deal with this kind of stuff later.

I remembered I needed more Apple Jacks, and oatmeal, and
pushed my cart into the coffee and cereal aisle. My phone rang again.
There were people standing around scanning the aisle. I walked past
them, turned the phone on, put my hand over the receiver, and
spoke quietly but sternly.

"Hello!"

"Chantell. Talk to me. How long are you going to stay mad at
me?"

I thought of how he disrespected me, and the hurt and anger resurfaced. No tears, Chantell, I told myself.

"You know what? You need to get it together, Eric. I don't have to deal with your mess, and I am not going to. Why don't you stop calling me?"

I hung up again and turned off the phone. I was trying to manage a lot. My head felt tingly and dizzy, and there was pressure behind my right eye. Between trying to keep an eye on my dad, work stressing me out, and Eric giving me the blues, I felt weak. I used to be anemic, really badly, and I remembered feeling this way. I wondered whether my iron count was low again. I held on to the cart and walked slowly.

Last week I'd gotten my annual exam at my ob-gyn and they'd taken my blood at the lab. I could find out what was going on with me very easily. I reached in my purse and called the doctor's number on the receipt in the envelope.

"Hello, Dr. Lun's and Dr. Parta's office."

"Hi. My name is Chantell Meyers, and I was there last week."

"Yes, hello."

"I'm feeling dizzy, tingly, and having headaches, and I was wondering if my blood work came back."

"Blood work. Oh, sure. Hold on, please."

I put a box of granola bars in my cart.

"Hi, are you calling about test results?" said a new voice on the other end.

"Yes."

"What's your name?"

"Chantell Meyers. I want to know if the results showed that I was anemic again, or if my blood pressure is up or something. I was anemic as a child . . ."

"Oh. Right here. Oo-kay, let's see, Meyers. Okay, we tested you for gonorrhea, chlamydia, TB, HIV, and hepatitis B and C. And they're all good . . . And your iron levels are good too."

"What did you say you tested me for?"

She repeated the list. "Gonorrhea, chlamydia, TB, HIV, and hepatitis. They are all fine."

"I didn't ask for an HIV test," I said, though truthfully that was a big relief to hear.

"No?"

"No."

"Well, sorry, but it's a good thing it's negative? Right?"

Being the control freak that I was, I told her, "Well, I didn't ask for it, and you can't just do anything to me without my say-so."

"Ma'am, all of your testing went well!" she proclaimed.

"Whatever!" I said. "That's illegal." I was going to take the test when *I* got ready.

"Huh?"

"You're testing me without my permission. That's illegal."

"Umm . . . You gave us permission!"

"No, I did not!"

The people in the aisle started staring. I wouldn't have really sued my doctor, but what if it had been bad news? Stranger things had been known to happen. I didn't like surprises. I didn't want to hear anything else. It was a frustrating day, but at least the HIV testing that I often thought about was done; that was one less thing that I needed to worry about. I paid for my groceries and left the store.

## 9

# operation: tiffany drop

When I got up in the morning, I was wide awake and ready to follow through with my plan to teach Mina a lesson. I would have gotten the Australian heifer too, except I didn't know where to find her. One of Tia's students had just braided my hair, so I pulled the back of my new braids into a ponytail and put on some sweatpants and a sweatshirt and went into the kitchen. I looked under my kitchen cabinet and took out a pair of yellow rubber dish-washing gloves and a plastic grocery bag, and put them in my pants pocket. I laced up my old Nike running shoes and left the house through the back door. On the way out the back gate I grabbed the poop-scooping contraption and ran with its rake-like handles at my side. I jogged around the block, and when I got to the park I started to walk.

The grass was really green and it seemed that each little blade had at least a drop of water on it. The sunrays from above hit the water sprinkles so that they looked like diamond chips sitting on the ground. It was a cold morning, and except for a few people running and a couple walking their dog, the park was empty.

I walked around some more. A breeze of cold morning air rushed past me, raising the loose braids on the side of my hair, and I thought I probably looked like a flying chicken.

"Good morning," I said to the couple with the little dog.

"Good morning to you," said the husband.

The wife just smiled and gave me a nod.

I kept walking around and soon spotted a pile of dog pooh that sat in the grass waiting for someone to come along and to clean it up. Some owners were so irresponsible. I put on the yellow rubber dishwashing gloves that I'd stuffed in my pocket, opened the handles of the scooper, and locked the fork-like jaws around the pooh. Then I took out the bag, placed the poop securely in it, and headed for home.

In the top of my closet was the Tiffany box that my tennis bracelet had come in. I took down the pretty aqua blue box with black letters and a white satin ribbon around it. I'd splurged one day and bought it for myself after Eric kept promising to get it for me, only to let last year's birthday pass. Instead he'd given me a Reebok sweatshirt.

I removed the blue pouch from the box and took it outside into the backyard. I put the yellow dishwashing gloves back on and retrieved the bag of poop. Tearing it open, I dropped its contents into the pouch. I placed the pouch in the box, put the top on, wiped it all down really well, and slipped the ribbon back on.

I placed the Tiffany box inside some bubble wrap and another box, then mailed it to Mina at the office that afternoon. Mina Everett was full of crap, just like her present.

# 10

# big payback

My job was sending me away for two days to an "Effective Presentation Seminar" in Sacramento. It was hosted by Les Brown, and some of the country's most influential motivational speakers would be speaking. The two days promised to be entertaining and the food was bound to be good. I was trying to get ready to leave the office, but by chance I was still there for the mail run.

I heard people saying, "Mina . . . Tiffany box . . . Propose." And people started getting up and heading over to the other side of the room where Mina sat.

"What's going on? What's going on?" the front receptionist came to our area and asked.

"Mina got a Tiffany box . . . Her boyfriend's proposing through the mail!"

"C'mon, I'm on my way over there now!" The women giggled and walked across our floor.

I looked down at my desk and cleaned it off real good. I opened my drawer and took out my keys to lock up the drawers.

The women came back past my area walking really fast. Their hands were on their chests and they were frowning. Some people giggled. Others laughed out loud.

I picked up my things to leave. Gary, the guy who sat next to me, raced back to his seat and sat down.

"What happened?" I asked him.

"Trust me, Chantell," he said with his palm extended outward like he was directing traffic. "You don't want to know."

I grabbed my briefcase, my cell phone, my DKNY watch. I asked Gary to water my plant and fought to hold a straight face; I was out of there.

# 11

# canun does chantell

The two-day seminar had been great, but when I returned, it seemed my entire office had gone berserk.

Both my phone and Canun's were ringing off the hook with calls from upper management in New York. They were calling every hour, it seemed, to see if Canun had gotten Skyway Modems to sign off on the deal yet. Canun Ramsey was stuttering and pacing the floor, and voilà! Enter Chantell into the scenario.

I didn't know the details of the deal, but was being congratulated by my coworkers. Canun was sweating as he gave me the full scoop: "Your account has agreed to do this large test, but I've got a meeting, and I'm on my way out the door." I nodded. He said, "Call your account. We need to get the creative elements from them to get it started right away."

Skyway Modems, it seemed, had agreed to spend $100,000 to let us test out the effectiveness of our new product soon to launch, called the "Sunday Disk Drive edition." This new product was simple, but a novel concept really. My understanding of it was this: We, the newspaper, would be willing to put a cardboard disk onto the front of our Sunday edition of the newspaper to promote a business. This sounded like a win/win deal. It gave the business, in this case Skyway Modems, an opportunity to put an attention-grabbing message right there in the highly sought-after consumer's face, and it made us at the newspaper innovators, pioneers even, of an effective and exciting new way to disseminate information. Management said it would be way more effective than a local TV commercial or radio station spot, and better than any billboard could do! Yep, the pressure was on, but the potential was there. Whichever newspaper office could pull this off, and be the first in the country to get this new product sold, would look like a superstar!

Canun grabbed his coat and wrote a couple of things on a yellow notepad on his desk. "Chantell, our CEO himself thought of and created this new product and he's super anxious to get it tested. They're ringing my phones every three minutes for the contract." He swallowed. "I got all of the major legwork done, Chantell. This will be a nice little bonus for you. So make sure you get the contract signed and everything turned in as quickly as you can."

I nodded as I took in his words. Canun was bidding on making VP soon and wanted to look good in the eyes of the top executives. He took a tissue, patted the back of his neck, and left.

I headed back to my desk happy. Canun was not a strong salesperson, yet he'd gotten my account, Skyway Modems, to agree to pay to test it out. This was major! I was impressed.

Although it was believed the disk drive product would be super effective, it was also very expensive to produce. Once we could prove its effectiveness, other advertisers were sure to pay top dollar for the Disk Drive edition without hesitation, at all the papers across the country. Now that Canun had sold it, I knew what I needed to do: I needed to get over to Skyway, get the artwork, get the contract signed, and get this deal all wrapped up.

The excitement was contagious. We were talking about an additional $7,000 on my next commission check, and though I hadn't been the seller, when your account agrees to do something like this, you shine too. After all, if it weren't for all of the relationship-building that I'd done with the account, then they would not have agreed to run with this in the first place. Right?

I called the CEO at Skyway, Mr. Strautimeyer. He was a ballbreaker. You had to have all of your ducks in a row when you approached him. Last year, I'd seen him make another sales rep cry.

Well, I certainly had a newfound respect for my boss, Canun. I guess he wasn't the "coattail rider" that my coworkers had nicknamed him after all.

Mr. Strautimeyer's assistant put me right through to him.

"Hello, Mr. Strautimeyer, it's Chantell Meyers from the *San Francisco Daily News*. How are you today?"

"Well, I am fine, Chantell. How are you?"

"I am just great."

"What can I do for you?"

"Well, I know that you've decided to promote your new modems via our new Sunday Disk Drive edition, and I wanted to swing by this afternoon to pick up the creative. What would be a good time for you?"

There was a silence. Then Mr. Strautimeyer cleared his throat. "I didn't agree to that, Chantell. Your manager, Canun, mentioned something or another, but I was not even totally clear on what it was. And well, to be quite frank with you, Chantell, you already know that I've allocated my entire budget for this year."

"Oh, yes," I said and rubbed my forehead. The deal wasn't closed at all. It was a little hot in there.

Already, Mr. Strautimeyer had spent over a million dollars with me this year promoting his new wireless modems. I held the phone to my ear and contemplated. Think fast. Maybe I should try to give him a tiny push. Maybe that would get him to give it a try. However, I was reluctant to risk the working rapport that we had built. I didn't want to push him too far. But Canun had already opened the door, it was my job to try. So here goes . . .

"Okay," I said. "Well, why don't I stop by and show you the prototype, and perhaps you can—"

"That won't be necessary. I am extremely busy." And he hung up without so much as a good-bye.

That was finicky Mr. Strautimeyer. In the time we'd worked together, I'd learned a few things about him. One, he never said good-bye. Two, he didn't ever want to feel like he was "sold" or pushed into anything. And three, he'd just stopped this supposed big Sunday disk deal dead in its tracks. I exhaled and sat back in my chair.

Why had Canun put me in that position? He made it sound like the deal was signed, sealed, and all that I had to do was deliver it. Little weasel was always trying to move up the corporate ladder on someone else's back.

Needless to say, after that the rest of my day didn't go so well. Not only did I have to deal with everyone coming over to my desk to ask, "What happened? What happened?" I also had to phone the VPs in New York and explain that there was no deal. What was I going to say to them by way of explanation—that my manager had never really had a deal? And oh, by the way, he's an idiot. I don't think so! I took the heat. I said that Skyway decided against going with the Sunday Disk Drive project. But of course, to them it looked like once I got involved, the deal went sour.

You were only as good as your last deal in this business. If things kept up this way, I was going to be looking in the paper for a new job.

# 12

## a better time

My California king–size bed was my place of solitude and comfort. It had three high mattresses and a stepstool next to it that I used to climb up into it. I lay under my goosedown comforter, which was encased in a cream-and-yellow satin duvet cover with little pink and yellow flowers on it. I looked over at the nightstand to check the time. It was 10:54 p.m.

I lay in bed and thought about the massive to-do list that I'd left on my desk. Even then as I lay in my bed, Mr. Strautimeyer's comments made me feel uneasy. He was truly a businessman's businessman, and if he thought I was trying to manipulate him into that deal, I could lose his business.

Two crystal picture frames sat next to my alarm clock on the nightstand, illuminated by the moon's light that came through my window and hit them just so. One was of Eric and me together; we'd taken it in a photo booth at a carnival. The other was of just myself in a little black dress, at a nightclub in the city.

I'd tossed and turned so much over my awful day that my head wrap slipped off again. I rewrapped my hair and tied it up again. When I had told Canun what had happened on the phone with Mr. Strautimeyer, he had said he was shocked that Skyway didn't sign the deal. The little rat even had the nerve to try and look at me like I'd done something to mess it up!

I sighed and put my hands under my head and tried to go to sleep, but I tossed and turned and was up again. Work was a mess, and my romantic life was a mess. I wanted Eric there with me, to hold me, to comfort me. But I knew that if he were here, that would only lead us to areas that I was trying to stay away from. I was convinced that we needed to get married, and even my new copy of *Glamour* magazine confirmed that the best way to get married was to not have sex with the guy. I twisted and turned in my feelings of emptiness and loneliness. I was on my back, then on my side, then my scarf came off again. I put it back on. I had to remember to write out my checks in the morning. Water, cable, garbage, phone. I'd get to them.

I closed my eyes again and dreamed, or I remembered, I don't know which. I was somewhere between dreamland and the place where your memories are stored. With my eyes closed, I remembered a better time for me. I must have been five or six years old. We were upstairs in the balcony at church. I wore a white ruffled dress that coordinated with my socks and the bows in my hair. I never liked dressing that way, but it gave my Grandmother Hattie such satisfaction to see me so proper-looking. I preferred my Big Ben jeans with the yellow patch on the back pocket. But Grandma said that I was a little lady and that I should dress as such. My ponytails were neatly combed and perfectly parted with barrettes that hit my neck as I ran. My bangs curled down and bumped under on my forehead. My caramel skin and almond eyes caused people who didn't know me to make comments.

"Mrs. Brumwick," the neighbor watering her grass from across the street would yell over, "your grandbaby is just precious! She looks like a dolly!"

My grandmother would beam with pride as I stood there with my best shy-coy look.

But at church, this look never worked. There, my appearance fooled no one. I could kick a kickball from here to Timbuktu and the congregation knew it. There, all of the members' children knew to stay out of my way because I was bossy as all get out. My personality was strong and even my demeanor said "Follow me." And that's exactly what lots of the children used to do.

But not asthmatic little Keith Rashaad Talbit. He was the goody-two-shoed, sickly little grandson of Sister Edna. She started bringing him to church just weeks after he was born. His parents died in a fire when he was just a baby, and Sister Edna raised him alone, with the help of the church members. By the time he was a year old, Keith Rashaad Talbit had become the unspoken godchild of every member of the church.

This little boy was always a runt for his age, and a bookworm. His semisweet-chocolate brown skin was usually dry, ashy, and itchy. He kept hive ointment handy in his pocket just in case he got too nervous.

Pastor Fields and the rest of the congregation always kept an eye out and an ear open to make sure the kids weren't teasing him. They did the best they could to protect him. But sometimes, the little girls made jokes with Keith as the punch line. More times than not, it was me spearheading the "make-fun-of-Keith" sessions after church let out, or during church, upstairs, after Mother Ola Rose Pearl had dozed off.

Some Sundays, Mother Pearl would bring a ten-pack of Freedent gum to church with her—the kind in the light blue wrapper that advertised it didn't stick to dentures. She'd open a few packs and give us all a stick. Those were some good times. The parents always dreaded those days, and they could tell them right off because they'd glance up to the balcony and see all of our jaw muscles working in tandem, almost uniformly, much like little cows grazing. After a couple of minutes, one of the parents would always come upstairs, get the wastebasket out of the corner, and make sure that every child made a deposit.

In my dream, I vividly saw Mother Pearl go to sleep. Her chin slowly lowered and covered up her neck, then she suddenly jerked her head back up again. Her silver, fluffy hair was parted in the middle and combed straight downward. She wore thigh-high stockings that she rolled down just below the knee.

Pastor Fields was speaking, and Mother Pearl sleeping. I pulled out a new deck of cards from my shiny little black purse. I gathered three other little girls from the pews and found a nice corner. We spread the cards out on the floor and proceeded to play my favorite game.

"Okay, ladies," I said, "let's play some Concentration."

I was darn good at it too. The best in first grade. I gave them the rules.

"Okay, whoever loses has gotta kiss Keith Talbit and wear his Coke-bottle glasses! Molina, it's you and me. You're first." I gestured my hands toward the cards like the ladies on Grandma's favorite show, *The Price Is Right*.

"I'll go," said Molina, "but I'm not kissing Keith, Chantell. Noooo-no!"

"Look," I said, "rules are rules, and if you're not going to play fair by them, then you don't get to play!" I looked around at the other girls to see which would take her place.

"Chanteeell," she whined. "I want to play, but boys are gross! They make me tho' up."

"I know, Molina. Life is hard, though. Sometimes we don't get to make the rules. Sometimes"—I shook my head—"we just have to live by them."

And I almost felt sorry for her. After all, we were talking about the always-coughing Keith Rashaad.

Molina stared at the cards on the floor. Resigned, she said, "Okay." She turned over a queen and a six of diamonds.

"Hah! No match. My turn," I said, as the two other girls watched.

We continued to play until we got down to the last six cards. Molina was happy because she had thirteen matches and I'd only had ten. If she got one more, then there would be no way I could win. I told myself, Forget that! I wasn't kissin' nobody.

Molina flipped over a three, then over another three. "Yaayy!" she said out loud.

"So what, Molina!" I said. "Anyways, I'm not kissing anyone, because you shouldn't be kissing people in church. That's wrong! We're here to learn about God and Jesus!"

Molina ignored me and matched up the last four cards to win the game. The other two girls, who had been watching quietly, finally chimed in. "Chantell, you said yourself that if you're not going to play fair by the rules, then don't play. And our parents kiss in church all the time."

"Yep, sho' do. And people even get married here, so you know they be kissin!" said that other little one with her head moving.

I inhaled deeply and rolled my eyes. Stupid girls. Why were they in my business anyway? I got up, walked over to the pew, stepped over Ola Pearl, and went over to where Keith was and sat down next to him. He was quiet, looking at the preacher with his hands folded in his lap. I took a deep breath, leaned over, and pressed my lips into his cheek. Keith adjusted his glasses with his fingers and looked at me, but before he could say a word, I whispered, "Oh shut up, Frog Face."

I still remembered how that little kiss made me dizzy.

I opened my eyes again. It was late, I was tired and groggy, but I was smiling. That was a memory that I had forgotten all about. I used to be so bold. I'd say whatever I wanted. I took nobody's mess. Not now, though. Nowadays, I was always fearful, and miserable even though I pretended that I wasn't. And when those weren't my concerns, I was worried about what people thought of me. Where had that fearless little girl gone?

I looked at the alarm clock. It said 3:37 a.m. I thought about the drama of work. I closed my eyes and tried to go back to sleep, but I couldn't. Canun had set me up, but I decided right then that I wouldn't be the fall girl for anyone anymore. I was sick of Mina, I was sick of Eric, and I was especially sick of Canun Ramsey! I must have dozed off for a few minutes, because when I looked at the clock again it read 4:10 a.m.

I adjusted my goosedown pillow under my head and pulled my arms out from under my new mint green sheets. I wiped the sleep out of my eyes. All my life I'd been Miss Courageous. All my life I would say or do what I thought was right despite what anybody thought. Last year, I was the top sales rep in that office, and what did I get for it? Set up! That's what.

I reached for the phone and dialed the number to my office. Canun Ramsey's voice mail picked up and I wondered if I should actually do this. The beep said it was my turn to talk.

"Hello, Canun." My voice sounded Macy Grayish raspy. It mattered not—I had some things to get off my chest. "Uhh, it's Chantell. Look, I am not coming in today." I was getting bolder by the moment. "No, I'm not coming in for a while. You knew that you didn't have that Skyway deal, and when it fell through, you let me take the fall for it. You need to grow up!"

I wondered if I had gone a bit too far. "Don't look for me tomorrow. Bye!"

There. I hung up the phone. I'd done some crazy stuff in my time, I admit, but I'd never quit my job without having another one. I was too mature for that. I had a townhouse payment and a new car! I should have been worried. In fact, I probably should have had an anxiety attack, right then and right there!

But I didn't. I just closed my eyes and went back to sleep.

## 13

## getting nowhere

When I woke up at 7:30, I first thought that I had overslept, then I remembered that I probably didn't have a job. I stepped out of the shower and put on my new camel-colored slacks. Lately I'd been eating even when I wasn't hungry, and today I noticed that they were a little tight in the stomach area. I slid on a long-sleeved, cream-colored shirt. After I finished getting dressed, I grabbed my keys and left the house with absolutely nowhere to go.

It was 8:43 a.m. and the sky looked dreary. I climbed into my black Jeep Wrangler, and tried not to think about its getting repossessed. My cellular phone started ringing as soon as the engine was warm. I grabbed the phone and looked at who was calling. It was Cameron, a cool white sister-girl who sat near me at work. Curious about what the folks in the office were saying, I answered.

"Yes?" I answered.

"Umm, Miss Thing, where the heck are you?" she asked.

"Chillin' at home. What's up, Cameron?"

"Chantell, Canun is mad as all get out! What are you trying to do? People in the office are saying that you are AWOL, and that you probably won't be coming back. Canun is passing out your accounts and everything. Girl, you'd better get in here!"

I didn't even want to hear this. I'd proven myself ten times over.

I'd brought the paper a ton of money over the last two years, and I still hadn't taken a vacation. I needed a break. I was tired.

"You know what, Cameron? I don't really give a rat's butt. I'm not going back in there until I'm ready. If I'm ever ready. And I don't have to explain anything to Canun. He needs to be explaining himself to me. I'm sorry, I gotta go. Bye!" I hung up on her. Let them fire me, if that's what they wanted to do. I was an achiever. The phone rang again. I turned it off. Now I was crying.

"I am sick and tired of this crap!"

I grabbed my wallet out of my purse and found a card for the EAP, the Employee Assistance Program. I dialed the number and a call screener picked up right away.

"Hello, employee assistance crisis line. May I help you?"

Did he say crisis as in C-R-I-S-I-S?

"Hello? Can you hear me?"

I was not in a crisis. I didn't use drugs. I was not a teen runaway, and I had never been married. What kind of crisis could I possibly have had?

I hung up the phone, started up the Jeep, and drove around until I ended up at Daddy and Charlotte's house. I figured they were upstairs, so I used my key and entered through the kitchen. I hoped she wasn't on a rampage today. I'd already been through enough. Charlotte stood near the stove in an oversize, yellow-flowered house dress. She was stirring up eggs in a white rubber bowl. Preparing Daddy an omelet, no doubt.

"Hi, Charlie," I said to her.

"Hey, Chawnee," she said, as her brown fingers poured the eggs from the white bowl into a shiny silver skillet. "How come you're not at work?"

She was accusing me right off. Jeez, lady, I had a lot going on, and I was trying to be in a good mood. I'd only been in the door for thirty seconds. Can you let me get in the house before you start digging?

"I'm going in this afternoon," I told her, biting the side of my lip. I knew what I was doing, and it was *my* business.

"Oh," she said doubtfully, like she knew me so well. She was always suspicious of me like that. I am full-grown, in case she hadn't noticed. I put her on the list of people that I was sick of.

"Is my dad up?" I asked.

"Yeah, he's up there watching the ball game channel."

My parents had just had marble floors and new white carpet put in. I stepped out of my new pointy-toed brown leather boots, set them by the front door, and headed up the stairs. Their bedroom door was cracked, so I pushed it open.

Daddy was sitting up in bed looking healthy, watching television. He was clean-shaven, as usual, except for his thick salt-and-pepper mustache. He had a big shiny bald head on top, and salt-and-pepper hair on the sides that he brushed downward from ear to ear.

"Hey, Baseball Ballerina!" Daddy was recovering well.

"Hey, Papa Doe's Pizza!" I said.

My dad and I got along great. We'd been calling each other silly names ever since I could talk.

"You're up and about bright and early. Why aren't you at work, babygirl?"

"Oh, I took the morning off. I'll probably go in this afternoon."

"I see. Where is your coat? It looks like it's going to rain. Did you go out this morning without one on? Chawnee, don't you leave here without a coat. You hear me? Shoot. Girl, it's colder out there than a polar bear's behind."

I laughed. "Okay, Daddio."

He was funny. He constantly compared stuff to everything's butt. No matter what the topic was, he found a way to make it into a lesson with a butt in it. If I told him to taste a spicy food, he'd say, "Girl, that food is hotter than a flea's butt running across a campfire."

"Here, Daddy," I said. "I brought you something."

I reached into my Prada backpack purse and took out a Monterey Jazz Festival baseball cap, to add to his collection. I went over and put it on his head. "Next February, when you're up to it, you and I are going to the jazz festival."

Daddy smiled. "Yep . . . By then, I'll be as good as new."

No prostate cancer or heart attack was going to get the best of my dad.

I thought about the coconut-shell anklet that I had on. It would make a nice bracelet for him. I took it off and grabbed his wrist to fasten it on.

"Aww naw!" he teasingly grumbled. "Here you come decorating me wit a whole bunch of barrettes and clamps and fasteners!"

"Aww, Daddy, this ain't no barrette, it's a bracelet for you. Hold still."

Daddy huffed and puffed, but I knew he secretly liked the gift. I giggled and closed the fastener. My daddy wouldn't leave me. He couldn't leave me; nobody cracked me up like he did.

Charlotte walked in the door with Dad's omelet and she started in on me. She waited until I got in front of Daddy to comment on my new braids. She was always trying to make him see the "real me," and she'd been doing it since I was little.

She pointed at my long black extensions that I'd gotten cornrowed down to my butt. "You've been going to work looking like that?" she asked.

I sucked my teeth and didn't say a word. My braids were something that I'd wanted to do for a long time. Ever since I'd seen Eve sporting some long blond ones in a video.

"Well, you won't make VP of advertising looking like that. That's not professional," she said.

"Charlotte, I don't really give a flying freak right now. Okay?" My chest started to feel tight again.

"Hey! Hey! Hey! Chantell, you calm down and watch your mouth!" said my father.

"Yeah, girl your mouth is somethin' else," Charlotte said. "You're so pretty, but that attitude just makes you ugly. You need to stop all that!"

"Now hold up on, you guys!" my daddy said sternly. "We're not doing that this morning. Okay?"

I rolled my eyes. Charlotte was always provoking me. I really didn't care what corporate America thought right then. Corporate America didn't care about me. I didn't care about corporate America. And what did *she* know about corporate America anyway? She hadn't worked in ten years.

I sat there and hung out with her and my dad for as long as I could. The three of us watched television together in silence. When I left it was still cold but the sun was out. I took my keys out of my purse and zipped up Charlotte's red sweat jacket. Daddy was right, it was too cold to be out without a coat.

In the car, I checked my voice mail; Eric had called. "Yes, Chantell. I just left a message at your office too. I guess you're in a meeting. Look, baby, I'm not sure why you're trippin'. Those girls weren't anybody to me. We were just talking, that's all," he said. "You know I want to be with you. So you need to stop acting like that, and come over here tonight . . ."

I took the phone from my ear. That was exactly what I didn't need to do! What I needed was for Charlotte to get off my back. What I needed was for my daddy to fully recover. I looked at my long fingers and the glossy coat of peach nail polish on the tips. What I needed was for Eric to marry me. That was what I needed! I hit the delete button.

# 14

# take a stand

I'd driven around thinking for a few hours before I heard my stomach grumble. A hot pastrami sandwich had been on my mind for a couple of days. I spotted a yellow Subway sign just off the freeway and pulled into their parking lot.

A buzzer sounded when I walked in the door and up to the counter. Metal edges outlined the glass, through which I could see green-and-white lettuce shreds, tomato rings, black olives, green peppers, and little pieces of paper that covered the meats and cheeses.

". . . Hey, sweetheart? I've got a customer. Hang on a minute," said the tall, thin guy from behind the counter. He set down the phone and put on a pair of plastic gloves.

"Hi. How are you today?" His skin was the color of peanut butter, and his face was still spotted with acne.

"Just great." I smiled my normal smile.

"White or wheat?"

"Um, wheat."

"Six-inch or foot-long?"

"Six-inch."

I ordered my hot pastrami sandwich, a bottled water, and a bag of Lay's and sat down at a table. Why did they put the sandwich in a plastic bag even after you'd told them that you were dining in?

The employee retrieved the phone and proceeded to talk. "Okay, we'll leave as soon as I get off work, and we'll get there about eight."

I unwrapped the paper from my sandwich.

"Don't worry, I'll just tell your father. It's between us men. Kristen, leave it up to me. I'll do the talking . . . Baby, we're not going to sleep in separate— We're not— I'll just explain. Honey, I am your husband. Alright? It's me and you forever."

I took a bite of my warm sandwich. It wasn't as flavorful as I thought it would be. I chewed slowly and glanced toward the guy, who looked to be about nineteen or twenty years old. Her and him forever.

I smiled as I remembered being a teen and struggling for my independence. I remembered how difficult it had been for my dad to deal with the fact that I had a boyfriend. He'd had a fit. He'd tried to scare the guy whom I thought I was in love with by saying that he'd grown up on the mean streets of Chicago and had mob connections. Then he'd changed our phone number and put me on restriction. I smiled remembering that awful day.

The guy behind the counter went on. "Well, we're adults, you know. We'll just say to them— Baby. I'll say it! Don't worry. We *are* going to finish school and everything will be okay. I'll be ready to leave here at four-thirty. I love you too. Okay, bye."

The kid behind the counter was willing to stand up with, and for, his girl. I needed to get Eric to see that he was supposed to stand up with and for me. I needed a lot of things. I needed Canun to know that he couldn't dump his issues off on me, and I needed Charlotte to stop attacking me at every corner. But right then, I needed Eric to want our relationship like the kid behind the counter wanted his.

I picked up my cell and dialed Eric back. It rang.

"Yeah."

"Eric, it's me. Eric, did you do anything with that girl on the boat?"

"What? No, Chantell. You know me better than that!"

"Then how come you left with her?"

He let out a long breath of air. "Chantell, I'm at work. And I can't talk about this now, okay?"

I looked over at the young man who was taking fresh hot bread from the oven. Then I said what I thought.

"Eric, I think we should get married."

"Chantell, I'll talk to you later, babe. Bye."

I hung up, and wanted to scream. Two long years I'd wasted on him. I'd given him over seven hundred days of my life! Why wouldn't he stand up for me? I took my sunglasses off the top of my head and put them over my eyes. What was wrong with me?

I needed to talk to someone. I looked in my purse and found the EAP card again.

The call screener answered. "Thank you for calling the Employee Assistance Program. My name is Mitch."

"Yes. Hi, Mitch, I need to talk to someone. Like a therapist or something," I added.

"Sure. What kind of concerns are you having, ma'am?"

"I don't know, I have a lot of bills and pressures, I think I just quit my job, my relationship is a joke. My stepmother picks on me . . . and I'm just tired."

"Slow down, slow down, it'll be okay. I'm here to help," he said.

He took my name and address and found two therapists in my area.

"Do they have a specialty area that they work in? I mean, I want to talk to someone who specializes in stress."

As opposed to someone who specialized in Tourette's syndrome, or someone who was afraid to walk under ladders.

"Ma'am, I'm no therapist, but it sounds like your issues are pretty common. All of our therapists and counselors are fully trained and accredited and can assist you with stress. I'm sure that we've got help for you, but I'll tell you something. Whatever your problems are, pray about them, it always works for me."

"Okay," I said and wiped away the tears that had been burning in my eyes and refusing to fall.

He gave me the two therapists' names and numbers and told me to call them. "If one doesn't work, try the other one. If neither clicks with you, call us back and get more referrals. Sometimes it takes a little work to find a good person for you to talk to. Okay?"

"Okay. Thanks."

I was lucky. I phoned the first one, and she happened to have a cancellation. She said that I could stop by that afternoon.

# 15

# san francisco's got a lot of birds

I arrived at the therapist's office that afternoon. I was the only one in the waiting room. It was a small, plain-looking office in a large building in San Francisco. There was an old beige couch in the waiting area, and two card table chairs across from it, with a wooden end table in between—on which lay a birdwatching magazine and a *Reader's Digest*. The pictures on the walls were dusty.

The therapist's door opened and she asked me to come in. She had long black hair with thin strips of gray throughout. I sat down on a hard chair next to her desk.

"So why are you here today?" she asked.

I said, "Well, I'm tired." I didn't know what to say.

"Please go on," she said.

"Well, I'm not sleeping good at night, and I think I don't have a job anymore."

"Why would you think that? What happened?" she asked.

Not knowing where to begin, I said, "Well, my boss keeps doing underhanded things to me." I then described a painful incident: "Last week he told me that he needed to turn in a report on the number of new business contacts that I had made within the last two weeks. I counted up all of mine and they totaled forty-eight. So I submitted forty-eight new names. When he got my numbers, he pulled me to the side and said with a chuckle that he didn't think that forty-eight was a realistic number to submit. He said that was an awful lot of new contacts even for me. He said that upper management wouldn't believe I had truly made that many contacts. So I said fine. He said he would tone down my number to something believable, like twenty-six or thirty. I didn't necessarily like it, but I said fine—whatever! He was my boss and knew what he was doing, right? Well, when all the offices around the country had turned in their numbers, headquarters put them all into a spreadsheet and sent them out to us. Everyone's numbers were displayed, and mine was near the bottom. The report showed that nearly everyone reported that they had made more calls than I had. Canun himself said that he'd made forty-one new contacts!"

"And how did that make you feel?" she asked.

Whoever said there was no such thing as a stupid question had never met this therapist. It had made me feel terrible, of course! I had been pissed! Really pissed! But to her I just said, "It made me upset." I must have looked like I was holding back because she looked into my eyes like she was trying to read me.

Then she said, "What are you thinking about?"

I said, "I don't know. I guess about how I don't really have anyone that I can talk to."

"You're not married?"

"No."

"Do you have any siblings?"

"No."

"What about your parents? Tell me about them," she said.

"Well, my dad is around, but he's been sick, so I don't want to burden him with all that I'm going through. And my stepmother, she likes to see me in turmoil. My real mother died when I was five."

The therapist said, "Chantell, do you ever have thoughts of hurting yourself?"

"What? No!" I said, annoyed and wondering where she was going with her questioning.

She was staring at me all hard. If she was going to start tripping, I was going to leave. She said, "Well I am just asking, because it seems like you're holding something back. And I wouldn't want you to do anything harmful to yourself."

Okie-dokie! This woman was a fully trained and accredited looney. I picked up my purse and said, "I'm sorry. This isn't really working for me. I have to go." I took my $10 copayment out of my wallet and set it in front of her.

She looked surprised. "Was it something that I said?"

I knew that going to see a shrink was a mistake! That kind of crap was the very reason I never told people my business. Why would I want to hurt myself? Was she trying to build up some kind of crazy case against me or something? I regretted telling her any of my business. Lord only knew what they did with their information. And what if they reported all this stuff back to my job? I could hear it around the office now: "Don't tell anyone it came from me, but Chantell called Canun in the middle of the night talking nonsense, now she's talking to a shrink, and I heard that her shrink thinks she is suicidal." The girls in HR would be gossiping about this for weeks.

# 16

# crawling back

After I recovered from my therapy visit, I spent the rest of the day trying to stay busy and move right along with my life; I was even praying when I remembered to. The phone rang as I went into the kitchen. I'd bought fresh flowers from a street vendor earlier, and they were sitting on the counter drying out and in need of water. I opened the cabinet under the sink and looked for a vase. The phone rang again.

"Hello," I said. I turned on the water and rinsed the vase.

"Chantell, this is Eric."

"Eric, I am not coming over, so what do you want?"

"I just want to talk. Why are you still mad at me?"

I took the flowers out of the plastic and untied the bundle. They were bright pink with long green stems. They sort of looked like sunflowers except for their big pink round heads. "I'm not mad at you, Eric. I just need some stability in my life."

"Chantell, we have to talk. I want us to move forward too. We have to pull it together. What about our trip to Mexico?"

I knew that he'd come crawling back sooner or later. And to be truthful, he was right. With everything else going on, I hadn't really thought about how we'd handle Mexico. But I wasn't going to let on that we were on the same page. Nope, first I needed to hear how much he needed me, and missed me.

"Hello!?! Eric?? You're not going to Mexico with *me*."

"Chantell, I paid my money just like you did. And I've taken time off work already. So, trust me, baby, I will be going to Mexico with you."

Look at my baby, I thought, all demanding to be with me and everything! I smiled. "Forget that, Eric! You're not—"

"Look Chawnee, let's stop playing games. You know that I miss you. I need to see you. We have a lot to talk about, and, baby, I've got you something."

This was working better than I expected! I took a paring knife from my wooden chopping block and cut some of the stem off of the three flowers. I tested the length and saw that they were long enough to fit in the vase perfectly.

"Chantell, let me come over."

"You must be kidding," I said, though in my mind I thought of how nice having company would be. And I did want my present! I hoped it was jewelry.

"You're not foolin' with that girl on the boat?"

"No, baby."

I leaned against the kitchen counter. The cabinet above me was slightly ajar. I reached up to close it, and something in it caught my eye. It was the Mason jars. I reached up and grabbed two of them. I set them down on top of the counter and put the vase back under the sink. I'd bought a box of jars last year when I decided that I was going to learn to make fruit preserves, like my mother used to.

"Baby, she wasn't anything to me. I'm not interested in her. I love you."

And there it was. He loved me. That's what I needed to hear. Loneliness was an ugly thing. I put the flowers in the two jars. They looked beautiful.

"Just for a little while."

"Okay, Eric," I said, "but don't expect anything from me. And you're doing all the talking. I don't have anything to say," I said. "And don't think I'm doing anything with you either," I added.

By this time next year, I would have a phat rock on my finger! I knew which one I wanted, too. I'd seen it at a jewelry store in the

Hillsdale shopping mall. It was a carat-and-a-half princess-cut diamond set in a platinum ring.

"Okay, Chantell, I'll see you this evening when I get off of work."

"Wait. Hold on a minute. What time? You can't just come over here whenever you want to, you know? So don't even think that." He needed to fully respect me as his wife-to-be.

"Okay." He laughed. "Umm, let's say seven-thirty?"

"Okay, honey. I'll see you then," I said.

I didn't have a job to go to, so I didn't know how I would spend my day until Eric got off work. I wasn't going to Tia's. I didn't feel like going back to Daddy's. I knew that I shouldn't spend any money, so any major shopping was out. I needed to get some fresh air. I already had fresh flowers, but I could use some incense, to refresh the house, and that was cheap.

I took my shower and went through all of my clothes in the closet. Gucci, Chanel, Dolce & Gabbana, INC, and all the others. They didn't matter at the moment. I didn't want to be alone anymore, and with Eric Summit fighting for us to be together, I didn't have to be. He loved me. I pushed past all of the clothes and put on a navy blue NYU sweatshirt and a pair of jeans. We were going to work it out—I'd make sure of it—and we could move on with our lives. Yes, that made me feel a bit better. I pulled my hair back into a ponytail, put on a bit of eyeliner and lipstick, and left the house to get my incense.

Berkeley was a place where the people were unlike any other folks. There was a sense of calmness there, yet it was, well, Berkeley. Home of the hippies, the revolutionaries, the homeless, the street vendors, the eclectic, the artists, the musicians, the insane, the extremely wealthy, and of course, the students of the university. And they all walked the streets together. I'd always liked Berkeley. It was an unusual retreat, a haven. It was a place where most people who were abstract enough to stand out somehow blended in and stayed a spell.

It was just the place to get my mind off my thoughts. I pulled into the Berkeley flea market. There were people there who were from all types of places and nations. Ethiopians, Indians, Asians, Caucasians, Mexicans, Panamanians, Cubans, Trinidadians, and African Americans. A perfect melting pot.

The smell of gumbo drifted through the air from one of the vendors over in the exotic foods corner. People were walking, chatting, selling old bikes, and applying temporary henna tattoos to arms, belly buttons, ankles, and nipples. There were people selling deodorant and toilet paper, eight-track tapes and old clothes. There were old framed paintings on velvet, and big wooden forks and spoons that used to hang on people's walls thirty years before. An antiquer's dream come true, that's what it was. People sold stuff on tables made of old sawhorses with wood paneling laid on top. The makeshift tables looked like they had been torn out of old abandoned houses.

I walked around until I found an incense dealer. "How much for these?" I asked the lady.

"Ten for a dollar, yaknow." She was a black woman with a hard accent. She was probably only forty, yet she had several teeth missing in the front. The woman looked tired, like she had seen very weary times in her life.

I grabbed a single bag off the little bundle of long plastic bags that lay on the table in front of me. Then I began to pick up different kinds of incense and smell them one by one.

"That one called Frombradi," she said. "It means 'let go, and let love.'"

I smelled it. Let go and let love was what I was talkin' about! It smelled thick and heavy, yet fruity. Like amber wood and mango fruit. I put some in the bag. I grabbed another and inhaled its scent.

"Oh my goodness," I said. "This is wonderful. What is it?"

"It's de lemongrass," she said.

It smelled very clean and citrusy. But not in a furniture polish sort of way—in a lovely grapefruit-and-lemon-spice-in-an-evening-bubble-bath sort of way. I loved the smell. I was very drawn to that smell. I hadn't done much of that lately—paid attention to things that I was naturally drawn to. I'd read somewhere that we should take notice of what affected us. What we gravitated to. I inhaled again. I was definitely drawn to Frombradi, and lemongrass. I added more lemongrass into the little bag.

I had maybe ten in the bag when I heard the sound in the near distance. Drums. A couple of bongos, then more joined in. It was exciting, and I wanted to go see. It was so—so Berkeley-like! I quickly filled up the little bag with twenty and headed toward the music. *Dun-du-du-dun, dun-du-du-dun-du-du* . . . People were gathering at the northern corner of the flea market. Four people played, then there were six, then ten, and before you knew it, there were as many as twenty players, mostly men. They were sitting on the ground. Their legs were crossed and they were having a real jam session. No other musical instruments, just bongos. And you could hear them finding one another's vibe in the air. And when they got it, you knew it. They all played together on some universal rhythm. People stood around tapping their feet and moving their legs. Everyone was vibing off of this feeling that was being expressed through fingers tapping on leather. At first I thought I'd watch. Then I started moving to the beat, and it was hard to resist. Without thinking, I "let go" like the Frombradi incense and moved my body in motion to the music, not knowing what my next move would be. I was not sure if others were staring at me. I didn't care. I danced. My eyes were closed. I moved and I swayed. Caught up in a zone, I grooved to the wordless thumps. If Charlotte could have seen me, she would have had a fit. To her, this was not ladylike. Here I was approaching thirty years old and acting like a vagabond, a gypsy. I moved my hands in the air. It was freeing. There was no fear, and no worry of what people thought of me. My clothes didn't matter. And had I been wearing old sweats, or stiletto heels, I still would have danced that way at that very moment. The only important perception of me was my own, I thought. I opened my eyes, and there was a whole group of people dancing. We were all just one, just us and one thud of the drum played by many people. I wondered if they did this every week.

That evening at home, I flipped through my closet again and wondered what I was going to wear for my premarital date with Eric. We hadn't seen each other in a month, and I wanted to look tempting. I lit a Frombradi incense.

I'd brought home more fresh flowers from the market. I took them into the kitchen and cut the stems down to fit in more jars. I filled some Mason jars partway with water. I put two big white flowers in one jar, some pink ones in another, and mixed up the colors in a third. The pink flowers had a hint of yellow on the inside and looked beautiful. To me, flowers looked much prettier this way. More pretty than if they were in some $150 vase.

I didn't need a therapist. I just needed to dance a little bit, see Eric, get some flowers, and a little bit of Frombradi. I put one jar on top of my glass and wrought-iron coffee table. I left one on the counter in the kitchen and took another to my bedroom, placing it on my nightstand next to the bed. I reassured myself that Eric would not be in there tonight, but he'd be here soon.

I'd just stepped out of the shower when my doorbell rang. "Just a moment," I yelled toward the door. I sprayed on some Vickie's Secret body moisturizer. I was a bit nervous about seeing Eric, and I tracked water all over my carpet as I stepped out of the bathroom.

I slid on a short, one-piece tangerine dress that I knew was too short to wear anywhere except in the house. I rationalized that I wasn't actually trying to seduce Eric or anything, I just wanted him to see what he would get every day if and when he stopped running the streets and committed to me exclusively. Besides, I'd just gotten out of the shower, and I needed to wear that dress so I could easily apply lotion to my legs and arms and still have clothes on. I dimmed the lighting and went to the door.

"I'll be right there."

If this worked out, I was going to see what he thought of honeymooning in Jamaica. "Who is it?" I asked.

"It's me, Chantell," said Eric.

I opened the door and my porch light helped me to catch a vision of masculinity at its highest. He wore a slightly tight gray shirt that emphasized his muscular body. It fit snugly over his ex-football-playing arms. He wore gray slacks and thick, heavy-looking black leather shoes that were cut straight at the toes and smooth all over. He smiled and his pearly whites glistened. His mustache was immaculate. It couldn't have been more perfectly lined. And he smelled like a hundred-dollar bottle of Issey Miyake cologne.

"So, can I come in?" he asked.

"Yeah, sure."

I stepped back so that he could come in, but the porch light allowed him to check me out first. He looked at my face, my legs, my dress. He looked at my French-manicured toes. Then his hand came from behind his back, and he handed me a hat-sized box.

"Here, beautiful," he said.

I squealed. He watched my every move. His mouth formed into a smile. He nodded his head a couple of times at me and walked in. I smirked—he was so arrogant, with his fine self!

"Open it," he said.

I smiled. "Okay."

I opened the medium-sized black-and-white box that was trimmed with golden ribbon. It was a new Chanel handbag, and it was cute, cute, cute! It must have cost $300! I could see that he loved me. I kissed him on the cheek. "Thank you, baby. Thank you!"

"You're welcome."

He was a sweetie. I went over to the television and turned it on for him. I was still dripping water from the shower. I could feel the heat from his eyes burning on me. I turned around toward him and saw the way that he sat on my couch. I noted how long his legs were. And tried not to lust. I would be Mrs. Summit soon enough. His elbow rested on the arm of my couch, and his fingers gently supported his tilted head. His gaze was so intense.

"Here." I handed him the television remote.

He turned on the TV to this soft music station. The screen went blank and Maxwell crooned out of the speakers in my entertainment center.

"I'll be back," I said as I grabbed the lotion that I'd brought out of the shower and headed toward my room.

"Where are you going?"

"To my room. I'll be right back."

He motioned toward the lotion bottle and said, "Let me do that for you." He held out his hand for the lotion.

"No," I said.

"Girl, stop trippin', and let your man do it."

"Oh, okay," I giggled.

He laughed, got up from the couch, and motioned his hands for me to lie down. I did and told myself that maybe it was just innocent when he was talking to the woman from Australia. I didn't stay and join them, so for all I knew, I'd probably jumped the gun.

My living room smelled of mango fruit and smoked wood as the incense curled throughout the house. Eric went to my room, brought back a pillow for me, and put it under my head as I lay on my stomach. He poured some Vickie's Secret lotion in his hands and rubbed them together.

He started with my feet, rubbing the lotion all over and pressing firmly into the arches of my feet with both thumbs. I cooed like a newborn. I needed to tell him that I was supposed to be his wife. He rubbed my calves, massaging the muscles and applying just the right amount of pressure.

"Eric, I don't want to have premarital sex anymore. We're getting older."

"Chantell, we have been dealing with each other for a long time."

I closed my eyes and gave in to this sensation that was how heaven must feel.

His strong yellow fingers went up my calves, rubbed my thighs. He raised my dress to get the back of my thighs, but I smoothed it back down. This was getting out of hand. He went up to my shoulders, rubbed in those creases. "Ohhhhh" was all I managed to say.

"I know," he replied.

I had to stop this. What about the promise I had made to God? I prided myself on keeping my promises. Eric went for more lotion, and I turned over and faced him. I slid my bright orange dress back down again and looked at him. I shook my head no. He leaned down over me and gave me a little kiss on the lips, and nodded yes. Lotion was still all over his hands. Now was the time to tell him.

I put my manicured fingers to his face and said, "Let's get married, Eric."

With his knees in my couch, he leaned his face down toward me and looked me square in the eyes. He said, "Okay."

I was so happy. "For real?"

"Um-hmph," he said.

We were engaged! I kissed his forehead and his cheek. I didn't need no therapist; there was nothing wrong with me. I was going to call Tia and tell her that I was joining her in the ranks of the married. Maybe I'd go over to my old church and see if my old pastor could marry us quickly. This was great. Me and my little dress were somethin' else!

Eric sat up and pulled his shirt from over his head. I kissed his chest. My husband. I knew that I'd made that promise to God for a reason. Now, look, I could be Mrs. Eric Summit as early as next weekend.

"Let's celebrate," he said in a thick voice.

"Okay," I said.

But he wasn't my husband quite yet. "Do you have a condom?" I asked.

"No worries, baby," he said as he pulled one out of his pocket. Good. We hadn't been apart so long that he'd forgotten the rules.

Man, I couldn't wait to tell Tia!

# 17

# thank you and good night

Later that evening, Eric and I lay in my bed, underneath my goosedown comforter. We'd been watching television, and he'd dozed off. We were wearing the matching pajamas that I'd picked up for us at Nordy's last Christmas. We were finally getting some use out of them. They were green-and-cream paisleys with ducks patterned on them. He had the pants and the shirt, and it was mostly green. I had the big nightshirt, and it was mostly cream. I watched television and listened to his nighttime sighs until I got tired. I grabbed the remote, turned off the TV, and moved closer to him. I stared. The waves in his closely cut hair could make you seasick if you weren't careful. I rubbed them in the direction that he'd trained them to grow.

I lay there fantasizing. We were going to make some pretty children one day. Tall, strong ones that were beautiful shades of brown. Little football players, like their dad. And little girls with perfect little preteen physiques and long hair. And they'd dance in leotards to jazz and ballet. I got closer and put my arm over his chest. He smelled good. The thought of us getting married made me feel comforted; I made a soft sigh as I exhaled. He felt me snuggling close to him.

"Night, Sabrina," he mumbled.

I sat there frozen. I didn't say a word. I took my arm from around him, put lots of blanket in between us, moved back over to my side of the bed, and closed my eyes. I was thinking that I must have heard him wrong. I kept trying to figure out what sounded like Sabrina. West Covina. A tambourine-a. The night scene-a.

As I thought about it more, my eyes started to fill with water. I wiped the tears away, cuz this wasn't a time to be weak. Besides, I now realized what he'd said. He hadn't said good night, Sabrina, he'd said, good night, sweet dream-a's!

I shook him. He frowned. "Eric! Eric, wake up," I said. I touched his shoulder with my hand, and he fanned it like he was shooing a fly.

I shook him again. "Eric Summit!"

He opened his eyes. "What?"

"Eric, if my old pastor, Pastor Fields, could marry us next weekend—you know, just a small little service until we could save for a larger shindig—could we do it?"

He yawned. "What? Naw, girl! Are you still on that kick? We ain't getting married just like that!" He rubbed his eyes.

"You're playing with me, right? Eric, you distinctly said that we could get married. I hadn't had sex in almost four months because I was trying to be faithful to God. And I broke that because—" My voice was cracking, and I wiped away a tear before it reached my cheek.

He shook his head and lay back on the bed. "You're just determined to tie me down, huh? Chantell, I am not ready to be tied down. So back up."

"Well, why did you tell me that we were going to get married, then? You said it like I could go get my dress."

I didn't know what to believe anymore, then the anger rose up in me. "You told me that we were getting married, then you lay in my bed, called me by another woman's name. How am I pressuring you, huh? How?" My voice cracked.

He shook his head like I was just pathetic. "Girl, I didn't say all that. What I said was—"

I couldn't take it. I slapped him upside the head as hard as I could. "Get out. Just get out of my bed!"

"Chantell! You'd better not hit me anymore. Understand?"

"No, I don't understand!" I wasn't afraid of him. Eric may have put me through a lot, but one thing that he didn't do was put his hands on me. "And who the heck is Sabrina?" I demanded to know.

He just shook his head and tisked, like I was a hopeless case, and looked around for his pants.

"That's right. That's right! Get out of my bed! Get out of my life! Who wants to marry your old cheating behind anyway!"

I did, but that was beside the point.

Oftentimes, when you lose something, it heightens your desire to have it. I hadn't given Eric two years of my life for nothing.

When he left, I put my head in the pillow where he had been, smelled his scent, and cried.

# 18

## sunday morning

Two days had passed and I was still moping around. Humiliated is a good description of how I felt. I could still smell Eric's scent on my pillow when the sun's rays came through my window and hit my bed. I opened my eyes when the phone rang, but I just lay there. My plan to get Eric to marry me had failed, and I felt both alone and ashamed.

I wanted to hear something good. I needed to hear something good. I clicked on my thirty-six-inch television, and a man on an infomercial boasted that he could teach you to make a fortune in real estate if you sent in $299.99. I clicked the channel again, and Andy Griffith and Opie sat in the front of a police car on the black-and-white TV screen. With another click, a stainless steel, state-of-the-art juicing machine sucked the juice out of an orange, making instant juice. I clicked again and a choir in electric blue robes sang as they held a high-pitched note uniformly with their mouths in an O. I thought about my old church with the brown wooden cross on top. I remembered they displayed a big banner out in front that read: "Come Fellowship With Us!"

The alarm clock read 8:52 a.m. I looked over at my walk-in closet and spotted a cream and blue two-piece suit with the cleaner's plastic wrap around it, one that I hardly ever wore. I took the suit out and turned on the water in the shower.

The Faith Center was a big beige two-story building that could seat more than two thousand people. As a child, I remembered my grandmother being involved in the building fund and new member service committee. Membership then was well over six hundred, but on any given Sunday there were three or four hundred people there. But now with all of the cars brimming in the parking lot, I bet it was hard to get a seat.

I was embarrassed about trying to go to church; I knew that Jesus forgave, but it felt like everyone in there was looking at me like they knew something was up. So I rushed up the big steps and into the front lobby with my head down, incogNegro. I hoped that Pastor Fields didn't recognize me. In addition to misleading God and getting my freaky deaky on Friday, I hadn't been to church in over a decade, and to make things really bad, I didn't know what I was thinking when I selected my apparel that morning. The suit was cute, it came from Bebe, but the three-quarter-length cream jacket fit me like a bustier, and the slit in the back of my cream skirt went almost all the way up to the jacket.

I was headed upstairs to the balcony to find a corner and be alone when an usher touched my arm. "Good morning, God bless you, sister, we're not seating anyone in the balcony just yet. We want to fill up the main sanctuary first. Please follow me."

Oh, great, I thought. I followed her over to the doors that entered the sanctuary, and another usher escorted me to a seat.

A woman that I knew, Sister Monica, was posted at the doors to the right. I remembered her from going to church long ago with my grandmother. She'd been a single young lady who'd had a set of twin boys, and found Christ when she was about twenty years old. I must have been eleven or twelve years old back then.

The inside of the church was decorated in blue and white. The pews were made of solid oak and the seating area was covered in a dark blue fabric. The walls were white and the windows were covered in stained glass that reflected the sun with different colors of blue, yellow, red, and green.

I recognized a lot of the faces, though I didn't speak to anyone while I waited for church to begin. I sat there quietly in my guilt and chewed on a piece of gum. There were people everywhere, black folks, standing and talking. Older ladies in hats. Deacons in the front row. Young ones, old ones. Tons of young people in jeans, all casualed out.

I thought about my little ploy on Friday night and wondered how I could have gone about it differently. A woman came up to the microphone and asked us to close our eyes and pray before service began. I bowed my head and tried to clear my mind.

I thanked God for my father's continued recovery. I asked Him to guide me. I asked Him for direction with my job. I asked Him to aid me in my relationship with my stepmother. I asked Him to bless my friends and family. I told Him that I'd gone for months without sex, and that I knew that I'd blown it, but that I knew Eric was for me. I asked Him to let Eric see that we needed to pair up and build our lives together. Amen.

"Excuse me, baby, are you Sister Hattie Brumwick's granddaughter?" said a high-pitched voice that sounded like a squeak. I knew that voice.

"Yes, I am. Hello, Sister Mable," I said and turned to the row behind me.

She looked the same as ever. She was a big woman and walked with a cane. She had gray hair that she wore in shiny silver curls. She wore a gray dress with a white collar and clip-on earrings with big teardrop-shaped pearls dangling from them.

"Come here, chile, and hug my neck! How you doin', baby?" She extended her arms to me over the bench.

I hugged her. "I am good. How are you?"

"Oh, good, good. I am good. I'm so glad you're here," she said, and held on to my hand. "How is your father and your stepmother?"

Wow, this woman had a memory on her!

"They are well. How is your family?" I asked.

"Everybody is blessed. Molina is up there. You remember my granddaughter, don't you?" she said and pointed up to the balcony.

"Yes ma'am, I do."

Losing the card game to Molina was the reason that I'd had to kiss the little boy, up there in that balcony. I looked up, and now the balcony was filled with as many adults as children.

"Yep. I am glad you're here, baby. You doin' the right thang. Just come on back to Jesus," she said.

I nodded uncomfortably and turned back around. I wasn't entirely sure that I should have been here in the first place.

Two minutes later, the church's double doors opened and the choir came in. *"Prais-es to your name, Lord! We'll sing prais-es to your name!"* They sounded like a band of angels. Extraordinary. *"Prais-es to your name! Hallelujah! Prais-es to your name!"* With glorious roars, and smiles on their faces, they marched in to the tune of the music. I watched in awe as they clapped their hands and sang their hearts out.

*Lifting you up!*
*Hallelujah!*
*Prais-es to your name!*

When they finished singing, the choir took their seats in the choir stand. Pastor Fields took to the podium. She looked pretty, in a long white robe and her hair all pulled back into a long gray ponytail.

She looked around and spoke into the microphone as she began. "Did you shut the door on yesterday when you got up this morning?"

I looked at her and stopped chewing my gum.

She said it again. "I asked you if you shut the door on yesterday when you got up this morning the way that God says for us to do in Lamentations 3:23? We are all human and we err sometimes, and when we do we can't afford to go around holding on to junk. Jesus paid the price for our sins, and all that He requires is for us to confess our sins with a clean heart and ask for forgiveness."

"Amen!" went the congregation.

"Let's talk a little more today about forgiveness. Is that okay?"

And before I realized it, I was yelling out with the congregation, "Yes, Pastor!" Whew, this message was right on time.

Then I heard Brother Jacobs give his trademark "All right now, Preacha!" from across the room. I looked around to see where he was. I couldn't see him but it made me smile.

Pastor Fields told us that God forgives, and that there is no need to dwell in guilt. She said that we have all fallen short of God's glory, and when we do, we just have to call on Him for forgiveness and pick ourselves back up again. My faith was being fed in a major way.

It felt good to be at church. The message made a lot of sense. The vibe was good, and I felt God's presence in the place. So when Pastor Fields asked for people to come forth and kneel at the altar to pray, I unashamedly stood up and walked down the aisle.

# 19

# business as usual

That evening, I realized it was high time for me to get back to work. So I phoned Canun and left him a message on his voice mail.

"Hello, Canun. It's Chantell Meyers. Look I umm . . . As you know, I've been under the weather. Ahem." I cleared my throat. "I have not been feeling well. But, I am ready to come back to work, and I'll see you tomorrow. Umm, well, that's it for now. Okay, bye."

I hung up the phone and patted the back of my damp neck, because quite honestly, I didn't know if I had a job or not.

Canun called me back early Monday morning and said that he would see me in the office around 8 a.m. That was promising. It was always hard for him to keep secrets, but he'd managed not to give me any telltale signs on where he stood on the matter of my absence. He simply said that he'd see me when I got in the office.

It was 7:50 a.m. when I walked into the office confidently and sat down at my desk. The other reps were staring at me with their eyes bugged out. I wanted to look at them and say "Boo!" to see if they'd scatter.

My coworker Cameron strolled over with a new pixie haircut and a pair of designer jeans. "Chantell, I am glad you're back."

"Thanks, Cam," I said and worked on my list of clients that I needed to contact.

It was obvious that my little absence was the talk of our division, because the other reps kept going over to one another's desks and whispering, smirking, and looking my way. Or they'd glance at me from over the cubicle. I sat there with pen to paper, making notes. I could smell my subtle perfume dancing on my wrist. My lips glistened with MAC lip gloss. I brushed my flyaway soft hair from my face. I was aloof, unaffected, and uncaring. A couple of times I met their stares, and smiled and said, "Did you need to say something to me? No? Oh, well, by the way you were looking at me, I thought you needed to tell me something."

I knew what they were whispering. They were asking one another who did I think I was. They were saying that the company was giving me special privileges, or that I was sleeping with Canun, or that affirmative action had saved my job or something stupid like that. I'd been there four years and I knew the type of things that were said when office drama reared its ugly head.

I had work to do. It looked like someone had been covering my account list, but there were a lot of little maintenance-type things that needed to be done on my accounts. I had to ignore the stares and the gossip. Michael Pearson, the rep who worked exclusively with car dealerships, had the desk across from me. He got an instant e-mail from the guy next to me and said aloud, "Yep, I feel the same way." They instant e-mailed back and forth a couple more times, and their computers dinged each time they received a message. They were going to get told off if I heard anything even remotely resembling my name or my situation come from them.

I had been at work going on two hours, and I hadn't heard from Canun yet. And I was beginning to wonder if he was just going to let it go when an instant message from him popped up on my computer monitor: CHANTELL, CAN I SEE YOU IN MY OFFICE FOR A MOMENT?

SURE, I typed back and hit send.

I grabbed a pen, a notepad, and my purse in case he was giving me my walking papers. I looked up at the awards and plaques on my cubicle walls and told myself not to worry, that I could get another job relatively quickly. My heart beat like a drum, and I almost believed that my nosy coworkers could hear it as I walked past their desks.

His door was almost closed so I tapped it lightly.

"Chantell. Hi, have a seat."

I sat down. Give it to me straight, Canun.

He shuffled papers around on his desk. "So, are you feeling better? You seemed awfully upset from your phone call last week."

"I'm feeling better. Thank you."

"That's good to hear. But frankly, I would have expected a little better communication on your part, Chantell. You're a professional. We can't have you MIA."

Yeah, well, I would have expected a little less backstabbing on your part too Canun, I thought. But I said, "I understand, and I apologize for the way that I handled myself. I was just suffering from a little burnout, but I am better now. At the time, I felt it was necessary to temporarily remove myself from the work environment in order for me to reenergize and be better able to do my job, for the team!" I smiled. "See, I needed to rejuvenate in order for me to come back at optimal performance. Now I am back, and I am rejuvenated, and I am ready to exceed all of my revenue goals." I stuck my shoulders back, and I put my chest out a little so that my body language showed him that I was an asset not just to the company but also to him. I knew how to speak Canun Ramsey speak. Canun wanted to make VP, and the revenue that I brought in made him look good. Darn good.

And that was it, that was pretty much all that I needed to say.

"Oh, absolutely! Chantell, we all need a break sometimes, certainly, we can all understand that. This could have been grounds for termination, however. We'll let this serve as a verbal warning." Then he whispered, "In the future, however, let's keep the lines of communication open, okay? I had to cover for you, you know. I told the big guys that you told me you were out ill."

"Oh, thanks, Canun," I said with a smile.

"Ahh, don't worry about it. I got your back."

I smiled and laughed. Yeah, I'll bet he did.

I was going to start back to my desk when I remembered the cruise. I turned around and went back to Canun's door.

"Oh, Canun," I said.

"Yes?"

"You remember my vacation a week from Friday. Don't you?"

"Huh? Oh, yes. Just make sure your desk is taken care of before you go. I don't want anything left unattended to."

"Sure thing, Canun, and thank you."

I stopped by HR, just to make sure that they knew that I would be out the next week, before I finished cleaning up my accounts.

## 20

# hello again

Tia and I sat in a booth at TGIF's in Jack London Square on Monday evening. We were laughing, chatting, eating appetizers while waiting for our dinner to arrive.

"So how was your mother-in-law's visit?" I asked.

"It was fine."

"Really?"

"Well, no, actually she got on my nerves pretty badly, talking to Ron like he was a five-year-old. But I got through it," said Tia.

I laughed.

" 'Ronnie, you want Momma to make you dinner? Ronnie, when is the last time you had a real sweet potato pie, baby?' " mimicked Tia. "Then she'd look at me and say things like, 'You know, Tiwina, when Ronnie was a teenager, his girlfriends were always on the thick side. He sho' changed up with you. Didn't he?' " Tia paused.

"What did you say?" I asked.

"I didn't say anything. I just smiled with my lips tight the whole weekend. Like this." She plastered a hard fake grin across her face.

I laughed.

"And Ron, he looked like a deer caught in the headlights the whole weekend. I was so mad at him," she said.

I cracked up. They were a mess. The waitress brought our food and we ate and got caught up on each other's lives some more.

My back was to a group of four or five at the booth behind me. I hadn't been paying much attention, but I heard someone say, "True. Very true. When you have little black girls and society tells them that they aren't beautiful, that their hair is not long enough, that their features are too much, lots of time they don't fly like they could. Their wings stay at their sides. They stagnate. But ohhh, when you make sure that they are aware of how beautiful and unique they really are, then, my friends, you have something different. Then you have little Venuses and little Serenas running around."

"True."

"Well said, Doctor," said another man's voice.

Tia looked at me from across our table and whispered, "Eavesdropper."

I smiled at her and shrugged. "I'll be back. I'm going to the little girls' room—I have to go pee-pee."

"Uhh, that's TMI, Too Much Information, and you know it! Just go. Please." Tia shooed me away.

I giggled and got up from the booth.

I started toward the bathroom at the back of the building. I looked good with my light pink slacks and matching soft pink wraparound shirt. It crisscrossed in the front and tied in the back. Apparently someone else agreed, because I could feel him staring at me. I didn't bother to see who it was, though, because it didn't matter. My heart was set; I was going to marry Eric, and that was all there was to that.

I came out of the bathroom, and a tall figure walked over to me. I sort of looked away, staring straight ahead, looking at nothing between his head and his shoulder. I was going to say to him, "Look, sweetheart, I'm sure you're fly and all that good stuff, but I'm already taken. Okay?" Then he had the audacity to touch my arm. Excuse you! I thought. I looked over at him and was going to speak, but I saw that there was something familiar about this face. I think it was the eyebrows—no, it was the lips. I couldn't place it. He was maybe six feet, with a thin yet muscular frame. He had smooth chocolate skin, like Tyson Beckford. He had a perfectly trimmed goatee and thick, perfect eyebrows. Where the heck did I know him from? Then he leaned over to me, kissed me on the cheek, and said, "Hello, Frog Face."

My heart started beating like crazy, and the wall had to hold me up. Breathe, Chantell, breathe. "Keith Rashaad Talbit?"

"Yeah," he said with a big grin.

"Oh my God, Keith Rashaad! I can't believe—what are you doing here?"

He laughed. "I'm glad to see you too."

I blushed and fumbled over my words. "No, I mean, I didn't know you were— I mean, you're here and you didn't call. Not that you *had* to call me or anything. I just haven't seen you in a long time."

Back then, years ago, after I'd kissed little Keith in the balcony on Sunday, he'd started shamelessly following me around. It wasn't like I had a ton of best girlfriends. Before you knew it, we were playing Batman and Wonder Woman on the steps outside of the church while our grandmothers attended committee meetings.

I guess I had a right to say all of this to him now. I mean, he was my childhood best friend.

My grandmother used to say that bad luck came in threes, and here I was staring at the third great loss of my life. I hadn't seen him in sixteen years.

We stood in the back of the restaurant near the bathrooms. There were pictures all over the walls. We blocked the hallway. I looked at his face. He had changed so much! As a little kid, Keith had been sickly. Eczema, broken arm, ear infections, you name it. Then as he reached middle school, he had acne galore. But he was so bighearted, and smart. And he had these eyebrows that were magnificent.

"Can I hug you?" he asked.

"Aw, man, can you?" I stepped closer to him.

Then he took his arms and wrapped them around me. It was a big strong hug, and my feet rose up off the ground. I put my arms around his neck, and felt him sway with me just a bit. When he let go, he looked at me, and with his index finger he touched the little mole above my eyebrow.

"Chantell, look at you. You've gone from ponytails and Band-Aids to beauty queen."

"Stop." I blushed.

"I'm serious, you look incredible."

"Well, thank you, Keith Rashaad. You look amazing yourself," I said.

I thought about when we were children and wondered about his asthma. I remembered a time when we were about twelve. We were racing in the street and Keith had an asthma attack. Keith was my acekoomboom, my buddy, my roaddawg, and I thought that he was going to die. So I ran. I sprinted, as fast as I could, four blocks to his home. I got his inhaler and brought it back to him.

A man was trying to get past us in the hallway. "Excuse me," he said.

"Oh, no, excuse us," said Keith. He put his hand to the arch of my back and walked with me a few steps, till we were out of the hallway. I still couldn't get over how he'd changed. It was like the story of the duck that turned into the swan. I tried not to, but I couldn't help it: I looked at his arms for hive marks from all those food allergies. I saw nothing.

Keith must have seen me looking, because he laughed. "It's all gone," he said in his smooth, deep voice.

"What?"

"The asthma, the hives, I outgrew it all. And I wear the Keri lotion every day."

He chuckled at his own joke. Because of the hives and lack of lotion, Keith often had looked chalky as a kid.

I stood there, looking at him in awe. This was amazing. He was hypnotic. Then I realized how ridiculous I probably looked staring at him, and I was embarrassed.

"Who are you with here? I mean, I'm here with my friend Tia. Are you alone?"

He smiled. "I'm actually here with the group behind where you were sitting. We're with the Boys and Girls Clubs of America."

"Did you move back to the Bay Area?"

"Oh, well, no. I'm here on a three-month project. But while I'm here, I am going to spend some time mentoring kids." He motioned over to his table with his eyes. "We were talking, and I saw you when you got up. I knew that it was you right off, when I saw the mole and those sad eyes."

I looked at him. He thought my eyes were sad.

"Keith, can you come and meet my friend Tia? Do you have time?"

He nodded. "Sure. I'd love to. In fact, we were just finishing up. Let me excuse myself and I'll be right back."

When he came back, I put my arm in his and walked with him toward my table. At the table I said, "Tia, this is a very old and dear friend of mine, Keith Rashaad Talbit. Keith Rashaad, this is my best friend, Tia Pardou."

Keith shook her hand and sat down next to me. "It's a pleasure to meet you," he said.

Tia said, "Keith, it's so nice to meet you too. I feel like I have known you because I have heard your name so many times."

"Good things, I hope," he said.

"All good things," Tia said. She looked at me and raised her eyebrows.

We chatted awhile and Tia and I learned that Keith was a new doctor, who had just completed his residency in Boston. He'd been granted the privilege of working on a special skin-grafting research team at the Oakland Children's Hospital. I was so proud of him. His parents had died in a fire when he was an infant, and so it was fitting that he chose to work with burn victims who were children.

"I am so happy for you, Keith Rashaad."

"Thank you, Chawnee."

And I was happy for him. His Grandmother Edna had raised him until she died. Then he got sent away. He'd never called. I used to wonder if he'd died.

"I'm glad that you are doing well, Chantell," he said after I told him what I had been up to. The three of us continued to eat and chat, until the waitress made her way back over to us. "Can I get you guys dessert, or something else to drink?"

"Can I have an iced tea, with no lemon?" I asked.

Tia ordered a hot tea.

"And what would you like, sir?"

Keith Rashaad said, "Um, how about a root beer?"

Tia's cell phone rang. She answered: "Hello? Oh, hi, honey!" she piped up. She held up a finger as if to say that she'd be right back, and slid out of the booth. It was perfect timing because I had something to ask that couldn't wait any longer.

"Keith, where did you go?" I didn't say when we were children— I didn't need to.

He took a long breath, then he said, "I couldn't call, Chantell. When Grandma Edna died it was . . . it was very hard for me."

There was a lot of energy bouncing from Keith to me, and from me to Keith. When Tia walked back, I was sure she could see it. Maybe she'd planned to sit back down with us a while longer, but that energy was unmistakable.

"Hey, look, you guys, I'm going to head home . . ." She picked up her coat from the back of the chair. "Ron's rented videos, and he's waiting for me." She gave us both a hug.

"I'll call you later," I said.

"Tia, it was nice to meet you," Keith said.

And before you knew it, we were alone.

"I tried to call you once, you know? I found a Chantell Meyers on AOL's directory with a phone number. And I was just so sure it was you. I left a message, but when I didn't get a call back, I figured it wasn't you . . ." He looked a little embarrassed. "I was going to just suck it up and go knock on your dad's door, once I got here. But I guess I don't have to."

I looked over the table at him and was reminded of those Sundays up in the balcony at church. "You have to come to church with me. It has grown so much, and Pastor Fields would be so happy to see you."

"Count me in. I rarely miss church on Sunday mornings."

I smiled. "Some things don't change, huh?"

"Nope." He smiled. "I'm still Keith."

"Hey," I said. "Remember Ola Rose Pearl?"

"Who could forget Mother Pearl?"

We laughed.

"She used to pass out gum to all of the kids in the balcony! While our parents listened to the church service we'd be upstairs smacking and chomping on Freedent, like little senior citizens," I said.

We laughed some more.

"You know, I still chew that gum sometimes," he said.

"I do too! Shoot, it's good!"

We laughed, hard.

"Remember when we'd sneak from Sunday school and go to the corner store for candy?" I asked. "Between the both of us, we'd have maybe sixty-five cents."

"Do I?" he said. "Spending up our Sunday school money. We'd walk into the store, and there would be mounds of candy. Now and Laters, Lemonheads, M&M's, Boston Baked Beans, Jolly Ranchers."

I cut in: "Oh, and don't forget the Heath bars! Them things was good too!"

Keith Talbit looked at me and smiled. "Chantell, you're funny!"

"What?" I said.

"Nothing." And he just looked at me. His stare made my face warm. I loved my friend so much, and I couldn't believe he was back and sitting next to me!

"All that candy," he went on, "yet we always seemed to go straight to the gum section first, and find the Freedent."

I smiled. "You want to go outside and walk around?"

"Yeah, sure," he said.

## 21

# sitting on the dock

We walked around past the closed, dimly lit shops. Keith thought Jack London Square was great.

"How long has all of this stuff been here?" he asked, stopping near a railing where we had a great view.

"For a while now. Oakland is really getting a face-lift."

Walking with him like that, at that moment, made me feel that everything would be okay, as long as he was around. I even caught myself wondering silly things, like was he attracted to me, and thinking what-ifs, like what if he lived here. I knew that I had gone too far when I started having feelings of fear. Like I wasn't worthy of such a good person as Keith Rashaad. He'd done a whole bunch of good. What had I done good? Nothing. Nada. Come to think of it, what did I know how to do well besides cut people with my sharp tongue and look cute? Keith's area of specialty was medicine; mine was just plain old sin.

I needed a reality check, so that my imagination wouldn't have me thinking of picket fences, children, and a dog named Spot.

"Keith, do you have an evangelist wife or a dentist girlfriend or something back at home?"

He laughed and stepped back. He said, "Chantell, you're funny. I am not a saint. I try to stay connected with God, but I am by no means perfect." He paused. "Let me put it this way. I'm just a work in progress, just like you. Just like every other Christian. I've made a conscious decision to try to stay close to Him." Then he said, "And the answer is no, Chawnee." He laughed. "I don't have an 'evangelist wife' or a 'dentist girlfriend' at home."

And I told myself that I wasn't glad. It really wasn't any of my business anyway.

We walked in silence for a while, then stopped by a bench near the water. We stood there together and looked out. Beautiful yachts were docked. We stared out and watched as the moon's reflection danced on the ripples. The ambiance was nice. I made a note to myself to tell Eric that we should come out here and walk some night.

Keith picked up on the story of his childhood departure, where he'd left off in Friday's. "After Grandma Edna died, I was so angry. Mad at God. Mad at the world. I felt like I didn't have any support. No real family left. Nobody to show report cards to. Nobody to wait up for me to see if I came in past curfew and put me on punishment. I felt like I had no one to hold me accountable."

I stared at him under the light. He kept talking, and I don't know when I grabbed hold of his arm and comfortably folded mine around it.

He continued, "I was sent to live with my Aunt Gertie and Uncle Tommy. I guess I should have been thankful that I didn't have to go to a foster home or juvenile. But I wasn't. I thought that if my aunt and uncle had really thought anything of me, then I would have heard from them before then. My aunt and uncle lived in Texas alone, with no children. And that suited me just fine, because I didn't want to talk to anyone anyways. I didn't pay anyone much attention."

Keith was always so even-tempered. I couldn't imagine him that angry with anyone.

"So what did you do every day?"

He turned and looked at me and said, "I started hanging out in the street. My aunt and uncle tried to sit me down and talk to me, but I wouldn't hear of it. I went from being a straight-A student to smoking weed and stealing cars for joyrides. My aunt and uncle threatened to turn me over to the police and let them handle me."

I stood there trying to fathom such a thing.

"Then, one day my uncle saw me. He'd turned onto the street where I was hanging out. I had a cigarette in my mouth and my pants were sagging. I was about fourteen or fifteen years old. Me and the fellas, we were tough like that."

He smirked and went on. "My boys must have seen him coming before I did, because they started looking at the ground with their hands in their pockets, whistling and fidgeting. I just kept talking. Boastin' and lyin'. The next thing I knew, the cigarette was knocked out of my mouth. My boys had run off, and these hands that I didn't know were so strong were holding me by my shirt and had my scrawny teenage body pinned to the ground, and I couldn't move." He chuckled.

"My uncle said, 'You are not going to f— up your life in my home, boy!' He said, 'I am telling you right now, come home. Come home and get it together. Be the person that your Grandmother Eddie said you were. Or come home and get your stuff out of my d**n house.' Then he got up, went to his car, and just drove away."

I looked at him. "So what did you do?"

"I walked around Houston the rest of the evening thinking. I had a choice to make. I realized that I'd come to a fork in a road in my life, and that I had taken the wrong path. So I made a U-turn and took the other road. I went home that evening and told my aunt and uncle that I was sorry, and that I would do better. I worked hard, and turned my grades around. I graduated from high school. I got a scholarship to study math from Harvard. After college, I stayed there and went to medical school. I did my residency in Cambridge, and that's where I've been up until this last week."

"Wow, Keith Rashaad. You're amazing."

"Thank you, but I'm not amazing."

"Yeah, but you've been through a lot, Keith, and you came through it."

"Yeah, but I had it wrong, though."

I looked at him curiously.

"About the support thing. I had a support system. God gave me

Grandma Edna, and He gave me my aunt and uncle in Texas, but Chantell, He carried me. He was my system. No doubt about that."

Keith was so sincere, and honest, and grounded. He was all of the things that I was not. I loved my old friend, and just wanted to squeeze him. Just talking to him was helping me to be a better me. I wouldn't lose contact with him again.

The cold night air hit me. I wrapped my arms around myself. "Brrr, it's getting cold."

He put his jacket around me and said, "Yeah. It's getting late. Where'd you park?"

"In the parking garage across from the theater."

"C'mon, I'll walk you to your car."

We headed out of Jack London Square and toward the big parking lot.

"So, Saturday," he said.

"Saturday what?" I asked.

"Saturday, do you have any plans? Can we hang out?"

"Sure. I'm open. What time?"

"How about five p.m.?"

"Okay. Where are we going?" I asked.

"Who knows? There's so much that I want to do while I'm home. Just be ready," he said.

I smiled. "Okay."

We stood on the corner and he said, "Let me look at you." He stared at me under the streetlight. "Yep, you're as pretty as the day you first called me Frog Face."

"Oh, here you go. Why you have to bring that up?"

We laughed.

"Because, Chantell, you were terrible!" Then he mocked me, in a little-girl tone: " 'Umm, excuse me. Excuse me, you guys! Move out the way, I need to go first. Cuz my daddy said that I was the princess.' "

We laughed again. "Stop exaggerating!" I said.

"I'm not!" he said. "None of the kids wanted to be your friend because you acted so awful."

I looked him square in the eyes and said, "Well, you were my friend."

"Yes, I was," he said, "and I always will be."

We took the parking lot elevator up to the third floor. When we reached my car, Keith saw how dusty it was and said, "Wash your vehicle, woman! Where've you been driving?"

"Hey, buddy. You just watch it! Don't start no mess wit' me."

"Come here for a moment," he said.

I walked over to him. He looked at me. I stared back and made a note of what I saw. Chiseled jaw line, chocolate skin, curly eyelashes, long physique, full lips, magnificent eyebrows, bald head, goatee, and the faint smell of a cologne that reminded me of trees. Lots of trees.

"What are you looking at?" I asked.

"I just want to look at you. I missed seeing your face, and your eyes."

"You think my eyes are sad."

"I think your eyes hold a lot of your feelings."

Then he kissed his finger and touched my mole.

When I pulled out of the parking lot, I could still feel his finger's touch above my brow.

# whatchu doin'

It was such a beautiful day! I had my curtains open and was dusting the shelves when my phone rang. "Hellooo!" I said.

"Hi, it's me." It was Tia.

"Hey, T! Whatchu doing, gurl?"

"Don't hey, T, whatchu doin' me," she said mockingly with a chuckle. "I've been wondering when your happy butt was going to call me and tell me what happened with you and Keith. That's what I'm doing!"

I giggled. "Tia, I don't even know where to begin," I said. "I think I am still in shock. I am so happy he's back. I don't ever want to lose contact with him again."

"Oooo. Somebody is whipped!"

"Stop it, Tia."

"Is he single?"

"I don't even know. I think so. It's not really important."

"Well, it sure looked important last night. You guys were intense!"

"No we weren't. It's not like that."

"Chantell, save it. Y'all was hotter than the jalapeño poppers that they serve up in there!" She cracked herself up.

"Girl, you're silly. That sounds like something my daddy would say. Anyways, Eric and I will be married by this time next year. That's where my head is."

"Mmm-hmm," she said.

"Whatever. Listen, Keith and I talked for a long time last night. I wish that you could have stayed and heard his life story. He's had a hard time, but his faith in God is so strong. That man is an inspiration to all."

"Wow. How long will he be here?"

"Only a few months. He's working on a special project at Oakland Children's Hospital, something to aid children's skin in healing when it's been burned. He's a mentor too, you know?"

"Chantell, listen to yourself. What did y'all do after I left? Did he put something on you?"

"No, Tia, you so nasty! It's not a romantic thing. I'm like his godsister or something."

"Girl, that man is not your family! I seen the way he was looking at you."

"He is not my type, Tia, and I have a man, remember? I've just gotten Eric thinking about our future. I am not about to abandon all of my hard work so the next woman can come along and benefit from it."

"You know what? Don't even get me started on you and Eric. I am not going to go there with you, Chantell. But what do you mean Keith Rashaad is not your type? What, he's a little too nice for you?"

I laughed. "Whatever, that's not what I mean. Sometimes I can't stand you."

She laughed too, with her brutally honest self.

"I like nice guys," I told her. "Remember my ex-boyfriend Trevor, that attorney?" Mentioning him was a mistake. I knew it as soon as it came out of my mouth.

"Ohh, I remember Trevor!" She laughed. "Every other minute he was reminding us of how prominent he was."

I burst into laughter too and mocked him: "'Well, you know, my family has a law firm. And quite frankly, we've always been really, very upper-echelon in the greater San Francisco Bay Area!'"

Tia laughed harder.

In my own defense, I said, "Hey, I was young! I know better now. I can't stand people like that."

"Chantell, I love you and all, and you're my girl, but, honeydew, you can act very ugly too."

"Forget you, Tia!" I laughed, but she was right. I could act awful. It wasn't that I was trying to be prominent, though: I just didn't want people knowing my fears, knowing my pain. I didn't want to be stepped on, and I didn't want to appear weak.

"Well, my friend Keith Talbit is not like Trevor anyways," I said as I walked over to the couch and sat down. "Keith is patient, and friendly, and goodhearted." I put my feet up on the couch.

"Then talk to him, Chantell."

I rested an arm back behind my head.

"Negative, capt'n. We're just friends."

# 23

# let's do lunch

I'd just finished a sales call when I pulled into the parking lot of Eric's workplace. If we were going to go on this cruise together, we needed to work out the details. I needed to talk with him face-to-face. Yes, we had our differences, and little arguments. And of course because Eric was so fine, there would likely always be women trying to throw themselves at him, just like when guys hit on me. The point was, it had been two years, and Eric and I loved each other. We just needed to hold on to each other and work out our issues. We were destined to be together, I knew that. That's why we kept ending up in predicaments where we had to be together. God wanted us together and happy.

It was twelve o'clock, and he should have been taking a lunch break soon. I got out of my Jeep and walked into the Safeway, and I thought about what I needed to say.

I found him in the break room in the back. He had on a long white butcher's coat over his clothes. I could see the collar of his striped button-down Ralph Lauren shirt sticking out of the top. I loved that shirt. My baby looked so fine, and his clothes were really clean. I always wondered how he kept them so neat, cutting up meats the way he did. He looked surprised to see me.

"Chantell, what are you doing here?"

"Hi. No worries. I am here in peace. I came to talk." I smiled and held up my hands. "I'm sorry for hitting you, Eric. I was just so mad at you. It sounded like you called me Sabrina, and I thought we were going to get married this weekend."

He looked around, then up at the clock on the wall. "You don't need to apologize, baby. And we are going to get married, but you have to stop sweating me so hard about it. Let's let it happen naturally. Okay?"

"Okay," I said; God had guided Keith Rashaad, and He was going to take care of me too. Then I asked, "But Eric, who is Sabrina?"

"Oh, I don't know. I think I was having a weird dream or something. Well, babe, you'd better head out. I have to get back to work."

"Oh, okay, honey. I don't want to hold you up. Oh Eric, one last thing."

"What's up?"

"Well, remember my friend Keith Rashaad Talbit from when I was a little girl?"

"Umm . . . Oh yeah, the little boy with the rashes. Right?"

"Yes, that's him. Well, baby, he's back in town for a little while. You have to meet him! He goes to church every Sunday! The two of you have got to meet—"

"Oh, okay, Chantell, sure. Look I gotta get back to work," he said, looking at his watch.

"Okay." I kissed his cheek. "One last thing."

"Chantell." He looked at me.

"Promise and I'm leaving. I wanted to talk about the cruise."

"What about it?"

"Well, I know that we're going to have a lot of fun. But I, uh, I think we need separate beds, though."

He rolled his eyes. "Why? I just told you I was going to marry you."

"I can't really explain it. I know that I slipped up recently, but my not having sex is kind of like my own little sacrifice that I want to make. It's a personal thing—"

He looked at me like I was ridiculous.

I said, "When it's time for us, He'll make sure we know."

Eric said nothing.

Then the door opened into the little break room where we sat. "Eric, baby? C'mon, let's go eat," said a checker as she walked in, removing her apron and hanging it up on a hook. Then she turned and looked at me and said, "Oh, hi."

"Hi," I said. She was a cute girl with long single braids pulled into a ponytail. She wore tight-fitting dark denim jeans and a little white T-shirt.

"I thought you had to get back to work," I said to Eric, while eyeing the woman.

"Oh yeah. But we're going to grab a bite to eat first."

The woman put out her hand to shake mine. "I'm Sabrina."

You couldn't have bought me for a nickel! I was so angry and hurt. I looked at Eric, then at her, and said, "I am Chantell, Eric's fiancée."

Eric smiled a nervous smile and scratched the back of his neck. "Well, baby," he said to me. "We're going to grab a quick bite. We only have thirty minutes, so I'll talk to you later. Okay?"

I left so that they could go have their little lunch.

## 24

# a change in plans

I went back to work fuming. If Eric thought we were going on a cruise together, he had another think coming. He'd better be glad I was trying to be a good person, because I could have easily knocked him in his head at his job. I sat up at my desk and pushed back my chair.

If the thought of leaving him hadn't always made me nauseous, I could have abandoned him long ago. But I hated quitting, I hated losing, and I hated good-byes! I wanted to scream! I put on my jacket and left the office.

Even though Eric always came back to me, I feared that one day some little hoochie momma was going to come along and lure him away from me for good. Maybe I feared too that if I left him, folks who knew us would come up to me and ask how he was, and I would be standing there, vulnerable, looking and feeling stupid and not knowing what to say. I took the elevator down to the first floor and opened the big brass-lined glass doors that led to the sidewalk.

I needed to face the facts. Eric had disrespected me with this Sabrina not once but twice in the last month. I was going to put a stop to all of this foolishness. And I was serious this time. Eric thought he was playing me. But I was going to play him.

There were people walking to and fro all over downtown San Francisco. I joined the crowd and walked down to the corner where a man sold Polish hot dogs and blue cotton candy from a cart. If he was going to shoo me away to go to lunch with another woman, then he was not going on that cruise with me! And he could count on that.

"Hi. How may I help you?"

"Yes, can I have a beef hot dog, a Seven-Up, and a cotton candy?" He handed me my dog, my soda, and a bag of blue cotton candy in clear plastic.

"How much?"

"Eight-fifty, sweetheart."

I handed him a ten and tried to smile. It was a challenge.

Let's see how funny and cute Eric was when he got kicked off the boat! Or if he found out that he couldn't take the cruise. I headed back to the building. Suddenly I remembered that I was the one who had actually reserved the cruise on my credit card. Although we'd both paid our portion of the Citibank bill months ago, maybe there was some way that I could fix it so that he couldn't board the boat.

I checked the confirmation letter as soon as I got back to my desk. Our ship departed from Pier 27 next Friday afternoon. I knew it was a long shot, but I left a message with the travel agency and asked if I could cancel one of the tickets. I told them that my cruise mate couldn't go, and asked them to call me at work to discuss how to go about canceling his ticket and refunding my credit card.

I could see Eric now. He'd be standing in line like people did on nighttime TV waiting to board the Love Boat. He'd look silly in a big straw hat, sunglasses, and a yellow rubber-duck inner tube around his stomach. He'd walk up with his boarding pass in hand, cocky as usual, and his flip-flops would flap as he walked up. And the lady who welcomed everyone would tell him that his boarding pass was no good, just like his old cheating behind. Now, I knew it probably wouldn't happen that way, but hey, he was always cheating on me, and I was getting pretty sick and tired of it.

I sat at my desk and did the paperwork for an additional $20K that I'd closed yesterday when one of my accounts, Perfect Auto Service, agreed to do a flyer campaign promoting their new quick oil changes. We decided to do the "drop" of the flyers in the Saturday edition in three weeks. I made all of the arrangements. Then I picked up a newspaper and looked through some of the day's headlines as I waited to hear from the travel agency.

There was a big storm coming in; the forecasters were calling it "El Niño's Sister." And a San Francisco man was found shot on South Van Ness Street. Migration to California was on the rise. And someone was trying to revise the Ebonics measure.

Revising the Ebonics measure—now, that was not going to happen, I thought. Living in Oakland, I was pretty familiar with that measure. I remembered it well. It proposed teaching children to speak and write using the dialect from which they spoke. It called for teachers to make the children aware of the differences in dialects, and it allowed them to expand upon standard English using their own individual dialect. I remembered being fascinated by it. The Oakland school district was one of the lowest-performing in the country, and it was a majority black district.

The measure seemed to be well-thought-out. It asserted, for example, that if a child said, "I'm goin' to the store," the Oakland public school educators were to reinforce the child by telling him, "Although you're saying 'goin','" understand that in standard English grammar, 'going' is always pronounced with a 'g' on the end." It sounded simple enough, but the problem was that the Oakland school board never explained it clearly. Then either the media or some individual started saying things like, "The nerve of that Oakland school board for trying to teach kids slang! How stupid! I'd never send my kids there. I don't want my kid being taught broken English."

Then the newspapers picked it up and had a field day, and the lie swept across the country. And everyone was making fun of that "stupid school board out in California" that advocated teaching kids how to speak street talk. There were skits on late-night TV making fun of Ebonics. The Oakland school board cracked under the pressure, and the next thing you know, the Ebonics measure was swept under the rug. That ship had sunk. Good luck trying to raise that sucker from the dead.

I was deep in reading at my desk, so it startled me when my phone rang.

"Hello, it's Chantell Meyers."

"Hi, Chantell, it's Betty Marks from World Travel returning your phone call."

I'd almost forgotten about my little ploy to keep Eric standing on the docks while I drank margaritas with men who looked like that boxer, Oscar De La Hoya.

"Yes, um," I said, "can I cancel a ticket?"

"Is it your ticket?"

"No, my boyfriend can't make it. Because, see, he's got the flu."

"Is the ticket in his name?"

"Yes, but I charged it on—"

"Yes, well, have him read the back of the boarding pass that was mailed out. Our policy says that the person the ticket is issued to must call us, then write a letter fourteen days in advance and he or she can get a full refund minus a hundred-dollar service fee. If it's between seven and fourteen days, then you're entitled to a full refund minus two hundred dollars."

"I see. Well, can I change our reservation and get my own room?"

"What is your reservation number?"

"It's, uhh, A-230-9456-MN."

I heard her typing through the phone line.

"No ma'am. There is no way. Your cruise filled up months ago."

I guessed we would be there together after all. "Okay. Well, thank you. We'll be there."

"Are you sure?"

"Yes. He's eating soup and drinking lots of liquids. I bet he'll feel better by then anyway. Thanks for your time."

"Sure. Bye-bye."

That is exactly what I was talking about. It seemed God wanted us together.

## 25

# dreaming of zarina

The day had been nightmarish, but at least I'd already hit my revenue goal for the next few months. I got home around 6:30 and set my computer bag on the floor by the door. Every time I thought of Eric and Sabrina, I'd get angry. I was tired of his mistreatment of me. He thought because he was handsome he could do anything that he wanted to and I'd just let him. He also knew that relationships were difficult for me, and that I liked the idea of being in a long-term relationship. But, contrary to his belief, I did have a breaking point. And I was almost to it too! I told myself that he had better let all of those other girls go, and marry me soon, or I was out of there, and I really meant it.

I felt completely drained and needed to relax for just a few moments before I started on the kitchen. I took off my shoes, drew my feet underneath me, and lay my head on the armrest of the couch. I wished I'd had some fresh homemade jelly on hot buttered biscuits. My mother used to do a lot of canning and preserving of fruits and jellies. She learned it from her mother, who'd learned it from her mother.

I was determined to get to a library and check out a book on making jams and jellies. When I was little, each season, my mom would go to the vineyards or the orchards and handpick fruit for her homemade preserves. I remembered going with her once. We put on old clothes and scarves on our heads to protect us from the dirt and dust. We left early in the morning and drove out to the fruit farm to pick apricots from the trees. There were lots of other families there. The sun was barely up. The people who ran the farm gave us big huge croaker sacks, which were really itchy-looking, although the hard, dry bags with fibers sticking out all over them were strong enough to withstand a great deal of weight.

My mother, Zarina Meyers, was a free spirit, and always smiling. She said she smiled because we were not promised tomorrow. She was in and out of the hospital all of her life. My mom said that we should live, and be thankful and be happy.

"Get out of that box," she would say, "and try something new." That was her life's motto. My dad, I think, was both in awe of and amused by her. She had a degree in sociology from Stanford, but she was an artist in her heart. In my father's eyes, she could do no wrong. To him, she was the greatest thing since baseball was invented. Some days he would come in the door from work and my mother, the artist, would have changed the house's interior to canary yellow with murals of beautiful blue-and-green waterfalls flowing. My dad would smile and shake his head and just say, "Z, you're something else." And we would enjoy our new yellow house, until she felt artistic again and wanted to try something else new.

I must have dozed off on the couch thinking of Zarina, because I dreamed of her. I didn't remember ever dreaming of my mother before that evening on the couch.

She looked the way I remembered when I was five years old. Long hair pinned up into a bun. Slanted almond eyes. Size six frame. Full pinkish brown lips covered with cool golden-chocolate-colored lipstick. She wore a sheer orange scarf around her neck that matched her golden skin. She'd just come in through the door and had on a tawny-colored leather jacket and heels. I was in the living room sitting next to my dad, watching a western on television.

She had a new eight-track tape in her hand. She was popping her fingers and singing out loud. She looked great, like a *Soul Train* dancer, and if you hadn't known that she'd just gotten out of the hospital four days prior, then you would have been convinced that she felt great too. She popped the eight-track into the player and pulled me up and my dad up to dance with her. Marvin Gaye blared from our speakers. I stepped from side to side and watched my parents. My dad had an Afro maybe three inches long. He had on a green ribbed turtleneck and thick forest green polyester slacks. My mom kissed my dad, walked over to the TV, turned it down, and upped the volume on the tape player. She pulled him in and moved her arms behind her as she popped her fingers and shook her shoulders. My dad's knees were slightly bent, and he swayed and looked at my mother with a big grin on his face. They were having a ball. I stood back and giggled and changed the weight on my feet, watching them dance. Mom pulled me in and we all danced in a circle. Dad just shook his head and played along.

When I woke up it was ten o'clock in the evening, and a tear rolled down my cheek and onto the arm of the now tear-stained couch. A long time ago, somehow, I'd managed to turn the tears off, and they never came back until this moment. I'd lost my mother, darn it! My mother was a good person. She was a wonderful person from what I could see. I wished I knew more. Dad never spoke of her. Zarina was different, and unusual. Not like Charlotte, who was all stuffy and conservative. I was stuck somewhere in between both of them.

I was the person who made sure that life appeared fabulous. That is what I did for the sake of others. I didn't want folks to know the truth, but did it matter if I, myself, knew the truth?

I got up from the couch and went into the kitchen. I grabbed the phone and called my father.

"Hello," he answered.

"Hi, Dad, it's me." I grabbed a pen out of the drawer and took an envelope from the stack of mail on the counter.

"Hey, pork chop," he said. I drew some circles.

"How are you feeling today?" I asked.

"Oh, I'm feeling fine, pumpkin. Just resting, and watching the news. How is my baby girl?"

"I'm good."

"Are you still saying them prayers for me?" I could hear him smiling through the phone.

"Yep, you know it! Every time I think about you." I added a couple of wavy lines. "Hey, Daddy, where's Charlotte?"

"Aww, she's gone to get her hair done. She's mad with me, you know, because I went down to the shop and did a transmission today, and the doctors think that I should be on bed rest."

I stopped doodling. "Well, Daddy, if the doctors say that you shouldn't be back at work yet, then you can't go. That shop isn't going anywhere, and Mike and the rest of those guys are capable of taking care of it for you."

"I know, baby, but it's hard just sitting here, doing nothing."

"I hear ya, Daddio, but just sit tight. Hang in there. It won't be too much longer and you can move around all you want to. Okay?"

"Sure. Fine."

I put the pen back to paper. "So, Charlotte, she's really hot with you, huh?"

"Hotter than a fried moth in the porch light."

I laughed. "A fried moth in the porch light, Daddy?"

"Yep. But she'll be alright. And I'm feelin' good."

Good. Now the question. I decided to just be blunt and come out with it. I cleared my throat. "Huh-hum. Daddy, do you have any of my mom's stuff?"

"Sure, baby, your momma has all kinds of stuff in there, just tell her what you need."

"No, Dad, I mean *my* mom, Zarina."

Silence.

"Hello?" I said.

"I, I'm here . . . baby. Baby, that was a long time ago . . . Boy, you kind of caught me off guard. Chantell, come around here tomorrow. Okay?"

That was pretty much all he said, but I could hear the pain radiating in his voice. I didn't like to hear my dad's voice strain like that. Zarina still made him weak. Daddy liked to make light of things. He liked to joke. We were alike in that respect. It was a mask. That was his mask of protection. My mask of protection was Gucci shoes, and Chanel body wash.

"I'll be there tomorrow evening."

"Good," he said.

Then he changed the subject. "Hey, Chantell where is Eric? I haven't heard you mention him lately."

"Oh, don't mention him, Dad, we're on the rocks."

"Oh, sorry, babe. Hey, don't y'all have a little boat thing that you are supposed to do together coming up?"

"Yes, Daddy, but I don't want to talk about it."

"Oh, okay. I'm sorry, baby. Chantell?"

"Yes, Daddy?"

"Make sure you make some time to come over here so that we can talk. Okay?" he said.

"Okay, Daddy. I won't forget. I'll be there tomorrow."

"Good. Good night, princess."

"Night, Daddy."

# 26

# trying to get a grip

Tomorrow hadn't come because I wasn't ready to deal with Zarina yet. I lost my nerve, I was chicken, whatever. I talked a good game, but not knowing who my mother was, was a big part of who I was.

I was trying to get that dream out of my head, but I kept playing it back. I kept seeing my mother. She looked so happy. I felt lonely. She left us. I felt abandoned, and nothing my dad was going to say could change that.

I went to work and felt like I was a hamster running on a wheel and not getting anywhere the entire day. It was the first time in months that I'd gone the whole day and not called to check on my dad. I was sitting at my desk shutting down my computer when I remembered the Wednesday evening service that night at the church.

Pulling into the Faith Center parking lot, I grabbed my Bible out of the backseat and made my way over to the church's doors. I had gotten there a little late, so I missed the first part of the message that was being taught. The speaker was a tall man who stood up front in a dark blue suit, with a pair of silver-framed glasses on. He told us that God wouldn't do for us what we could do for ourselves.

"God's not going to brush your teeth! God's not going to comb your hair! He will supply food for the hungry, but He isn't going to put the food in your mouth!"

I sat there listening to the tall man with the tiny crowd, then something clicked in me, and I almost bit my lip!

God had given me the resources, I just hadn't used them. I remembered my conversation with the guy from the Employee Assistance Program, when I kind of quit my job. He had said, "Sometimes it takes a little work to find the right person to talk to." I remembered that he'd even advised me to pray. I said, "Thank you, Jesus," because even though I was in honest-to-goodness turmoil, I was starting to think maybe God was trying to get through to me.

After church, I took out the number of the second therapist that was given to me. At this late hour, I'd probably get a message machine, but I dialed anyway. The therapist actually picked up, and we set an appointment for next Tuesday at 2 p.m. I'd be there, but in the meantime I went home and crunched on a bag of Spicy Doritos for dinner.

# 27

## a confession

I just needed to talk, okay? I was trapped in this cycle of shame, and guilt, and pretending that nothing was wrong when I really felt awful, and I was determined to find a way out. I phoned Tia during work at the beauty school. There was always some drama going on with the young students. Tia was a stick-in-the-mud, but she knew every Nas and Nelly song. She and Ron owned the college together, and Ron worked there part-time when he could.

The school's phone rang, and I was surprised when he answered. "Hey, Chawnee Chawn, what's up?" he said cheerfully.

"Hey, Ronnie Ron, how is the barber college going?"

Tia's husband, Ron, was a lot older than her, and while they both had a great sense of humor, they were as different as Top Ramen and chestnuts. Tia was a thin, relatively quiet and conservative woman with a pageboy haircut. She was very pretty and quite elegant. Ron was kind of on the husky side, loved to laugh, and was a keen businessman.

In his regular day gig, he was a real estate investor, and he owned probably ten businesses in the Bay Area—mostly dental complexes and things of that nature. He was also part owner of a big construction outfit in SF. He was Creole, short and kind of stocky. His eyes were hazel, and he had black curly hair that he wore all combed back.

I thought Ron was smart, country, and funny as all get out.

He said, "I'ma tell you right now . . . Don't be crying when your friend is gone. We're packing up and moving our behinds to Nebraska if things don't get no better around here!"

"Oh no, what happened now?" I asked teasingly, sounding disappointed.

"I'm telling you, Chawn, I'ma sell this d**n school cuz these little Negroes don't know how to act! I ain't got the time or the patience to deal with they little behinds," he said only half jokingly. Tia loved teaching hair care, and the school was her mother's school from back in the day. They kept it for sentimental reasons, but Ron was not a sentimental businessman.

"Tell me what happened," I said.

"One of the girls done had a razor in her head, like she fresh out the jailhouse. And when the student washed her head, she unknowingly shaved a patch out of the top of the girl's hair. Correct me if I'm wrong, if you put a razor to hair, the chances are pretty good that it's going to cut the hair, right?"

I laughed. "Yes."

He said, "Boy, I'll tell you. Then some fool name Jimmy done snuck and took it upon himself to do a d**n Jheri curl. That fool messed up and forgot to put on the neutralizer on some dude name Big Red's hair."

"Aw naw!" I said, egging him on. "So what happened?"

"Well, Big Red asked Jimmy why he ain't got no curls. And Jimmy done told the boy that he had done a new kind of curl on his head; he tole Big Red to give it until tomorrow for the curls to take."

"Well, was it?" I asked.

"Was it what?"

"A new kind of curl?"

"Naw, you know that boy ain't know'd how to do no curl! He just started Tuesday." He paused. "Now Big Red done said he go come back to whup on Jimmy."

I put my hand over my mouth and tried not to laugh.

"You should have seen him. Big Red was 'round here looking like a wet mop!"

"Oh naw!" I yelled.

"Yep, and I'm supposed to keep an eye out and call the police if I see him around here. But he is not going to come up in here fighting. I'm telling you now. I am not having it!"

"Is everyone okay?" I asked.

"Yeah, these knuckleheads is fine," he said with a chuckle. "Tearin' up folks' stuff."

"Well I'm glad. Where's Tia?"

Tia then got on the phone and said, "What's up, girl?"

"Girl, your husband is a mess!"

"I know he is," she said. "How are you doing?"

I dove right in. "Not bad, but I have something to tell you."

"What?" she asked.

"You have to promise not to tell anyone."

"Chantell, I would never tell or repeat anything that you told me in confidence. Now spit it out! What's up?"

I took a deep breath.

"Hello?"

How was I going to say this?

"Chantell, what's wrong? You're scaring me."

"I, ahh, I'm going to see a psychiatrist."

"And?"

"That's it. I'm going to see a shrink, because I need someone to talk to about stuff."

"Chantell, honey. That ain't nothing. It's a good idea to talk to someone."

"I guess I just feel embarrassed, or ashamed."

"Girlfriend, the shame is in needing to take care of yourself and not doing it cuz you embarrassed. That's the shame. I've seen a therapist off and on for a couple of years now. It's one of the best things that I've done for myself and our marriage."

What? I couldn't believe it. "Your life is ideal. Rock solid!"

"We do have a wonderful life, but it's because we work at it, we are honest, we pray, and we're true to ourselves."

"Wow, Tia."

"Chantell. This is a good move for you. You find someone that works for you and work on yourself. And I don't have no advanced degrees in psychology, but if I can do anything, tell me. If you just want to talk, tell me. Okay?"

"Okay, Tia, I will. Thanks."

# 28

# good stuff

Keith Rashaad Talbit said that he would call and confirm our plans for Saturday, but he hadn't phoned me. Maybe he was just being nice and wasn't planning on calling. Maybe he'd gone back to Boston. I went into the kitchen and made myself a cup of tea and told myself that everything was going to work out. Besides, even if he had left, he'd probably call me from Boston to give me his number. Oh well, at least I knew that he was okay.

I told myself not to worry about it. I needed to think only of the homemade preserves that I was going to prepare. I washed my hands and started removing the skin from the apples that I'd placed in the sink. I wore a red-checkered apron folded in half and tied around my waist, because I knew that looking the part was half the battle. The cookbook was open on the counter and it said to measure out a cup of sugar. I'd just reached in the cabinet when the phone rang. I really needed to call Pacific Bell and get caller ID.

"Hello?"

"Chantell? This is Keith Talbit," said a smooth, deep voice.

I sighed; he'd called.

"Hi, Dr. Keith."

"Did I catch you at a bad time?"

"No, I was just cooking a little."

"Oh, what are you making?"

The warmth of a smile moved over my face as I spoke. "I was making some apple jam."

"Really? I remember you talking about learning to make jellies, when we were young." Did he remember everything about me?

"Yep. Well, actually, this is my first batch, so don't ask to taste any just yet."

He laughed. "I'm sure it will be delicious, and I'll be the first in line when you need a taste tester."

"Deal. So what's up with you? How've you been?"

"I'm doing well, working an unbelievable amount of hours, but it's all good," he said. "I'm just confirming our date for tomorrow. Please tell me we're still on."

"You know that we are. What time?" I asked.

"Great. Five o'clock?"

"Sounds good. I'm looking forward to hanging out." I hung up the phone and put the apples in boiling water. I smiled and nodded. Keith Rashaad. I had to remember that sometimes patience was everything.

The next afternoon I flipped through my CD collection and stumbled across Erykah Badu. She did her thing in my CD player while I took a shower and got ready for my "buddy date" with Keith Rashaad. I was glossing my lips when the doorbell rang.

I opened the door, and Keith said, "Hello, Chantell." His subtle fragrance drifted through my doorway.

"Hello, Keith Talbit."

Keith stepped in my front door and kissed my cheek. I took his coat in my one hand and waved my other hand around the room to present my little living space to him. "Tah-dah!"

"This is great." He looked around at the custom-fitted wooden shutters on each of my windows, and my super-soft Italian leather sofas that I'd just paid off in August. "This is very nice, Chantell. It fits you."

"How do you know what fits me?" I asked.

"I just know." And he smiled like the allergic little boy that he used to be.

I almost giggled.

"It smells great in here."

"Thanks, it's lemongrass," I said.

"I like it."

I smiled. "Please have a seat."

Erykah Badu sang from the speakers softly.

"I love her music," I said.

Keith grabbed my hand. "Me too. You can finish getting ready in a moment. Hang out with me." He held my hand as we walked over and sat on the couch, below my mother's painting of a little girl and boy, and listened to the song.

My eyes closed. We sat there, feeling the song. Not saying a word, we gently rocked from side to side, while Erykah belted like only she could. And without sex, or groping, or grinding, Keith Rashaad Talbit quenched my thirst.

"So where are we going?" I asked finally.

"You'll see," he said. I grabbed my purse and followed him out the door. We cut across the lawn and out to the carport. He'd parked in my extra car space—a dark blue Lincoln Town Car.

"Your car?" I asked.

"Nah, this is the chief of staff's extra car."

"Oh," I said and headed toward it.

Keith turned toward me and asked, "Chantell, do you trust me?"

"Yes, of course, Keith Rashaad."

"Good. Then give me your keys."

"Huh?"

He held out his hands. "Give me your keys."

I reached into my purse and handed him the keys. He walked over to the passenger side of my Jeep, opened the door, and motioned for me to get in. I sat down, and he went around and got into the driver's side.

"Where are we going?"

He smiled and said, "You'll see."

We went to a little family restaurant and grabbed a bite to eat, then stopped by Merritt Bakery. "Wait here," he said.

"Okay," I said, in what I'm sure sounded like a confused tone. I sat there and looked around. The sun was starting to set. The temperature was nice, like lukewarm water. People in spandex were walking toward Lake Merritt. It was a fine evening to be outside.

I'd just changed the radio station when Keith came back with a little pink box just big enough for a piece of pie. "Here," he said. "Hold that."

I held on to the box and we were on our way once again. It was about 7:30 and the sun was going down when Keith drove us to a do-it-yourself car wash.

I laughed. "Dude, what are you trying to say?"

He put his finger to his lips. "Shh!" He was so cute.

The sky was orange and blue, and the car wash's night lights were already on. He pulled into the end stall, then turned on KBLX, the Quiet Storm, and Anita Baker's voice filled the air. He stepped out of the car and went over to the quarter machine. I turned up Anita so that we could hear her.

When he returned he had a handful of quarters, which he started to put in the machine. I walked around to the back to check to see if my gym shoes were in there. I opened up the back of the Jeep and looked.

"Just what do you think you're doing?" he asked.

"I'm going to help," I said.

He closed up the back of the truck and turned to me and said, "I got this."

"Okay." Yes indeed, he was very cute.

He went to the front, opened the door, reached in and took out the pink bakery box and a black plastic fork. "Here. Make yourself useful by working on this." I opened the box and looked at the huge piece of cake topped with a ton of fresh strawberries and whipped cream. The strawberries were deep red and pressed into the mountain of cream.

"Ohhh, this looks wonderful! Eat some with me."

"Negative, mate," he said. "I've got a Wrangler to wash."

He went back over to the machine and continued to put quarters in. I stood back and the machines revved up. Keith rinsed off the Jeep. I stood just feet away and watched him go to work. I'd never been on a date like this before. Ever.

I yelled over the machine's noise, "Sure I can't do something?"

"Yeah," he said, "you can eat your cake."

I sliced into the cake with my fork and delighted in the sweetness of the berries and the fresh whipped cream. Oh my goodness. I didn't realize that I'd closed my eyes. When I opened them, Keith was looking right at me.

The cinnamon in my skin hid it, but I'm sure my cheeks were red.

"Good stuff, huh?"

"Yeah," I said.

# 29

# change goin' come

I admit, I didn't know how to feel. I'd started to wonder if God had really spoken to me at church about this appointment, as I gave the cab driver the address.

We drove to a neighborhood of beautiful San Francisco homes. They were huge old houses that sold for a million dollars or more. The driver stopped at the address, and I scoped the place out. I walked up the set of steps shared by the renovated Victorian that had been split in half. The porch was huge and each door had its own mailbox. The house was a light brown, trimmed in black. The door seals around each entranceway and the edgings around the windows were black. Neatly shaped and trimmed green shrubbery made a perfect rectangle outside the window on one side. On the other side there was a rose garden.

I was about to knock on the door of the side that matched the address I'd written on the card, but a sign on the door said: "Please open the door and come up the stairs." As I entered, the first thing I noticed was a black wrought-iron flower stand in the corner and a huge set of narrow and steep stairs that led upward. As I walked up the stairs I could hear music playing. Music with no words. Violins played with the sound of waves crashing though them; incense burned, and I continued up the stairs and found a sparsely decorated waiting room. A couple of pictures hung on the walls. One was a black chalk drawing, the other an abstract painting of many colors. There were a couple of bulletin boards that held flyers, and a poster was pinned to one of them. There was a little waiting area with four chairs.

Someone else was sitting in the waiting area. He looked nineteen or twenty. He had a square face and wore round glasses. His hair was a bright red and his fair skin bore tiny freckles. He was holding an instrument, perhaps a trombone. He didn't look like he had any issues. I figured he was a teenage rebel, whose parents had forced him to come here by threatening to throw him out of the house if he didn't get his act together. I wondered if he had a drug problem and abused crank or ecstasy.

I was plenty nervous about being here. I shook my head as I thought about the last time I'd "spoken" to someone and she'd asked me if I was suicidal. What the heck was I doing here? This wasn't for black folks. We didn't talk to shrinks, we worked out our own problems. We'd had enough labels and stereotypes about us. I wanted to leave. But I sat there with the teen, determined to see where all of this led.

I didn't see a place to sign in, so I grabbed an issue of *Good Housekeeping* magazine out of the rack and pretended to read, but really I watched water float through a little fountain in the corner.

A lady came out one of the doors.

"Thank you, Tammy. I'll see you in two weeks."

"You're welcome. See you then. Bye-bye."

The doors closed again, and I asked the young redhead, "Am I supposed to sign in somewhere?"

"Nah, your person will come out and get you."

"Oh. Thanks," I told him.

I got up and went over to the message boards on the far wall. A small plaque on the outside of one of the doors read: "Mary Higgins, Licensed Massage Therapist." The bulletin board next to it had postings for different types of services. People had put their flyers and business cards up advertising everything from tutors for your child to massage therapy training to obedience classes for your dog.

A moment later, a black man with brown hair and green eyes

opened a door on which the sign read, "Fredrick Brown, Ph.D." He said, "Chantell Meyers?" I walked over to him, and he opened his door wider for me to come in. He was maybe five-seven or five-eight, and about fifty years old. He had a short Afro and black plastic-framed glasses. He wore a blue plaid lumberjack shirt and jeans. He wasn't dressed the way that I thought a nut-counselor should be. There was a beige tweed couch against the wall near the door. I went and sat down. He sat at his desk and turned toward me. His desk faced the wall, and above it was a bookshelf with probably five hundred books. I looked at the titles. *Cognitive Behavior. Communication 101. Depression Therapy. Attention Deficit Disorder in Adults. Heal Your Marriage. Yoga. The Benefits of Running and Exercise.* He smiled at me. I felt a little more comfortable.

"Ms. Meyers, I'm Dr. Fredrick Brown. What brings you in to see me today?"

"Oh, I don't know." I kind of smiled. "I guess I'm not sure where to begin."

"Start anywhere you'd like."

I closed my eyes and breathed through my nose. Then I looked across the room, over to his degrees and certifications on the wall with the big window. I wondered what I'd say. I had nothing to lose, so I tried the truth.

"Okay, the other night, I had a weird dream. And in real life, I am always playing the person who is unaffected. And I know that this is probably not good for me, but I don't know how to stop."

"Hold on, hold on," he said. "Let's just break it down."

Did he just say break it down?

He looked at my expression and chuckled. "Ms. Meyers, I have a question for you."

I looked at him.

"Do you believe in God?"

I nodded. "Of course."

"Good. Then why don't we spend a moment and ask God to be present with us before we go on?"

"Sure," I said. That sounded like a good idea to me.

Then he closed his eyes and held his hands open before him. I did the same. "Dear Heavenly Father," he said, "we ask for You to guide this session, and to give us wisdom. You know this young woman's heart, Father, but we ask for You to give her courage to open up and see herself and what direction You'll have her take. Please, Father, allow her to walk out of these doors with a new perspective. All of this, we ask Lord Jesus in Your precious name. Amen."

I opened my eyes. Fredrick Brown seemed like a good man, but I'd never heard of a psychiatry session going like this before! Then he said, "Tell me about your family. I'd like to know where you come from."

I told him my story and he listened. You'd think that I would have been hesitant, blabbing all of my business to this complete stranger, but somehow, once I started talking, things just tumbled out of my mouth. I told him about my ever-joking father. About the cancer. I told him about my grandmother, who said I was just like her.

I looked over at him, and he was just nodding his head. Shouldn't he have been taking notes or something? He kept listening, so I told him about my successes at work. And about that Mina Everett woman, and how we kept our distance from each other at work so that we could keep our jobs. I told him how I never cried in front of people. I told him about my mother, whom we never discussed in my family as though she'd never existed. And that my father and I were going to get around to discussing her soon.

"Stop right there," he said with a finger pointed at nothing in particular. "If you will, I'd like to ask you to just stay there for just a moment. Tell me about your mom."

"Sorry, there's not much I can tell you about my mother. I don't know much about her." I needed to tell him about my incompetent boss.

"Well, try," he said. "Tell me what you *do* know about your mother."

"But that's just it!" I looked him in the eye. "She died when I was five, so I don't know anything!"

The little black man just stared back at me. Like he didn't believe me. What was his problem? I guess I'd decided that I liked him a little too soon. I looked at him sternly, silent. The first one to speak lost. I folded my arms, because like I'd already said, I didn't know my mother. He didn't budge. He must have been stupid or something. If a person didn't know something, then she just didn't know!

His green eyes were on me. Trying to pierce me open. After what felt like thirty minutes of silence, they did. I was there for my benefit, and nobody else's.

"Okay," I said. "I'll try." I took a long breath before I began. "Umm, I know that my mother was a painter. She made beautiful artwork. She never thought she could have kids because—" Oh God, what was I doing? "Because she had sickle-cell and she had fibroid cysts in her cervix. She had them so bad that before I was born, the doctors removed one of her fallopian tubes. She often said that I was her miracle baby, and she always said that I was supposed to be someone great." My voice cracked as I said, "She should have never had me, though."

"Why do you say that, Chantell?"

Emotion swept over me and caused my face to contort into what was probably an awful expression. I tried to contain it. I tried to regroup, but there was no turning back.

The therapist took a tissue out of the box on his desk and gave it to me.

"She shouldn't have had kids," I said. "She was too sick to have children. She'd probably still be here."

"Chantell, have you ever told anyone that you felt this way?"

"No," I said.

"How did she pass away?" he asked.

"The sickle-cell. She neglected her body. She was a real go-getter, and it put her in the hospital pretty often. Once she started feeling even a tiny bit better, she'd demand to go home. She didn't like sitting in hospital beds, but she didn't like laying up in the house either."

"You sound a lot like your mother. Being driven and all."

I liked hearing that. It made me smile. "She was patient, and a wonderful mom. We'd often go to street fairs together, and explore the world on the weekends."

"Chantell, do you think that you're the reason that your mother isn't here?"

I looked at the floor and nibbled at the side of my lip. He was going too far. Why was he asking so many questions?

"I don't know."

"Chantell, you're an intelligent woman. Surely you know that if your mother was sick, and if she didn't find the time to take good care of herself, then her getting sicker is not your fault. How could you have made her sick?"

I just looked at the floor and jiggled my knee.

He fired away again, "When was the last time you talked about your mother?"

I shrugged. "I never talk about my mother."

"Do you remember how you felt when she died?"

I looked at him with a blank expression, then I said, "Like someone had pulled the rug out from under me. That's a stupid question!"

He didn't seem affected by my lashing. He just kept going. "Listen to me. You know that life is not always fair. When it's not, there is nothing wrong with crying. God did not promise us fairness, Chantell. And we don't know why things happen, but the Bible does teach us, in the book of Ecclesiastes, the third chapter, that 'To everything there is a season, and a time to every purpose under heaven,' and Chantell, you're not responsible for your mother's not being with us."

Well, I sure felt responsible, and I felt alone. Trying to get ahold of myself, I wiped my eyes and folded my arms.

"Listen, you don't have anything to prove to any of us. It's okay to say, 'This hurts me' or 'I feel bad when that happens,' or to just cry."

We were both quiet.

"Let me ask you this: Let's say you've had a bad day at work, or better yet, let's say you've had a disagreement with a friend. How do you handle situations like that?"

"Oh, I don't worry about things like that. I don't depend on anyone. I make my own money. I make my own mortgage payments. I take myself on vacations. I don't have to worry about that type of thing."

It sounded stupid after I said it. But I'd said it so many times before that it just came out. In the past, I'd been proud to say, "I lean
on me." But I wasn't so certain that it was the answer to my life's
problems anymore.

I was quiet.

It shocked me when Dr. Brown said, "Chantell, you know what? I
think you were right to spend some time away from work. You took
off work in a rather colorful way, but it sounds like you were burned
out and I think it was a good thing. You were trying to spend more
time with yourself. You should do more of that. Feel your feelings.
Do you understand what I am saying to you?"

With a balled-up tissue in my hand, I nodded. I think I understood what he was saying, but I had another question. "Doctor, do
people really change? I mean, if you've been doing something for a
really, really long time, then aren't you just that way?"

He smiled and said, "What a wonderful question. People can
change and they do change all the time. You can change because God
will allow you to change. Second Corinthians 5:17 states very
clearly, 'Therefore if any man be in Christ, he is a new creature: old
things are passed away: behold all things are become new.' You just
have to believe God, and want to change."

That was good to know. I thought maybe I wanted to make some
changes.

Then there was a small chime of a bell, and he said, "Well, that's
our time for today. I think that you've done a lot. What do you
think?"

"I think I agree," I said.

It didn't feel like a whole hour had passed. "Thank you, Dr. Brown."

"You're quite welcome. Would you like to make another appointment?"

I thought for a moment. "Maybe." I needed to absorb all of this.
"I'll call you."

"I sure hope you do." Looking at me, he added, "And remember,
through Him, anything is possible."

I left the big old house and walked down to the Church Street intersection to hail a cab.

## 30

# go fly a kite

I had to walk out of the residential neighborhood to find a cab. On the way, I saw a homeless man. San Francisco had a serious homeless problem. There were homeless people everywhere.

The man had on a beige tweed hat with a snap in the front that reminded me of a duck's bill. He had on a dirty tie-dyed T-shirt with the sleeves ripped off. Clearly the shirt once had been bright purple and blue and yellow. His long straggly brown hair hung wildly past his shoulders. He had a stocky build and he wore black sweatpants and no shoes.

He pushed a shopping cart that was filled to the rim with stuff. In it, I saw a Hula-Hoop, and five or six different pieces of cardboard that were smashed up against the wall of the cart. The most visible one read, "54 cents will make my day. God Bless." He also had a rolled-up sleeping bag, a smashed painting that was missing the top side of its wooden frame, a bag of cans, and a worn brown leather shoe. I wondered if its match was in there somewhere among the stuff.

We walked down the tree-lined street, and eventually we crossed paths. He looked straight ahead, rambling on to himself. Then, like a town crier, he yelled deliriously at no one. He spoke passionately, as though he was sent by a royal family from a faraway land to awaken everyone and bring them to their senses.

He said, "Dear Fellowmen: It is with great pleasure that I inform you that you all must carry kites. Carry your kite with you, and fly it on windy days. We have a wise king who knows what is best. This simple pleasure will make a world of difference in your lives. As simple as using your son's picture as a bookmark or holding on to your daughter's childhood toy. So take heed I say, and have your kite near, for it is the law!"

He yelled, "So again, everyone, *everyone* must carry a kite! . . ."

Once we'd passed each other, I looked back at him. He pushed the cart with one hand and made big gestures and hand motions with the other. Each time he took a step, I could see the bottoms of his oily feet.

I walked a few more paces, then stopped. My dad and I have always had a thing about the homeless people. I reached into my purse and took out some money from the side pocket. I put my shoulder bag over my head so that it hung crossways like an old-fashioned newspaper boy would carry his papers. I turned and ran back to the babbling man.

"Excuse me, excuse me," I said, panting like I'd run a marathon. "Here you go." I handed him two twenties. "Go eat," I said, "and buy yourself a pair of shoes."

"Thank you," he said.

"No sir, thank you." I turned around and continued back down Church Street to the busy intersection.

"Come now," he called after me. "It's an order. Everyone must carry a kite!"

# 31

## what is love?

I pulled into the residency dorms behind the Oakland Children's Hospital and blew the horn. Keith came out of the building wearing a pair of antiqued faded jeans and a white button-down shirt with a blue pullover sweater. He opened the door and got in.

"You ready to do this?" he asked.

"Yeah," I said. "Let's roll."

We arrived at the Faith Center a few minutes early. We walked into the church arm in arm and found seats in the back center pews.

"It feels good to be back in here," Keith said.

I had to agree. The church filled up quickly, and in no time at all, we were shoulder to shoulder with other members. A little girl, maybe a year old, was in front of us. Her mother held her so that she stood up in her lap and faced Keith and me. She had little brown chubby cheeks and four black, cushiony ponytails. She smiled at us and babbled. Keith smiled, and I waved my index finger at her.

"Look, there's Pastor Fields!" he said excitedly. "I want to say hello." It seemed he had no inhibitions. He looked at his watch and said, "After church."

Keith was so much more open than I was. He didn't care if people saw his emotion, be it happy or sad. He just put it out there for the whole world to see. I loved that about him.

A gentleman announcer in gray slacks, a gray shirt, and a black plaid tie walked up to the microphone and welcomed everyone. "Are there any first-time visitors here with us today?" he asked.

Several people stood up. Keith whispered, "Maybe they'll ask for members who haven't been here in fifteen years to stand next, huh?"

I laughed. "Don't hold your breath."

The greeter told them that they were welcome and asked if anyone would like to say a few words.

One man said, "Praise God. I am Charles Mathers here visiting from Missouri. I belong to Missionary Zion Baptist Church in St. Louis, and I just wanted to say that I saw this church on my way to my hotel on Friday morning, and the Spirit led me here. I'm very happy to be here with you all today." Another lady spoke: "I bring you greetings from Love and Friendship Community Church in Sacramento . . ."

A few more people commented while the little girl in front of us kept reaching over and trying to pull the flower off the hat of the lady next to her. Her mother was busy listening to the speakers and hadn't noticed what the baby was trying to do. The mother listened and rocked from side to side. The baby's eyes would light up with excitement as she drew near the flower and the netting that sat on top of the lady's hat. Her little fingers would open and close as if she were practicing how she would grip it if she just got her hands on it. But her mother always seemed to pull in the other direction just in the nick of time.

Pastor Fields got up and began to give the sermon. Everyone was quiet. I was still a little shocked by the number of young people who were present. They took in every word like each one was a vitamin or a nutrient. There were young ladies with blue braids and tattoos on their backs, and rings in their lips and eyebrows. There were guys there with their pants four sizes too big, with cornrows, and twists, and Afros, and dreads. The scenery was a far cry from the frilly dresses and the polyester-pant-wearing church days that I remembered.

The pastor spoke about the twelve disciples of Jesus, and how He chastised them about keeping their faith, and not doubting. The message was helpful, practical, and for me educational because I'd always thought those guys were near-perfect.

Pastor Fields asked us to turn our Bibles to Jeremiah 29:11. I swished the pages of my Bible with an expression on my face that said I knew where all of the books were.

She read it aloud:

*For I know the thoughts that I think of toward you, saith the Lord, thoughts of peace and not of evil, to give you an expected end.*

"Did you hear that? Read it with me." And the people did.

"Memorize that, and get it in your spirit," she said. She told us that God wanted good things for us, and that he gave us what we expected. I found the right page too late to read along, but I heard the message just the same. Well, actually, Keith set his Bible down and showed me where the passage was, and I bookmarked it.

The baby girl in front of me smiled and made a little gurgling sound while eyeing the bright cloth flower. Her mom swayed to the left a bit too much, and before anybody realized it, the toddler had a red cloth flower in her hand and was munching on it. The mother immediately apologized and tried to get the flower out of the little girl's grasp. The baby refused. The mom had to pry the flower out of her baby's tight little grip.

The choir stood up and sang a gospel song that sounded like reggae. In a really deep voice, the tenor sang, *"Clap ya hands for Je-sus. Give him all de praise! Clap ya hands for Je-sus. Oh ya, clap ya hands. Bouyaka! Bouyaka! Bouyaka! Whoooo!"* The congregation clapped their hands, and everyone was up and praise-dancing, including Keith and me. It was spiritual. It was exuberant. It felt great. And it made it very easy for me to close my eyes and talk with God.

After church, when everyone was leaving, Keith went over to Pastor Fields and reintroduced himself. Her eyes lit up when she recognized him. She gave him a great big hug. I smiled, remembering how she used to love little Keith Rashaad. Then he pointed over to where I was sitting, and I waved. They motioned for me to come over. I'd been back at the church for over a week, but I had been too ashamed to go up and say hello. I walked over to them.

"Hi Pastor Fields," I said with a huge grin.

She looked at me above her glasses, then pulled me to her. "Little Chantell, oh my goodness! Look at you! It's so good to see you. It's so good to see the both of you. I am just overwhelmed with happiness." We talked a bit more before we left the church.

Keith and I strolled down the sidewalk and talked.

"Keith, church was great. When did church get like that?"

"What do you mean?"

"I mean, all the young people that go to church nowadays, it's amazing. I remember church being for grandparents. A place where kids went because their grandparents forced them to go."

Keith chuckled. "Yeah, I know what you mean. It seems there are lots of churches these days that are reaching out to young people. It's like there's a spiritual revolution going on or something."

"Yeah, and it's pretty cool."

I opened my car door, put my Bible in the backseat, and said, "So, where are we going now?" I surprised myself with how comfortable I was getting with him. I guess I just assumed that we'd hang out together a while longer.

"Wherever you want, princess," he teased. He knew that Dad used to call me that. I smiled.

He didn't go over to the passenger side, but stood near the door of the driver's side with me. He stared at me. "I want to put my arms around you."

I looked down at the cement.

"Remember when I asked you if you trusted me?"

"Yes."

"I asked you that because it's important to me that you do. I love you, and I have loved you all of my life."

I didn't know where he was going. "You love me *how*, Keith Rashaad?"

"I love you enough to want to build up our friendship, and nurture the connection that we share."

I told myself that I didn't know what he was talking about. I was trying to remember the oath that I had made to myself, so that I wouldn't get confused. What the heck was it?

Keith said, "What I am saying is that I don't want to lose you again, Chantell. And I'm wondering how you feel about me."

I thought Keith Rashaad Talbit was the most real, most grounded, most handsome, and most loving man that I'd ever seen.

But then it came back to me, my oath that I'd taken. I didn't intend to be left again. Keith Talbit was the third great loss of my life, and I had absolutely no intention of being left again. Period dot. And with careful planning, I wouldn't be. I had a boyfriend, and things wouldn't get any more serious than they had when we were kids.

So I said, "Let's see, how do I feel about you? I feel we are tried-and-true friends."

"Hmm" was what he said, and I thought he might have looked a little disappointed. But he put his arms around me and hugged me just the same. And, for just a moment, I lay down the oath and felt his arms around me, and life was good.

# 32

## the key

E ven though the ride wasn't the smoothest, riding with the top off of the Jeep always relaxed me. The sun was going down, and the breeze from the Pacific Ocean was making the temperature in the Bay Area nippy. I drove up and down along the familiar San Leandro streets where I'd grown up. There were children playing on sidewalks and in driveways. There were houses that had lights on in the kitchen, and you could see mothers making dinner for their families. I parked in the cul-de-sac on the sidewalk in front of my parents' house.

There, four teenage boys played basketball with a hoop on a large black pole maybe as high as an official court. They played hard. They seemed unaffected by the cold. They were running and sweating intensely. Their shirts were off and their backs were shiny. Two teenage girls stood nearby on the sidewalk watching. One had all of her hair pulled back into a ponytail that swung each time she laughed. The other had her hair parted and pulled into a ponytail at the top and let loose in the back. They wore short jean shorts that barely covered their little behinds. And they had teenage figures and little white tops on, which matched with their clean white sneakers.

One girl stood with a hand on her hip, yelling things to the boys in the street.

"Dunk it, Anthony!"

"Uh-ohh, Taj, here it comes. Here it comes!"

"Ahh, that was tight!"

"Y'all tight! Do that at the game, Anthony."

I watched and listened. Then someone said to me, "It's cold out here. You coming in?" It was Charlotte.

"Oh, hi, I didn't even hear you walk up."

Her expression was stern and serious as usual. "I see, come on in. Your dad is upstairs."

I got out of the car and headed past Charlotte's Ford Tempo toward the door. Her backseat was full of groceries. She opened the door on the driver's side and I went around to the door on the passenger side. She filled her arms up with bags and said again, "Your daddy is upstairs." I opened the door, wrapped my arms around three bags, and closed the door. I wondered if she knew that my daddy and I were going to talk about my real mother.

"Okay," I said.

We came into the house through the garage. I stepped onto the marble floors, headed into the kitchen, and set the bags on the counter. Their kitchen was always immaculate. Never any crumbs on the counter. Never any tomato sauce splashed on the can opener. Never any dust between the stove and the refrigerator. I'd never say it, but Charlotte was excellent at cleaning. I wasn't this way. While I did what needed to be done, I was far from the perfect homemaker. I grabbed the bananas out of the bag and placed them in the fruit bowl. Then I rinsed off the apples and put them away too.

She must have thought I was stalling because she asked, "Are you going to go upstairs?" She didn't say it in that "I'm trying to start a fight with Chantell" tone that she sometimes used, the one that got on my nerves so badly. No, her voice sounded cracked and an octave deeper, like she wanted to cry.

I put the fruit down and followed the shiny marble floor to the front door. I looked around the living room at all of the white French provincial furniture that never got sat on. I looked down the hall toward the den area, where everyone who came over relaxed. Then I looked up to where I was supposed to be headed, up the stairs.

I took off my shoes and put them near the front door next to the big wicker basket that housed new socks for visitors who didn't want to walk around barefoot. I didn't know what to expect. I headed up the stairs slowly. For a moment, my mind went back to the day I found my father collapsed in his room. I looked down at my newly pedicured feet. My toenails were powder blue, and I'd had white butterflies painted on the nails of both of my big toes.

I tried to ignore the rapid pace of my heart. I put one foot in front of the other, and I looked at the white butterflies. I imagined them flapping their wings and flying up the stairs as I walked.

I peeked in and there was Daddy. He lay in his bed half asleep and half watching the news. I gave him a kiss on the cheek and sat on the edge of the bed. He looked good. I said another quick thank-you to God as he sat up and turned down the volume. Daddy had a big, strong voice and so my suspicions were aroused by his lowering the television's volume. He was really making me nervous.

"Hey, Daddy."

"Hi, Chantell. I am glad you finally made it. I really want to talk to you."

He reached over to the nightstand, grabbed his water bottle, and took a sip. He removed the eyeglasses that he always wore and looked at me very seriously. Daddy always tried to make everything okay for me, and this demeanor was one that I rarely saw. We were going to talk about my mom, but was he going to tell me I'd hurt her? If I'd done something to her, then I was sorry.

"Daddy, what is it?"

Daddy held up his hand at me as if to say, Don't speak.

"After your mom died, I used to pray for strength and knowledge as to what to do." He looked away from me and at the dresser in front of the bed. "You was a girl, and I used to worry if I was doing the right things for you. Did I hug you enough? Did I comb your hair nice like the other little girls? Would your mother agree with the bedtime that I'd set for you? But you turned out real good, so I must have did okay."

I smiled and nodded. "You were a good parent, Daddy."

He held up his hand again. "Please, baby, let me finish. I'm trying to say, I'm so very proud of you, baby."

He paused and chuckled. "I worried about you, though. I had reason to be concerned. Some of the things that came out of your little
mouth sometimes made me nervous." He laughed.

It felt like Dad was going to drop a bomb on me. Like maybe my
mom hated me, or maybe his checkup at the hospital didn't go so
well.

"Please, Daddy, what's the matter?"

"Honey, just let me finish talking. Anyway, you were just like your
mom—smart, pretty, and creative."

The door opened and Charlotte came in. I don't think we'd ever
spoken about my mother in front of her. I swallowed. Oh boy.

She sat down in the chair next to the bed. Daddy just kept on talking.

"You look just like your mom now," said Daddy, gazing at me
again. "I knew that one day you'd want to talk about Zarina. I've
been waiting for it. We've been waiting for it." He looked over at
Charlotte.

"Your mom was energetic and full of spirit. She loved life almost
as much as she loved you. She had a magnetic vibe about her. People loved her. She always meant what she said, and if she made a
commitment to you, then she would kill herself trying to keep it."

Daddy looked as though he might cry. "I remember when we
moved into our first home. One year, on Thanksgiving, your mother
invited the entire block to our house. All of the neighbors came over
before they sat down at their own tables to eat their meals. There
must have been fifty people in our little living room standing together. We all held hands and prayed as a whole. Then everyone took
turns and said something that he was thankful for. It was beautiful.
It became a routine too, Thanksgiving at our house. We did that
every year from the day we were married, up until the very end."

How beautiful. I closed my eyes and tears fell.

Dad continued. "Your mother was ill often, and when she was
pregnant with you, the doctor asked what to do if he was forced to
choose between her living or your living. I told him that we'd go
home and we would discuss it. But she said that there was nothing
to discuss. She told the doctor that if life had become a game that

would result in a coin toss then he should just count her out. She said she refused to play heads or tails with her child."

I covered my eyes and cried. I cried because my mother was beautiful. She was more than physically beautiful; she was truly beautiful.

"She went to the hospital on a Wednesday afternoon," said Daddy. "For two days she lay in the hospital bed in labor. I felt like I was losing my mind. Her pain, my guilt. It was torturous. But on that following Wednesday"—Daddy's voice cracked—"the three of us, we went home as a family."

I mourned some more for my mother the way that I should have long ago. I cried tears of happiness because I felt whole and fortunate to have come from two good people. And tears of sadness because of a longing that I'd held hidden deep inside of me for so long.

Then Dad took Charlotte's hand and held it. I looked at both my dad and Charlotte. I had one more question. "But Daddy, through the years you never mentioned my mother. You guys acted like she was never here. It seemed like nobody cared that she ever even—"

I couldn't swallow. The knot in my throat was huge. It was right there at the bottom of my throat. The tears rolled down my cheeks fast. I cried until that longing feeling that was hidden away in the base of my stomach surrendered. It covered me from my head to my toes. And Daddy and Charlotte let me go through it.

I was still sitting on the edge of the bed when I looked up, and Daddy motioned for me to come closer to him. He reached out and hugged me. Charlotte sat next to me and rubbed our backs.

"I'm sorry, baby. I cared. We cared," he said. "We just couldn't do nothing about it." He took a deep breath and said, "At first, I couldn't talk about it. I felt so sorry for you, Chantell. Losing your mom hurt me to the core of my being. Watching you interact every day, without her, that just ripped me up. Then you got really quiet, and it seemed like you just closed up. We tried counseling. I tried talking to you, but you never budged."

I wiped my eyes with my knuckle. I didn't remember counseling.

I cried for my mother. I cried for my father. I cried for all of us. Too many tears for my knuckles to wipe away. I let them fall freely. I looked over at Charlotte, and she was crying too. "We've just been waiting for you to ask about her."

My father got out of bed. He wore the brown-striped pajamas I'd bought for him last Christmas. He didn't move like someone who just had surgery a couple of weeks prior. He was getting around pretty well. He put his brown feet in his slip-on brown leather house shoes and went over to the dresser. He opened the drawer and took out an old crinkled manila envelope. Opening it, he took out a single key on a chain.

"This is a key to a space at Darryl's Mini Storage downtown. Go to space number seventy-seven." He handed the key to me.

"What's in there, Daddy?" I asked.

"Things for you. Go see."

And that is all that he would say. I took the key and put it in my purse. In a little bit, Dad would start clicking the channels on the television and telling me about how many games were left in the Raiders football season.

It was getting late. I hugged them both, thanked them, and told them that I should get home so I could wake up for work in the morning. Tomorrow, I thought, I'd go to the storage and see what was in there. My parents walked me outside. The crisp night breeze hit me and it felt cold. Very cold. I'd gotten a lot of information about my mom that night. But soon, I'd have more.

I was anxious to see what was in there. What kind of storage place was it? What would happen if I lost the key? Was this the only copy? Could I still get in? Was it like a safe-deposit box? I took it out of my purse, slid it into the front pocket of my black jeans, and walked to my Jeep.

"Pull the truck into the driveway," said my dad when he saw that the top was off. I got in and turned on the lights. The orange lights in the dash were very dim. I turned the knob, and the temperature, gas, and miles per hour gauges glowed. I maneuvered a U-turn in the middle of the street and pulled into the driveway. Dad went into the back of the Jeep and took out the soft-top and started to put it on. I got out of the car and stood in the driveway with Charlotte. Goosebumps rose on the back of my arms. We didn't say a word. We'd never been friends, but we stood in the driveway side by side. I touched the key in my pants pocket, just to make sure it was still there.

"Everything there is for you," said Charlotte. I don't even remember driving away.

I drove around in the blue velvet night with the intention of heading for home. It started sprinkling a light mist. Cars' white headlights came toward me on the opposite side of the street. Red rear lights stopped in front of me. I made left turns and right turns. Finally I pulled in to the mini-storage place called Darryl's. There was no one there. The parking lot was empty except for a big iron gate and me. I got out of the car and went over to the phone pad that was stuck into the beige cement wall next to the gate. It sat there suspended in concrete with no directions and no instructions. It was late. It was damp and chilly. I got back into the car. What was in there? I turned on the lights and the radio. Warm streams of heat hit my face and ankles as I sat there.

My dad, who never talked about my real mother, said he'd been waiting for me to come to him about her. How come he didn't just bring me here? Why was the stuff in storage and not at their home? How long had it been in here? And I couldn't believe that Charlotte, my evil stepmother, who acted like I was here by some immaculate conception by my father alone, was crying over me, and my mother. She was so phony. I bet she was the reason that the things weren't at the house in the first place. This was about the time that I remembered that I was to leave for vacation the next day with Eric. I wouldn't be able to get back over here for almost a week. I started my car and pulled out of the parking lot.

# 33

## getting nowhere

Everything was happening in my life at the same time, and the timing couldn't have been worse. My stepmother was acting like she liked me, I'd just inherited a storage room full of probably some very important things, and I still had a cruise to pack for. I was tired. It was late, and I didn't want to go home. I didn't want to be alone. I reached over into the seat next to me and grabbed my cell phone out of my purse. I dialed Eric's number.

"Hello," said a groggy voice.

"Hi, Eric. It's me."

"What's up?"

"I phoned you earlier, you didn't call me back."

"Oh, I haven't checked my voice mail."

"I need to talk to you."

He was quiet. He probably had somebody over there now. "Come on," he said at last.

"What?"

"Come over."

"I'll be there in a few." I didn't give it a second thought. I hung up the phone and headed toward the lake.

Eric lived in Oakland, just next to Lake Merritt. Oakland was an unusual town. It was one of the few cities that I'd known of where you could go downtown and find a lake smack dab in the middle of it.

Around the lake there were lots of houses and apartments. Some Victorian, others recently remodeled. Hundreds of them, it seemed. No two alike. To live by the lake showed stature. It was a haven for up-and-coming single, black twenty- and thirty-somethings. The rents in this area had skyrocketed, doubling twice in the last two years.

By the time ten minutes had passed, I had pulled onto his street. I parked, checked my makeup, and put on some MAC brick-colored lipstick. I walked up to his building and rang the intercom to his apartment.

"Chantell?" he said.

"Yes, it's me"

He buzzed me in, and I took the elevator up to the eighth floor.

"What's up?" he said when he opened the door.

"Hey. I need to talk to you."

I went over to his white leather couch and sat down. He stood in the hallway that led to his bed looking like he wanted to sleep.

I began, "I've got this key and my dad says for me to go to this storage place called Darryl's with it."

"Chantell, can we do this in bed?"

"Yes, sure, Eric. But listen to this. For months now I have been asking myself how can I make my life better. Now I realize that I haven't been living for me. And how can you be happy if you're living for other people? I don't know. Anyways, everything is just weird right now. I had this dream of my—"

His lips pressed into mine. "Let's go to bed. We can talk more there," he said.

He walked me into his room with his arm around my waist. Eric's bedroom was beige and cream and black. And it was all clean except for the chair in the corner with all of the clothes in it. That's how he cleaned up. He took everything that he had tossed around the room for the last couple of days and put it all in the chair. And it stayed there until it could hold no more, or he or I could stand it no more. It was about this time that I realized that Eric was wearing just his dark blue checkered wool Eddie Bauer boxers and a crisp white T-shirt that looked as though he'd ironed it. He tugged at my Donna Karan blouse, pulling it out of my black pants. This was not what I came over for. He got closer to me, and I had to stop this.

"Eric, I am trying to talk to you."

"I'm listening."

He wrapped his arms around me and walked me backward to his bed. The warmth from his body felt really good. Everything wasn't about sex. He rubbed his hand through my hair.

"Eric, I am trying to say something."

The backs of my calves were against his mattress. He stepped forward again, with just a bit of force. I fell back onto his bed. His chest pressed against mine. It always came to this. I needed to be strong.

"Eric, I've just come over to share my news." There was a kind of control that I gave him, or that he could take at will. But I didn't come over to give myself in that way.

He started whispering in my ear. "Chantell, it's me. Your man. Your husband-to-be." He kissed my neck.

His warm, Aqua Fresh–smelling breath was gentle to my nose and warm on my ear. But my heart said for me to look, listen, and open my eyes. Husband-to-be wasn't good enough. And I said, without yelling, "No."

"What?"

"I said no, Eric." And I rolled him off of me. We were not communicating, and we were not married.

"This is not how I want to live my life. I came over here to tell you about the key. To tell you that my father had something in storage that pertained to my mom. But you don't listen! Eric Summit, I am precious, and worthy of a guy who wants to build a life with me."

We sat up. Eric put his hands to his forehead, like maybe I was giving him a headache, and moaned.

"I am trying to talk to you, Eric! I want you to listen. And I want to talk to you about real issues. We can have a real good life together! That's what I want for us. That's why I ordered separate beds for us on the cruise. Cuz we have to do it right."

"Chantell, we were fine the way that we were. What is wrong with you? What are you trying to prove?" He walked over to the door. "Look, you can sleep on the couch if you want to."

I got up. "That's okay."

He shrugged his shoulders. "Fine."

I fished my keys out of my purse. "I'll just see you tomorrow at Pier 27. We've got a whole week to talk about this."

"Yeah."

# 34

## pack your bags

I got back to my house after midnight, and I was exhausted. Sure, my body was tired, but all of the things going on in my soul were what had me begging for rest. Old doors were revolving, and new doors were opening. I never really got the chance to discuss the key with anyone. I'd had no time to really reflect on my thoughts.

There were a ton of things that I still needed to do before I left. Cruises were supposed to be about fun and relaxation, but all I was feeling at the moment was a lot of pressure. I didn't know what the key would lead to, and I wasn't even finished packing. I imagined this was what the therapist was talking about when he said for me to slow down and feel my feelings. I was going in every direction, and not getting anywhere. Burning all my candles at both ends.

I managed to finish the last of my packing and prepared for my morning shower. I passed my collection of shoes all carefully boxed and arranged. I had belts and slacks and trousers, and blouses by Donna Karan, Prada, Anne Klein, Liz Claiborne, BCBG, and Jones New York. I grabbed my almost knee-length black skirt and a snug-fitting burnt orange sweater. I went back to the shoe area and grabbed my matching burnt orange pumps.

I walked toward the shower past the vanity mirror and chair. I had probably forty types of toiletries and perfumes neatly arranged on the countertop. I looked in the cabinet and found the cleansers that I wanted to use. I smiled when I thought of how I'd stood up to Eric last night. Thank the Lord for that. I was getting stronger and stronger every day. I looked around at all of the bath oils, body creams, and shower gels that I owned.

I turned on KBLX, the Quiet Storm, wrapped my hair up in a huge white towel, and got in the shower. I put on my bath gloves, poured some body polishing cream into them, and cleansed. Luther Vandross blared from the radio, but I was deep in thought. I thought about my mother being in labor and how she'd told the doctors to pick me if they were forced to choose between the two of us. That was her unmoving position, and it came from deep within her heart, from her interior. I thought about the money that I was spending decorating my exterior. It was amazing. I had done everything that a person could do to show the world that I was priceless. But what had I done to decorate the person inside? What had I done for my spirit?

I got out of the shower, trying to settle into this new mind-set. I put on my clothes and makeup. I looked like a million bucks, but I didn't think it was the most important thing in the world. I put the key to the storage room in my purse, loaded up the Jeep with my luggage, and headed for the office. I had more healing to do, but at least I was making progress.

Later, at work, I pushed myself back away from my desk and headed a few rows over to my coworker Cameron's desk. I handed her copies of my accounts that she'd agreed to keep an eye on. "Here's everything. I believe that I have taken care of everything, so there shouldn't be too much maintenance involved."

"Don't worry about it," she replied. "If something arises, I can handle it. Go have some fun, girl."

I went into Canun Ramsey's office and gave him the duplicate copy of the list. Remembering my last fiasco, I cringed at the thought of him calling on my accounts again.

I grabbed my purse and left the building. This time away would prove beneficial, I was sure. I went into the underground parking lot and retrieved my Jeep. I had three suitcases packed and ready to go in the backseat. I left by 11:30 a.m., and had a little over an hour before the ship would depart. I was supposed to find long-term parking and meet Eric at Pier 27.

At 12:05 p.m. I was still driving around San Francisco, looking for a long-term parking garage with space available that didn't cost a million dollars. I drove past the pier. The traffic was heavy, and I was at a standstill, almost directly in front of the boarding area. I spotted Eric in the crowd of people, waiting in line to board the ship. Cars drove in both directions on the busy street, separating me from the line of passengers, but I could see Eric chatting with people, his wandering eyes looking for me. When two big doors opened and people started taking their places in line, I knew that I needed to park, and fast.

My light turned green, and the traffic started to move. I made a quick left turn and swooped around the Embarcadero Center. I was racing against time, and the screech of my tires proved it. I spotted a garage on my left and pulled into it. The sign read: "Daily Parking Rate $40."

The twenty-something attendant wearing Converse walked up to my car and asked, "How long will you be?"

"Do you have long-term parking?"

"Are you a tenant here?" he asked, looking down at my form-fitting orange shirt.

"Umm, hello, I'm up here," I said. "No, I'm not."

"Non-tenant long-term parking is fifty dollars a day."

"What?" I asked

"Fif-ty dollars a day."

We'd be gone for five days, I thought. "That is going to be two hundred and fifty dollars!" I said.

He raised an eyebrow like he wasn't impressed that I could count. "Sorry, ma'am," he said unsympathetically.

I gave him my keys and he gave me a ticket.

Thankful that I had rollers, I lugged my suitcases out of the back, put my carrying bag over my shoulder, and pulled.

As I hurried along the sidewalk, I could hear jazz being played on the patio above the department storefronts. The saxophones and trumpets hummed. I could hear people laughing. The San Francisco

Lunchtime Jazz series happened in the Embarcadero every Friday, all month long. I walked past the commotion and around the corner.

There were several people waiting at the crosswalk, businessmen in dark suits and London Fog trench coats, and women with silk blouses and slacks or jeans. My boarding pass was in my purse. I was dragging my suitcases with a handle in either hand. My carry-on was heavy and uncomfortable over my shoulder, which must have been obvious.

"Can I help you carry your bags?" asked a man wearing a soiled blue ski jacket and with dark black hair that looked like it hadn't been combed in a very long time. Seeing homeless people always did something to me.

The light chirped for us to cross, and people started walking in both directions.

"No, but thank you for asking."

"Then do you have any change?"

I believed that homeless people were homeless because they had lost something. I'd lost a few things in my life too. "I'll see what I have when I get across the street," I said.

I let go of my suitcase handles to check my watch—12:30. I was sure Eric must have been having a fit by now. I stood in front of the pier and unzipped my carry-on while the man waited. He stood close to me, and I could smell his scent. It reminded me of meatloaf. I hunched over, trying to ignore it, and kept digging. Eventually I found a dollar, and as I stood straight up to give it to him my head bumped his chin because he'd moved in even closer to have a look in my pocketbook with me. I was a bit startled. Okay, I was scared, but I looked at him and said in my best don't-fool-with-me tone, "Could you get your nose out my purse?"

"Oh, I'm sorry," he said. I handed him the dollar.

"Thank you," he said and went on his way.

I ran over to the pier. I checked my watch—12:37. Dang it. Where there once had been a big crowd of people, there was now only a short line left waiting to board the ship. I couldn't see Eric anymore. I walked in baby steps toward the ship, thinking of my daydream about leaving Eric on the pier as I and my other shipmates set sail. I thought of my talk with the therapist about feeling my feelings. What did I want? Was I being true to myself?

I walked through the boarding area and continued my self-examination. In the past, I'd felt a sense of pride when guys came on to me, and I would always smile when I saw women envying my legs, or my waist. And if the truth were told, I even used to giggle when women came on to Eric, because this showed me that it was always my grass that looked greener than my neighbor's. That all seemed trivial now.

What was my and Eric's relationship really about? We'd been together a long time, yet we spoke maybe twice a week. And when we talked, it was only about where we were going that week. Or to confirm which one of us was to come over. I wasn't happy. Then I thought about the dream I'd had of my mother and father dancing. What was that about? Had I learned anything at all from the stories my dad told me about Zarina?

I approached the ramp to board the ship. "May I see your ticket?" said a woman in a white uniform with black bars on the shoulders. Then a man's voice called over the speaker system, "Last call for cruise number 754 to Cabo San Lucas, Mazatlán, and Puerto Vallarta. Again, Crystal Cruises number 754 will be departing in ten minutes."

There was so much going on in my life right now. The truth was, I didn't know what the truth was because I didn't know what I wanted out of life. I'd put so much energy into my image and into Eric and me. But was it positive energy? Truthfully, I was obsessed. I did not want to be ignored. I wanted to be as beautiful and carefree as the starlets I saw on television. I wanted children that looked handsome like Eric. But right then, for the life of me, I couldn't figure out why. What was it all supposed to prove, and who was I trying to prove it to?

"Ma'am, may I have your ticket?" the woman repeated.

I looked down at my bag, then up at her.

"I—I don't have a ticket."

The lady looked at me strangely. She glanced down at my big suitcases and the black bag slung over my shoulder.

"Where are you going, then?"

I mumbled, "To get a life I guess."

I turned around and lugged my stuff back to the car.

The parking attendant who had liked my sweater looked surprised to see me back so soon. "Miss your ship?" he asked.

"No," I said. He looked like he was waiting for me to say what happened. "How much is it?" I asked.

"Daily rate is forty dollars."

"What? That's robbery! I just left the car not even thirty minutes ago."

"Look, ma'am, I don't make up the prices. The standard daily rate was posted on the sign when you drove in. I can't give you your keys until you give me forty bucks."

I looked in my bag, found a fifty-dollar American Express traveler's check, and held it out to him. In an instant I'd forgotten my personal inward journey. "Here!"

"Sorry, ma'am, we don't take traveler's checks."

Was he just having fun at my expense? I wasn't in the mood. "What do you mean you don't take traveler's checks? They are the same as cash!"

"Sorry, ma'am."

"Well, can I leave my bags here while I go to the ATM machine?"

"I'm sorry, ma'am." Now he was smirking.

"You know what? You need to get a life too," I said and walked out of the garage with my three now very heavy bags on me.

That guy really got on my nerves, to the point that my newly forming perspective just went right out the window and I watched it go. Maybe I'd join that yoga class at the Y; I kept seeing flyers posted all over our building about it, and maybe it would help me to put things into perspective again.

When I got back, the attendant's radio was blaring classic rock from the 1980s. I walked in to give him the money, and found him in the office where the keys were stored. The song was ending, and the generation X'er was deep into it. He was sitting in a chair, playing his imaginary guitar and shaking his ink black dyed hair everywhere.

"Here," I said, pushing two twenties across his desk. He pulled my keys out of his coat pocket, and they rattled as he kept playing. He certainly wasn't trying to please anyone. I got my keys, went to my Jeep, and pulled up to the exit to leave. He smiled and waved good-bye like we'd been the best of friends. "You have a good day, ma'am."

# 35

# off to darryl's

I was back in San Leandro in less than an hour. Filled with both hesitation and adrenaline, I drove down Estudillo Street to Darryl's Mini Storage. I pulled into a stall and parked. There were two other cars in the lot. I went into my black shoulder bag, found my purse, and headed toward the now open electric gate. Through the big office window I saw a man and woman, both with dark hair, sitting behind their desks reading newspapers. I opened the door to the modern storage facility, and a bell made from noisy metal trinkets let them know someone had entered.

"Hello," I said. "Can you tell me where storage number seventy-seven is?"

"Hi. Sure, what's your name?" asked the woman.

"My name is Chantell Meyers, and my father gave me this key." I held it up.

"Oh, Meyers. Right," said the man. "I'm Steve Peterson, and this is my wife, Jeanne. We live here on the grounds, and your things are never left unattended."

"Oh, okay," I said, and wondered what "things" I had. I wondered if homemade jelly kept for twenty years. Maybe there were photos of me and my mom and dad together. I hoped so. I would love to see her face again. Maybe she'd be in her *Soul Train* wardrobe. Maybe it was pictures of her asleep in the teal casket that I remembered from the funeral. Oh God, please help me get ready for this, I thought.

I followed the Petersons past a long line of orange metal rolling doors. One man had his storage door opened, and I saw an old bike and a badly splintered canoe. He sat in there in a lawn chair with his legs crossed, smoking a pipe, in the midst of elk horns mounted on plaques and fishing poles, like it was his own garage.

"Hello, Mr. Michaels," said Jeanne.

"Hello," said the old man.

Jeanne and Steve led me to stall number 77. "Here you are," said Steve, patting me on my hand before they walked back to the office.

"Thank you," I called back to them. "I guess."

Alone again, I wondered if there was something awful in there. If my dad hadn't been sick he surely would have come here with me. What if there was someone in there? If I thought about it too long, I was liable to turn around and go home. I took a deep breath, found my key, and opened the padlock at the bottom of the roll-up door.

The huge door creaked as it disappeared upward. First I saw what looked like tall packages with sheets over them. It was dim except for the welcomed light from the open door. The place was darn near dustless. I might even have thought that I was in the wrong storage space except that something told me this was where I should be. There was a huge old bookcase filled with books. I walked over to it. It was mahogany, and big and heavy. It had six planks lined with books, mostly authors that I'd never heard of. A few I'd read in college—Phyllis Wheatley, Dorothy West, Harriet Jacobs.

There was a huge old Bible with cracks all over its leather cover, and papers sticking out of it. There were trinkets and a big blue stuffed bear that looked familiar, but I couldn't place where I'd known it from. There were tons of dried flowers in bunches tied with what looked like strands of straw or hay. I spotted a light switch on the wall. I flicked it and suddenly the dim room was well illuminated. I lowered the rolling door halfway, for a bit of privacy, and continued to look around. The room was neatly kept. There was a beautiful quilt that I definitely remembered from long ago. It was neatly folded and stored in a clear plastic bag. I went over to it and tore open the plastic. It was made of yellow, cream, black, and green scraps of fabric. My mother used to lie under it on the couch. It was folded and tucked so neatly. I put it to my face and inhaled it.

My eyes were busy moving, scanning all of the objects along the wall, and I bumped into a trunk. It was old and black, with metal edges and a big ebony handle. I released the clasps and lifted the lid open. Inside I found old pictures, letters, and postcards. I felt both sad and intrigued. I picked up a postcard that was from my grandmother. She was visiting her sister in Little Rock, Arkansas.

It read:

10/04/74

*Dear Zarina,*

    *I hope you're doing well. Your Aunt Mae is recovering just fine. The doctors said she should be up and about in two weeks or so. I am glad for that. As for you, my beautiful and stubborn daughter— Promise me right now, that you will get at least eight hours of rest every day.*

    *Send everyone my love, and I'll see you next week.*

    *Love you,*

*Mom*

    *P.S. How is my little Chantell doing? Tell her not to forget that her Nana is going to take her to Bible study on Wednesday, as soon as I get back.*

I sighed and closed my eyes. Putting the postcard to my nose, I inhaled deeply. I thought of them. I remembered my grandmother; she was prim and proper, but feisty. Her hair was never out of place, as she went to the beauty shop every Friday. She was a brown-skinned woman, prone to moles. She had them all over the back of her neck. She had long, thick, coarse hair, which she wore straightened with big soft finger waves in it. Each night she took these huge hair clips and clipped about five of them in her hair, and she slept like that. The next day she'd take them out and magically she would have perfect huge waves in her hair. My grandma liked to look immaculate, and she dressed me that way too. She bought me Carter's dresses from JCPenney, and Stride Rite leather shoes. My dresses were full of buttons and bows and pink lace and she took me to church with her every Sunday. She never really asked my mother, or my father, or— after my mom died—my stepmother Charlotte. She just said for them to have her little debutante ready by 10 a.m. on Sunday for church. She'd say, "My grandbaby isn't going to be a heathen for anybody."

My grandmother's name was Mrs. Hattie Brumwick, and she died when I was twelve years old, almost exactly seven years after my mom. She was the second big loss in my life. She always used to say that bad luck came in threes. So when she died I knew that it was just a matter of time before I lost someone else. Then Keith left the next year. I sat down on the dusty floor and put the postcard in my purse.

I saw a large brown leather book pressed against the inside of the trunk and pulled it out. I recognized my Grandmother Hattie's handwriting, and realized it was a logbook that sometimes doubled as her journal. In it, beneath grocery lists, my grandmother had written: "That Zarina is so stubborn. My sister Mae says that we were wrong to tell her that she was too sick to do anything but be conservative. Maybe she was right. I don't know how to make her be still!"

There were notes like that all through it. Near the back, beside a list of monthly expenses, she had written: "I have tried to do the best that I could for Zarina and her family. She's just got her own way about her. Always has. I'm so worried about her. All I can do is hold her up to the Lord."

From what I could make out, my mother, the first big loss, was quite a little rebel. My grandmother had tried to keep her prim and proper but she thought that Zarina acted like an Oakland Raiders fan. It seemed that people, my grandmother included, always told Zarina that because of the sickle-cell, she was too sick to be anything but very conservative. And apparently something happened where my grandfather, her father, had stopped talking to her for two months once he found out she was pregnant with me. Her father, according to my grandmother's words, was just an ornery and bull-headed man. He flat out told Zarina that she should not try to have children. My mother said that my grandfather was a darn fool, and that people should do what was in their hearts.

I didn't know him at all, my grandfather. He and my grandmother divorced and he got remarried and moved away. My grandmother wrote that he loved my mom dearly; she said, however, that he was too stubborn to say it, and that Zarina was just as bullheaded as he was. Grandma Hattie said that she knew that the mysterious gifts that my mom received in the mail each year with no return address, up until the day they made amends on his deathbed, were from him.

I placed the book at my side, reached back into the chest past a half-full Chanel No. 5 perfume bottle, and grabbed a handful of pictures. I looked them over. There were pictures of me, my dad, and my mother, standing in front of our new root beer brown van. I recognized myself right off because even in the distance I could see the little black mole above my eyebrow. I must have been a year old, and I stood in front of the two of them leaning against my mom's leg for support. I had on white sandals and a yellow sundress with big white bloomer underwear showing underneath. My mom looked great. She was younger than my present age, and her black hair was down and hung freely around her shoulders. She wore a gold outfit that looked something like a woman's space suit. It had gold-flecked trim around the sleeves, and the same shiny ornaments down her pantlegs' stitching. She had her arm around Dad, who looked ultra-1970s. He wore a black tank top with some letters on it and a pair of jeans. His hair was styled in an Afro parted on the side, with big sideburns, and an Afro pick bearing a fist logo sticking up in the back.

I put the pictures near my purse and my grandmother's logbook back in the chest. I walked back toward the big tattered Bible in the bookcase. I pulled it from the shelf. It belonged to my grandmother. The first page read: "This book is presented to Hattie Brumwick, from Joshua Brumwick." I flipped through it and there were bulletins from my church that dated back to 1979. There were family pictures in there, and things written in the margins.

Someone had written: "Thank you God for working on me. Thank you God for healing me and preparing me." And "I can feel you comforting me. I can hear you reassuring me. I can see your blessings ready to pour upon me."

I opened the Bible and read to myself from the fourth chapter of Mark: "And he rose and rebuked the wind and said unto the sea, Peace be still. And the wind ceased, and there was a great calm."

And I can scarcely explain what happened as I sat reading. A gentleness came over me and rocked me and held me for a while.

When I was ready, I flipped through more old family pictures of us at places that I recognized, places that I sometimes visited now like Big Bear Lake and Yosemite Park. I examined the photos closely; we were camping in some, and roller skating in others. My mother and father and I had had a short but beautiful family life.

I was still sorting through pictures when I heard someone knock on the partially rolled-down door. "Are you all right in there?" I heard a man's voice call.

I rolled the door upward and saw that it was the man with the canoe. I was crying like a baby and hadn't even realized it. I was embarrassed, and surprised that I had been loud enough to alarm anyone.

I wiped my eyes. "Yes, I am okay. Just going over some old stuff." I smiled.

"Yes, well, I do know how that is." He rolled the door up a bit more and peeked in. "I'm Chuck, and I am your neighbor." He held out his hand. "So if I can do anything, you just let me know." He sounded like he lived there.

"Chuck, I'm Chantell Meyers." I shook his hand. "Thank you. I appreciate it."

"Well, you're alright. So, guess I'll be getting back to my place." He turned and walked away.

He made me smile.

I glanced around the space. There were sheets everywhere covering both big and little rectangular squares. I walked over to one sheet and whipped it off. My eyes opened wide. There were three huge pictures in slots on a rollaway bed. The first was a painting of sunflowers in a Mason jar. It was soothing yet strange, because it looked like the pink flowers that I had cut and placed in a Mason jar and set on my coffee table a few weeks back. I reassured myself, "See there! I knew my mom! How could I think that I didn't? We like the same flowers!"

The second painting was of a little brown girl and boy maybe five years old. They wore loincloths and were kneeling over a little stream. The little boy's hands were cupped and the little girl was drinking from them. The young boy looked stern and determined. The young girl's eyes were hollow. To me, she looked tired, like she had no more fight in her. The entire painting was done in earth tones—browns, greens, beiges, creams—except for the water, which was a beaming, riveting blue. The frame was made from heavy oak.

The painting was the most beautiful thing that I'd ever seen. I wondered what had inspired this. I looked at the back and saw written the words "Quenching My Thirst." In the bottom right-hand corner my mother had signed it with a big Z, and a squiggly line.

I was determined to get some of that stuff home with me today. I drove my Jeep inside the big black gate and around to storage space number 77. In the storage room, I had my very own historical, personal library or museum or something. And I was determined to hold on to it. It would take me a while to go through everything, but the little that I had seen gave me a new sense of myself, a realness about me. I recited some of the things that my grandmother had written in the old Bible. "Thank you God for working on me. Thank you God for comforting me." I experienced a certainty that I'd never felt before. And I was going to work harder on my relationship with God.

It felt good to know that my mother existed, that I hadn't dreamt her up. And I asked God to show me more of my true self. I tried to get the paintings into the Jeep, but stopped when I heard the scraping sound of a wooden picture frame. I stepped out of the room and rolled the big door down and locked it. Then I ran around looking for Chuck, my neighbor with the canoe—maybe he could help me to get them into my vehicle. He was nowhere to be found. I ran around the narrow alleys to the front office and it was locked. I didn't know where the couple lived, so I'd just have to come back and take the paintings another day. I went back to space number 77, retrieved my purse, grabbed the Bible and the stack of pictures, and headed out.

The big electric gate opened slowly, so I grabbed my cell phone from my purse. I looked down at the pictures that were sitting on my seat. I wanted go to the craft store and get a photo album. Since I had the week off, I could mount the pictures into a scrapbook in nice chronicles.

Trying to be "right" was hard. I waited for a light to turn green and regathered the slipping stack of pictures. Charlotte was the only person missing from them. She'd probably been the one that kept me from my mom's stuff. She wanted to have my dad to herself—I bet that was why she picked on me like she did. She was the one who wanted to act like Zarina never was.

Charlotte needed an attitude adjustment, and I was going to tell her to go get one. I dialed the number. The phone rang.

"Hello," she answered.

I let her have it. "Charlotte you've been keeping all of this stuff from me because you didn't want me to know my mother! You never gave two cents about me. All you wanted was my father's hard-earned money!"

"Chantell . . . Where are you? Come over here right now!"

"You know what, Charlotte? Don't you tell me anything. You are not my—"

"Chantell, you little spoiled, ungrateful heifer! You get over here right now! Do you hear me? *Right now!*"

She had never spoken to me like that before. I was shocked. And for some reason, I listened. And I went.

# 36

## setting the record straight

I pulled into their driveway and went into the house. Charlotte was sitting in the dining room, at the table, flipping through an *Ebony* magazine. She wore a yellow jogging suit, and her legs were crossed and shaking in quick little movements. The television was on and tuned in to *Forrest Gump,* but the volume was off. Charlotte, who didn't look up to acknowledge me, must have just gotten a haircut, because her hairline at the nape of her neck was sculpted into a V. I walked in and sat down beside her.

She was still flipping the pages when she said, "I knew Zarina."

Oh brother. What a crock! This was the last thing that I expected her to try to pull. "Okay, whatever, Charlotte." How could she have known my mother? My parents were soul mates, and they never even knew her when they were together.

"We were young adults. Your mom and I were good friends and we lived across the street from each other. Your father, Harold, was my boyfriend."

This woman needed prayer! "Oh yeah. Tell me another one," I said. "And did you know that I used to go out with Denzel Washington?" I laughed and rolled my eyes up in my head. I'd heard enough of her foolishness for one day. Like my mother needed to go around stealing people's boyfriends. My mom was so pretty, she could get her own man.

"I don't have to lie to you, Chantell! When have I ever lied to you?"

She hadn't really.

"I'm rehashing this story for you, not for me. So just shut your mouth and listen."

She continued, "One day Harold came over to my house and saw Zarina. And instantly he just became a whole different person. Just like that. I tried to hold on to what we had, but it got to a point where I knew that I just needed to let it go. To let them go."

Wow, I was speechless. I looked in her eyes and saw pain, and it was obvious how real this secret of hers was.

"So that's what I did. I let them go. And they got closer and closer. They were living their lives, and I was trying to live mine. I was dating a fellow, Manfred Washington, when I heard that Harold and Zarina had had a baby girl. It still hurt something awful, but I wished them the best."

She paused. "Then one day Zarina came over to my house. She said she had to speak with me. Said she was sick. Really sick. She said that she didn't know how much longer she had. Your mother asked me to take care of you, and to take care of Harold."

She fumbled through the magazine with glassy eyes. "That is what I have tried to do."

"I am sorry, Charlotte," I said. "I didn't know."

"You didn't know because you're too busy rolling your eyes and talking smart. You think the world revolves around you," she snapped.

I couldn't say anything, because she was right. So I just looked straight ahead at the television and watched Forrest and Jenny run through the water to each other.

"I haven't purposely tried to keep anything from you, Chantell!" Her voice cracked and the tears fell freely. "You think you know everything, but guess what? You don't. Your mother's passing away hurt both you and your dad so much that we decided we'd just as soon wait until you asked about her to discuss her. What you don't know is that it hurt me too! Maybe not telling you wasn't the right thing to do. But we didn't know."

She said, "Am I perfect? No, I am not. But I love you, and I love your father. And that's something that you act like you don't know anything about. I go to that storage every month and pay that bill, and I keep those wooden picture frames polished for you. That *is* love. That is unconditional love. Sooner or later, you're going to have to learn, girl."

I put my arms around her. "I'm sorry, I'm so sorry. I am learning. Forgive me, Charlotte."

"I love you, Chantell."

"I love you too, Charlotte."

# 37

## coming out

I almost choked on my tea when I heard the mess Tia was saying. "Chantell, I can see right through you. Admit it!"

"Tia, you're ridiculous!" I laughed and changed the phone to my other ear.

"Say that you don't! I know that you want Keith Talbit!"

If this was what having siblings would be like, then I was glad I didn't have any. I rolled my eyes, sighed into the phone, then admitted, "Okay. Keith is different. And I love him, but it's not the way *you're* thinking."

"Well, why not?"

"Well, because for one, he and I are not the same type."

"What do you mean, the same type? I think he's digging you. And you said he washed your car while you ate cake! Why else would a man do that?"

"Oh, I don't know, Tia, maybe because . . . it was dirty!"

"You know what I mean."

I laughed. "Well, he does look at me strangely. But it's not romantic love. He's never tried to kiss me or anything."

"Well, Chantell, if you like him, tell him. Honesty is the best. It's so easy too, all you have to do is come right out and say, 'Keith I really like you. And I want to know how you feel about me.'"

I couldn't help it. I burst out laughing. "Girl, that's corny. Tia, you've been married too long. If I did that he'd think that I was some desperate little gold-digger trying to land a doctor. Heck no! He is just my friend. I'm not saying that mess to that man! Matter of fact, I'm not saying anything."

My girl had lost her mind. What did I look like? I was not going to hang around him and have him thinking that I wanted him to jump my bones like a half-naked extra in a rap video. I laughed some more. "You a fool, Tia."

"You laugh, but Chawnee, if you like him, I think you should be honest and speak how you feel."

"Okay, Dr. Phil."

She continued, "You know what? You're a trip, Chantell. When it's business, you're all over it like gangbusters. Schmoozing, getting the deal closed, getting the contract signed, handling your business. But when it comes to your heart, you shy away and scurry around from any attachment, unless of course it's a negative one like Eric."

Oh, no, she didn't go there. "Tia, what is that supposed to mean?" I was getting upset. She sounded like I was some low-self-esteem reject.

"Chawnee, slow your row, alright? I am just saying that, if you like him, he seems like a good guy. Express it. I want you to be happy, so don't get funky with me, homechick!"

"Well, thank you for your thoughts, Mrs. Married Woman, but you don't know what it's like out here." Hopefully my tone let her know that I loved her but I wasn't doing anything of the sort.

"Okay, you stubborn little wench, do as you wish. I ain't telling your butt nothing else," she said, pretending to be through with me.

"Yes, my darling best friend, I love you too." I laughed.

My phone clicked. "Oh, hold on a minute. That's my other line."

"Oh no, Chawnee, I've gotta run. I actually have to head up the school. Are you coming by Tuesday to get your hair done?"

"Yes, I'll be there."

"Okay, see you then."

"Bye."

"Bye."

I hurriedly clicked over. "Hello?"

"Hello, Chantell, it's Keith."

"Hi, Keith."

"Are you busy?"

"No, I just hung up with Tia."

"Oh, how is she?"

"She's good."

"Good," he said, then he was quiet.

"Keith," I said, "thanks again for the strawberry cake and for the car wash."

"Oh, anytime, you're welcome. I just wanted to say something."

"What's up?"

"I, uh, I meant it when I said that you could trust me," said Keith. Where did that come from? "I know," I said.

"We'll see."

"What do you mean?"

"I just mean that I really want you to know that I'm here for you. And that I don't want to lose contact with you again."

Keith was a true gentleman. He was both simple and complicated, and masculine. And so real that he scared me to death. And I knew that he, unfortunately, was likely too good to be true. I wouldn't allow myself to get wrapped up. I couldn't afford the disappointment. After all, he had said that he was only going to be around for a few months anyway.

I could write a book on being left. Too much. I was just going to pretend we were little-kid-best-friends again.

"Hey, what are you thinking about?" he asked.

"Oh, I don't know." I stumbled back into the conversation. "Do you ever feel like you're wearing a mask?"

"A mask?" he asked.

"Yes, you know, like, for example, one moment I have to be an advertising expert, and the next moment, I'm . . ."

"What? Diva extraordinaire, or little spoiled Chawnee, with the sad angel eyes?"

I chuckled. "Yeah, something like that."

"I'd guess that we all have roles in life. The trick, I think, is to stay humble and not get lost in them."

"How do you do that?" I wanted to know.

"Well, I don't know, Chantell . . . I guess you have to know what you value. Me, I value jazz music. I value sunsets, and waterfalls. I value God, who is the head of my life and whom I trust completely. Do you feel me?"

Mmm-hmm, I thought, but it didn't come out. I was speechless.

"You there?"

"I'm here."

"Can I see you again?" he asked.

"Umm, no, Keith, I can't." My life was a little too heavy right now.

"Why not?"

"Well, I have a lot going on at work, and you have a lot going on until late hours. I'm helping to take care of my daddy. I am not getting home until late. And you know that you're leaving soon." Oops, I didn't mean to say that last part.

"Huh?"

"I just mean that you have so much work to do before you leave, and I've been really tired, you know. Stuff like that."

"Well then, we don't have to go bungee jumping or anything. We can rent videos and eat popcorn. C'mon, Chawnee, it's me."

Why was I afraid of him? He was my friend, and he just wanted to spend a little time with me. Renew our bond.

I was quiet. "Okay. When?"

"That's my girl."

## 38

# on the road again

After the hectic workday I'd had Friday, I thought Saturday would never come around. I was looking forward to my little date with Keith. I wasn't sure what we were going to do. Keith said it was a surprise, but that I should dress casual. He told me to wear something that I could move around in.

I was excited, and rechecked myself in the mirror. I wore a cotton Gap T-shirt with a red number 52 on the front and long red sleeves. My jeans were cuffed up to my calves and bent with me as I moved, and my new K-Swiss sneakers were a beaming white. Tia straightened my hair, and I combed it in an off-center part, then bumped the ends upward into a semi flip at my shoulders. I thinly lined my eyelids sleek black, thanks to my swift hand and my new black liquid liner. I topped them off with a smudging of white eye shadow. And of course, my ever-shining lips looked great. I had on a new nude lip gloss that dazzled and was outlined by a soft pink lip color. Simple but pretty, I hoped.

The doorbell rang. When I opened it, Keith's six-foot frame appeared and the gentle scent of spices drifted through my doorway, delicately teasing my nostrils. I smiled and thought of the fun that we would have together. Keith's head was freshly shaved. His goatee was perfectly lined. His chocolate skin shone. He had on a silver watch, a white shirt with big blue and beige stripes. He also wore beige khaki pants with pockets on the sides down by his calves.

"Hi." Keith looked at me. "You look good, Chantell!"

"Thank you," I said. "So do you."

His brown skin radiated like he had bathed in milk, and his eyebrows looked like they had been groomed with care, the way they had since he was born.

"Are you ready to go?" he asked.

"Yes, are we taking my car?"

"Nope, not today." He grabbed my hand.

I locked the door and we left.

When we got into the borrowed Town Car, Keith put the key in the ignition and the car dinged, reminding us to close the doors. He took a deep breath and said, "Chantell, I've always thought the world of you."

He is so sweet, I thought. "And I you," I said. "Shoot, for a while there, you were my only friend, remember?" I laughed at my joke.

He smiled. Then he put his hands on both of my cheeks, gently turned my head toward him, and kissed my forehead. "Now let's go have some fun." He started the car, and we were off. I looked straight ahead and tried to gain control of my chest, which was rising and falling uncontrollably.

I could have taken his kiss for more than what it was, but I knew better. I thought about Tia's ridiculous comments. "You shy away from attachment when it comes to your heart." That girl didn't know nothin'. The divorce rate was over 50 percent, spouses cheated, they ran off, and they died. I had no intention of getting caught up in any unnecessary pain. With relationships, you should be cautious, and you should plan them out. Then you know what you get. And when it's over, it's over. No hard feelings. And when Keith Rashaad left, it would be the same way. I'd just give him some dap and say, "Alright, dude. I'll see you when I see ya!"

With Keith behind the wheel, we rode for nearly two hours. We found an oldies station that played James Brown and the Jackson 5. We laughed, and danced as much as we could in the car, which mainly consisted of us rolling our heads from side to side, doing "the snake," and shaking our shoulders doing "the shamrock."

# 39

# k-i-s-s-i-n-g

We ended up at the Santa Cruz Beach Boardwalk. All my life I'd lived in the Bay Area, and I'd never stopped in Santa Cruz for any time longer than it took to gas up. We got out and I surveyed the place. It looked just like it did in the commercials. Before me stood an amusement park on a beach, with a huge Ferris wheel, and skateboarders. Lots of families. Kids running around. Popcorn. Cotton candy. People with surfboards under their arms. The sun was shining on everyone. The sound of roller-coasters zipped through the air. To me, it looked unreal, like at any moment a director would come from behind a scene and say, "Cut! Okay, that's a wrap!"

I faced in the direction of the boardwalk, but Keith took my hand and led me the other way to a little nearby bike shop. The "shop" looked more like a hut from *Gilligan's Island*. Leaning against it were surfboards, bikes, roller skates, and baby strollers.

Keith looked around at the ten-speeds and mountain bikes with special gears. Then he went over to two very old bikes tied together, one orange, one black. They had no fancy gears. They had big fat tires, maybe three or four inches wide, with thick whitewalls on the sides, and big fenders that covered the top of both the front and back tires. The handlebars looked like straws that had been bent up into a U. Keith picked up the orange one and motioned for me to come and sit on its heavily cushioned black triangle seat. I complied. It felt comfy, like a favorite old housecoat. Keith went into the shack to rent the bikes, while I practiced ringing the bell on the handlebars. *Ting-ting, ting-ting,* it rang. I kinda liked the thing. "Hurry up, Keith Rashaad, your putt cycle's awaiting," I said.

He came out, got on the old black bike, and we started our journey. Keith's bike had a horn made of a black rubber bulb. "Push it!" I said. "I want to hear how it sounds." *Honk-honk*—it sounded like a duck on the water. I laughed. This could really be fun. He looked at me, smirking, and shook his head. I put my feet on the pedals and rolled down the walkway. I was a little wobbly at first, but then it all came back to me.

We rode along the beach and past the people. We rode until we came upon a group of surfers, three guys and a girl. We rode as close to them as the sidewalk built on the sand would permit. I stood there, one foot on the ground, the other on a pedal, while we looked out at them. They would swim out with their boards, wait for the right wave, and then jump on the boards and let it take them in. Unfortunately for them, there wasn't a whole bunch of breaking waves this day. Nevertheless, their group, and Keith and I, would get excited each time a wave broke, hoping that the water would swell up enough to bring them in stronger than the last.

"Look, here comes one, Keith," I would say. Or he would say to me, "Okay, this is a big one!" Only to have it never materialize into much.

I rested on the seat of my bike and sneaked a glance over at Keith. He wasn't sneaking, he was looking at me directly. I stood up and walked, straddling the bike, toward him. He sat on his bike and watched me come closer and closer. I was feeling bold, and silly, and when I got close enough, I looked at him dead square in his eyes, and I sucked my jaws in and made a fish face.

Keith just shook his head and laughed. "Little Chantell. You are so funny!"

"Why, thank you, sir, I try . . . Hey, Keith," I said, "remember how we first started talking?"

"Do I? You were really fast, and you walked over and kissed me in the church."

"No!" I cracked up. "No!"

"Yes, you did! Then you tried to cover it up by calling me a name."

"I told you it was because of a bet," I said, grinning from ear to ear. "Keith, I was six years old!"

"Umm-hmm. That's what you say."

"Stop!" I laughed. After I'd kissed him that day, I remembered feeling dazed and starry-eyed. It was his positive vibe, his energy. It was good even when he was a child, and he was delightful now.

Keith Talbit stood next to me and rubbed my back through my red T-shirt. He ran the tips of his fingers gently back and forth over my shoulder blades. I closed my eyes and felt his touch. I inhaled the scent of beach water. There were seagulls chirping and flying nearby. I thought about his kiss in the car, and wondered what it meant. I closed my eyes and absorbed the peace. I wanted to lock this moment in my long-term memory forever. Because if there was one lesson I had learned in life, it was that all good things come to an end. After Keith's project was over and he was long gone, I wanted to remember this moment forever.

"It's been so long since we just broke bread like this. Just me and you," he said. I opened my eyes and looked at him for two seconds. I really loved being with him. I really loved that he was a goal setter. I really loved that he spent time at the local Boys and Girls Club talking with teenagers. I really loved that he loved God and put Him first in his life. I put my lips on his and kissed him just as a big wave hit the shore.

"Thank you," he said to me in a whisper almost.

"Why are you thanking me?" I asked.

He said, "Chawnee, I know it's not your thing to show people your feelings. In fact, it's not your thing to let your heart show at all." He paused. "But your eyes, they tell on you."

I really loved Keith Talbit. I drew close to him and put a thousand gentle kisses on his lips.

"Wheew! Look-it, Mommy! They're *kissinn'*!" said a little voice that passed around where we stood blocking the sidewalk.

"Yes, Alexis," said the mother. "That's because they are in love."

The little girl giggled and squealed some more as she walked hand in hand with her mom. Then she started singing: *"First comes love, then comes marriage, then comes the baby in the baby carriage!"*

"Oh, Lexy!" said the mother.

Keith laughed, and I tried to smile too. I wanted to, but the truth was, she reminded me of what I was not supposed to be doing.

Keith must have felt the tension in my body. "Are you okay?"

"Uh-huh."

But I wasn't. I'd made an oath to protect myself. "Can we ride some more?" I asked.

"Sure," he said. "Let's go."

He led and I followed. We rode until we came upon another sidewalk. We followed it out of the beach area and through a neighborhood. We were famished when we came upon a little pink building that was a Thai restaurant.

"Do you eat Thai food?" asked Keith Rashaad.

"Yes, I love it."

"Good, me too. Let's go eat."

We parked our bikes and went in to eat. Though small, the restaurant was elegantly designed.

I tried to stick to my guns and block out my feelings, but it had been a whole hour, and I'd forgotten about my little oath again. We were laughing out loud, like kids in puberty.

"Your Grandma Edna was a wise woman," I said.

"Yeah, my Grandma Ed was a straight shooter. She taught me so much."

"She taught me a lot too." I thought about her. "Hey, remember when we were nine years old, and you said that we should steal the Lemonheads?"

"Nope! And don't try to blame that on me," said Keith, laughing. *"You* said we should steal the Lemonheads!"

"I don't think so!" I said.

"Yes." Keith pointed at me. "You said that we should put them under our shirts, and they were rattling around like marbles. And we tried to walk out of the store like that!"

I laughed. "I remember. I was so nervous, I let go of my shirt, and mine fell out! Dude, I think that was your idea."

"Yeah, whatever, I remember it all. Then the store owner called our parents, and I got a beating, and your daddy gave you a good talking to!"

I was in tears laughing.

"I will never forget what Grandma Edna said to me either," Keith said, staring down at his napkin. "She said, 'Boy, I love you dearly, but if you gone be stealin' you need to know that Momma ain't comin' out to the jailhouse to visit you.'"

We burst out laughing again.

"Oh, I loved your grandmother. She was no joke."

We reminisced some more until our food came.

"Keith, thank you so much; I haven't had this much fun in I don't know how long."

"You're welcome, Chantell. I'd do just about anything for you."

I played with the fork on the table in front of me and waited for him to laugh it off, but he never did.

"You know what? When I was little I used to always say that you were my girlfriend, and that when I got big, you'd be my wife. Then one day you just kissed me."

I spun the fork around and respread the napkin that was on my lap. I smiled and tucked my hair behind my ears. I hadn't realized before how hot it was in there. Before he could go on any further, I said, "Umm, excuse me. I need to go to the ladies' room."

In the bathroom, I paced. I wanted to say, "Keith, people I love always seem to leave me." And he thought he knew a lot about me, but did he know that I never cried at my own mother's funeral? What he saw was an infatuation, an illusion. I played with the little diamond studs in my ears. I wouldn't let it get any further. We weren't really dating anyway. Plus, he was leaving soon. I reapplied my lipstick.

A middle-aged lady came into the bathroom. She had short brown hair, tawny slacks with a matching belt, and a peach angora sweater. She was maybe sixty years old, with a string of freshwater pearls around her neck and pearl earrings. She stood next to me, took out a toothbrush, and rinsed it off in the sink.

"Handsome guy you got out there," she said.

"Thank you, but he's just my friend," I said.

She applied toothpaste to her brush and said, "Hmm. Well, it looks like he has more than just friendship on his mind to me."

"How can you tell?" I asked.

She laughed and set her toothbrush down. "Well, honey, for one, his eyes followed you all the way to the bathroom. He's got that look that my Jim gave me for over forty years." She blushed.

I did the same.

I went back to the table and sat down.

"There you are," said Keith. "I was wondering if you were coming back. I thought you made a mad dash out the window and skirted out on your bike."

"Nope, I'm still here." I smiled.

I sipped on the orange slushy Thai iced tea and ate my dinner. My soup and curry prawns were delicious.

We enjoyed each other's company throughout dinner, keeping the heavy talk to a minimum. Then we rode back to the grass hut, returned our rentals, and walked back to the car. Keith's cell phone rang. He looked at it. I wondered if he was going to have to get back to the hospital quickly. But Keith never said we had to hurry home. In fact, he didn't even answer the phone call. He simply closed the phone and put it back in his pocket without saying a word. I knew that it must have been a female acquaintance. I'd been treating Eric, who had been calling me constantly since he returned from the cruise, in much the same fashion. I knew that Keith was too good to be true. When we got back to Oakland, the sun was starting to set.

# when it's over, it's over

I walked into my house with a bagful of groceries and my cell phone at my ear. Tia was venting to me about her mother in-law, who'd sent Ron the secret recipe for her red velvet cake and told Ron to make sure that he "kept it in the family." Tia was hot, so I tried not to giggle. My head was tilted to one side and my arms were full of groceries. Eric had called me a couple of times and left messages, but we hadn't spoken yet. While walking over to the counter, I heard a knock at the door. It startled me, and a jar of salsa fell from the bag and almost hit my toe.

"Ohhh my goodness!" I said.

"What?"

"Oh, it's nothing. I just almost dropped something on my foot. I'm going to have to call you back. I just got in the house and someone's knocking at the door."

"Alright, bye."

I set the bag down, went to the front door, and opened it. Eric stormed in.

"What's your problem!"

"Hi, Eric."

"Where've you been?" His left eye was twitching.

"Nice to see you too."

"You can stop with the sarcasm. Where have you been?"

"Learning, Eric. And growing," I said, turning toward the groceries.

"Chantell, you're playing some kind of silly little girl game, and it's not funny."

I said nothing. His attitude didn't warrant a response.

"At first I thought maybe you'd missed the boat by accident," he said.

I turned back around to face him.

"But I've been calling you and calling you, and you haven't returned one call." He tried to sound tough, but he looked sad. "What's going on?"

I tried to explain. "I'm sorry. Look, Eric, I just think that we're together for the wrong reasons. Have a seat. Can I get you something to drink?"

He just stood there and looked at me.

Okeydokey.

"Okay, let's think about this for a moment," I said. "What were we doing anyway? Did we offer any emotional support for each other when we were together? No, because—"

His voice lowered seductively. "Chantell, you don't have to talk to me using the in-vogue psychoanalytic jargon from all them women's magazines. Of course we supported each other emotionally. Come here, babe."

He slid his arms around me, pressed his stomach to mine. I pushed back from him.

"See, Eric, this is what I mean. Let's tell the truth. Either you're not ready for a commitment, or I am not right for you, or something. Or I am not ready for a commitment. We've been caught up in a one-dimensional relationship. But now I'm really learning, and I think I am really, really growing."

"Me too," he said with his smirk.

I pushed his arms from around me. "Eric, listen, I can't do this anymore. I know that there is more to me than this."

"Than what? You're too good for me now?"

"No, Eric. More to me than designer clothes and being together for appearance's sake. I can't be with anybody right now. I just want to work on me and my issues for a while."

Eric looked so frustrated. He stepped back, threw up his arms, and said, "I don't know what the heck your problem is, but you're sounding really silly right about now."

He was trying to make me think I was being ridiculous, but the more I talked the more I was sure that I was doing the right thing.

"I'm trying to say that as a couple you and I *look* like we've got it all together. But a friend of mine's grandmother used to say that you should never judge books by their covers. How we looked together, what people thought of us, how much status we had, that stuff doesn't mean anything. There comes a time when you just have to say bye-bye to superficial stuff, and it's okay."

Eric looked at me like I'd shaved my head bald and was walking around in the rain naked with Birkenstocks on. Then angry creases appeared in his forehead, and he said, "You know what? You're trippin'. You ain't nothin' but a migraine-hoochie, but you will not drive me to Vicodin. So if you want to break up, fine." He even laughed. "I ain't worried about that. I got women fighting to be with me. Aright? I'm out."

And that was it. He turned and walked right back out my door. Determined to do better for me, I didn't go after him.

# 41

# focusing on me

I lay there nestled comfortably in my own little safe haven. The covers warm up to my neck, I chatted on the phone with Tia. I was trying to do the right things; spending less money on clothes and saving a little more in the bank. At church I was learning that faith came by hearing the word, and so I kept my grandmother's Bible sitting right next to my bed.

"So you didn't have to get on a cruise ship to find your buried treasure?"

"You thought that was cute, huh?" I said, laughing at her corny little joke. "Yeah, I have a lot of my mom's belongings. Girl, you have to see everything with your own eyes to believe it. And the paintings are just wonderful. Picasso had nothin' on my momma."

"Chawnee, I can't wait to see them," she said.

I sipped my orange, strawberry, and peach juice concoction and warmed my feet at the end of my bed with my mother's quilt. It looked great in my room and was perfect on those cold stormy nights.

"And you actually broke it off with Eric?"

"Yep. That's over."

"Al-righty." My girl didn't sound 100 percent sold. She'd soon see, though. I was certain that I wasn't a part of his future.

We talked about my dad, about her and Ron's upcoming trip to

Aruba, and the latest beauty school stories. Then she brought up Keith Rashaad, and I started getting fidgety.

"Well, what's up with him?" she asked.

"Well, we went on a date a few days ago, but because of the hours he is keeping at the hospital, I haven't spoken to him in a couple of days."

"A what? I know that you didn't say 'date'?" She giggled.

"Yeah. Tia, we went to the beach, and we had the best time," I whispered. "It was great. We rented bikes. He kept looking in my eyes when he spoke, and his breath was warm and sweet . . . Have you ever stood in front of someone, and when he spoke you just wanted to inhale him?"

I could hear Tia tapping on the phone. "Hello? Is this my friend Chantell on the phone? Hello?" she said, laughing. "Listen to yourself! This is great."

I laughed. "I know. I am trippin'. It's all very innocent, though. He's going back to Massachusetts soon. But we'll keep in contact."

"Well, I'm not one to gossip, but I think I could spot this relationship coming a mile away." She giggled.

"No, Tia, I've had enough of relationships. The only one that I am focusing on is between me and God, so don't get your hopes up on us."

"You know, you really know how to rain on my parade."

I looked up above my bed at the painting of the big yellow sunflower in the Mason jar that my mother created. The smell of lavender drifted from my pillowcases and into my nose.

"So are you going to church with me this Sunday?" I asked.

"Nah, not this Sunday. I've got too much to do. I'm going to go with you soon, though."

Tia was raised Catholic, and believed in God and prayer, but she preferred to do hers at home. Before we hung up, I was able to tell her a little about my and Charlotte's candid, serious conversation.

"So I think that we've resolved our differences."

"That's good, because you guys need each other, Chantell."

"I know."

As I reached over to grab my glass, my hand bumped a photo that

I'd framed, and it fell to the floor. I picked it up and made sure it wasn't broken. It was the photo of me, my mother Zarina, and my grandmother outside of church. I really liked this one of the three of us. My mom had written on the back of it, "Three generations of Brumwick women." I set it back on the table.

I'd put snapshots of my family all around my house. It was nice to come home and see my family's smiling faces. There were pictures of Dad and Charlotte, and me. There was a picture of my mom and dad out dancing somewhere. There were pictures of her pregnant with me. There was a picture of my mom in her teens all dressed up in a ball gown with my grandfather on her arm. It all made me smile.

I took another sip of my orange juice concoction and set the glass back down. I picked up the picture of the three of us and examined it again. Dad had taken the picture, while my grandma, my mom, and I all smiled. I smiled like I was at the dentist with cardboard in my mouth, getting my teeth x-rayed. I remembered that day. It was one of the very few times that my parents attended church. And they were only there then because they wanted to see their four-year-old stand in front of the church and recite her Easter speech.

I picked up the remote, hit CD #4, and Yolanda Adams sang from out of the speakers. I sank back in my bed and took it easy.

# trying to stay fed

Bible study started at seven, and I was still at the office. I finished cleaning my Tupperware dish, grabbed my briefcase, and headed back over the bridge to my neck of the bay. By the time I made it into the Sunday school classroom where it was being held, Pastor Fields was doing what my grandmother used to call a "cool cat walk" from the seventies. She said, "Like the young folks say, 'Don't be sleepin' on your spirit!' "

I laughed with the congregation. You could always count on her to put things in layman's terms.

Then she said, "We can laugh and joke, folks, but seriously, don't take care of everything else and neglect your spirit. Instead, be led by it. It will fuel you—if you let it. Turn with me now to Psalm 51:10. When you have it, say Amen." I got settled in and turned my attention to Pastor Fields' teachings. The congregation read: *"Create in me a clean heart, O God; and renew a right spirit within me."*

"What is that passage talking about?" She went on, "David is talking about your spirit . . . It's not wise to feed your body, pay your light bill, pay your car note, get your hair cut, and not be able to reach in here," and she pointed to her heart. "Let's look at another passage. Turn with me if you will, to Ephesians 5:14, and let's look at what it says."

I found Ephesians in time and read with the group, *"Wherefore he saith, Awake that though sleepest and arise from the dead and Christ shall give thee light."*

"Any ideas on what that scripture is saying?" she asked.

Someone in the second row said, "It's saying that we can't walk around asleep, we have to let our spirit come to life."

"Thank you. That's right, you need to be able to connect with God and have a relationship with God. And you do that through your spirit. Let's look at Ephesians 3:16 . . ."

I nodded my head and listened, though my stomach was growling.

# slowly opening

The next day I walked up to the hospital's complex where the new resident doctors stayed. Keith lived in number 59 of the dark brown, woodsy-looking apartments with a lighter brown trim. I located his apartment and knocked. The curtains moved at the door by the window, then the door opened.

"Hello, Chantell," he said with a smile.

"Hi," I said, raising one hand.

"Come on in," he said and opened the door wider.

The apartment was dim, and the furniture was minimal. But it was very clean. There was a heavy-looking tweed couch in the center of the floor. It faced a twelve-inch color TV with rabbit ears sticking out, and a fireplace. There was no carpet; instead there were beige tiles on the floor all over the apartment, and a big rug that started under the couch and ended under the television stand. The curtains by the door were made of a thick off-white material, with a rubbery backing.

Keith looked wonderful. He sported a newly bald head and cleanly shaven face except for his crisp, fresh goatee. He wore khakis and a dark blue T-shirt.

"Please make yourself at home."

"Thanks."

"I'm just about ready, give me a moment."

"No problem," I said, smiling back.

While he got ready, I looked around and spotted a huge corkboard that he had hung on the wall in the living room. There were pictures of him and his fraternity brothers. There were pictures of him with a white coat on, a stethoscope around his neck, with three other doctors. There was a very old picture of his Grandmother Edna. There was a picture of him and me at about seven or eight years old, at a Halloween party. He was a blue Rock 'em Sock 'em Robot, and I was Superwoman. We held plastic masks in one hand and our pillowcases with candy in the other.

"Hey, look at us!" I said out loud.

Keith knew exactly what I was talking about. "Yes, Superwoman. I have had that picture a long time. I don't have very many pictures from our childhood, but I always keep that one nearby," he yelled out from the other room.

I was flattered.

Keith came out in a striped button-down shirt over a T-shirt. He smelled good, which relaxed me. Keith relaxed me.

"Okay, I'm ready."

We left the house, crossed the street to where I was parked, and got in my black Wrangler.

"Okay, where are we going?" he asked.

"It's a surprise. I'm not telling," I said, "but you can try to guess if you want."

I started the car.

He smiled. "Okay, I'll play. But if I guess correctly, what will you give me?"

"What?" I asked, pulling out of his parking lot.

"Yeah. If I am going to be the one guessing, then you have to let me make up the rules. And the rules are, if I guess correctly, you have to give me something."

"Okay, but what do you want?" I eyed him suspiciously.

He smiled, sucked his teeth, his eyebrows moved a little, then he said, "How about dinner?"

"Okay, that's easy. You're on."

"To dinner?"

"Huh?"

"Are we going to dinner?"

"Oh. No." I laughed, because I actually was going to take him to dinner, but since he guessed it so easily, I was going to have to find someplace else to take him first.

"Is it to the park?" he asked as I stopped at a stop sign.

"Uhh, nope." Where was I going to take him? That wasn't a bad idea.

"To a mall?"

"Nope."

"Is it to your parents' house?"

"Nope." I entered the ramp to get on the freeway.

I kept driving, and Keith's answers kept getting sillier and sillier. "Is it to get the VCR cleaned? Is it to mow the grass? I washed your car, but I'm not mowing the grass in my good shirt!"

"No!" I laughed.

"To Paris? To get LASIK eye surgery?"

"LASIK what? No!" I laughed.

"Okay, I'm sorry. I get really silly around you, Chantell. Still."

He took me back to the fifth grade too.

I kept driving all that way until we got to Darryl's Mini Storage. The parking lot was filled up, and there were no nearby parking spots on the street. So I drove around the corner to a residential neighborhood.

"So. Where are we?" he asked, crinkling those eyebrows.

"You'll see," I said.

We stepped off the curb. I smiled when I thought about what he had said in the parking lot. He'd said that he'd always loved me. He proudly displayed my picture on his corkboard. We walked and he held my hand firmly. I was going to show him my hidden treasure. I wanted him to see it. And like a child, without thought, I stopped and spun around so that I stood smack dab in front of him. I put my arms around his neck and pushed up on my tippy toes and kissed his lips. A real kiss. A good kiss. He looked shocked, as I pressed my lips into his and kissed from one side of his mouth to the other. When I pulled my head back to look at him, a huge grin spread over his face. Then Keith leaned down and helped me to reach him. He gently rubbed his lips on my lips, while pecking me. Our lips parted and we gently touched each other's tongues. We stood there in the street with our lips locked until someone laid on the horn with full force.

We came up for air, and there were three cars lined up waiting to get by. Keith Rashaad locked his fingers in mine and we ran over to the sidewalk. A man in a black Jetta, whose bumper was just two feet in front of us, smiled and gave us a thumbs-up. Keith raised one eyebrow and waved apologetically.

A lady in the third car, a little green Tercel, rolled down her window and yelled as she drove by, "What's wrong with you two? Can't you do that behind closed doors!" She sped off.

"She was serious," Keith said as he looked at me. I looked at him and we burst into laughter.

"I guess so, huh?" We laughed some more.

"So, Chantell, tell me. Where are you taking me?"

"Top secret. You'll see."

We walked past some houses and up to Darryl's Mini Storage. I used the keypad in the cement wall to open the gate. We walked to storage space number 77.

"Why are we here? What's in here?"

"My lost world, my history, my past."

He looked at me, confused. I took out my key and unlocked the orange door. Keith helped me to push the rolling door upward.

When Keith saw the sheets draped over the big squares, he asked, "What's all this?" I held out my hand, inviting him to step in and look around. He unveiled painting after painting and examined them. I'd come here one day to count just how many there were. Zarina had painted thirty-nine of them.

"Chantell, these are incredible."

"Thank you. My mother did them all. She was really talented, wasn't she?"

Keith walked over to another sheet and unveiled another three pictures. "Yes, she was! Growing up, Chantell, you never mentioned her. You never spoke of her."

I still felt a hurt. "I know, that's pretty sick, huh?"

"No, I didn't mean that. It's not sick. It was just hard for you and your family."

Keith knew me so well. I almost told him that it was because people only want to be around you when you're doing well, but I showed him another painting instead.

"I love you, Chantell, and I care about you. I bet we'd be a great support system for each other."

This was the second time he'd mentioned the word love. Did he know what he was saying? Apparently he didn't, because he was talking like he was going to be here for a while, and we both knew that wasn't true.

"Hey," I said, "look at the books."

He walked over to the shelf and looked. "Wow, Zora Neale Hurston, Frederick Douglass, Langston Hughes, Maya Angelou, and James Baldwin. Your mother had some heavy hitters in her repertoire."

I smiled. "Yeah, she did."

I had so many emotions running through me. Confusion, happiness, sadness, fear. I grabbed a book and sat down on the floor. Keith sat next to me. He leaned over to me and kissed me on the cheek.

"Thank you for sharing all of this with me," he said.

I kissed him back. "Thank you for coming here with me." I was glad that he was the first person whom I had shared this room with.

He sat down on the cement floor next to me. "Read me something."

"Alright. I'll read you some poems written by my mom." It felt good to say that.

He uncrossed his legs and I sat between them, resting my back against his chest. It was nice, and dinner could wait a few more minutes.

The poems were handwritten in black ink:

*As long as I feel loved, I'll stick around.*

My voice made the words resonate like an echo in the small room.

*I crave your attention, your uplifting praise.*
*A phone call now and then, your touch on my face.*
*As long as our souls dance every now and then,*
*Then what we share won't come to an end.*

*Safe with you, I feel at ease,*
*So I long to inhale you like a gentle breeze.*
*As long as I feel loved,*
*I'll stick around.*

We absorbed that.

"Hummm," went Keith Talbit.

We sat there reading poems for over an hour, before I felt my tummy grumble. I looked up at him as I read a last line.

*. . . It feeds me. It fuels me. Passion. 'Tis my reason for living.*

I lifted my head from Keith's chest and looked up at him. His eyes were closed and he had the sweetest smile on his face. When I stopped reading, he opened his eyes.

"Keith, we had better get ready to go," I said. "I owe you dinner."

He looked at me with squinted eyes. "Okay. But first, I have to ask you something. What made you bring me here, Chantell? I mean, I'm glad that you did and all. But I was wondering why you choose to share this with me?"

He was asking a lot of personal questions. "For a lot of reasons," I said. "Mostly because it's a private part of me that I am embracing, and exploring. Because you are a big part of my past. And I wanted to share it with you."

I looked at him and wondered aloud, "That was okay with you, wasn't it?"

"It is more than okay with me."

We left Darryl's Mini Storage with our fingers interlocked.

With me driving, we rode to dinner. The freeway was crowded. Keith's phone rang. He picked it up and looked at it. Then without so much as a hello, he just put it back on his waist. Had it been the hospital, or one of his buddies, I was certain he would have answered it. I knew it was silly, but I thought about my past relationship with Eric. I remembered the way he left me and went with the Australian-accented woman from the boat. I know I shouldn't have, but I thought about how Eric had called me "Sabrina" in his sleep. Then I wondered who had been on Keith Rashaad's phone.

"You can get that you know," I said.

"I know. But there's no one else on earth that I want to talk to more than you right now."

I didn't know how to feel, so I was quiet.

"So, Chantell, tell me, what do you want for your life?"

"I'on' know."

"What's wrong?"

"Nothing. I was just thinking of stuff."

"Tell me."

"No, it's nothing. Just work-related . . . Umm, okay, I'll play, what do I want out of life . . . Maybe moving to a bigger house. I don't know, maybe to start my own business. I just want a nice life."

He nodded. He was going to have to answer the same question.

"What about you? What do you want?"

"Well, I've been thinking about it a lot lately. I want to be a good husband, good doctor, and good father. I want good conversation, and good sex."

"Whoa! You went there," I said.

"Hey." He chuckled. "I'm just being honest."

I laughed, yet I realized that I wasn't being honest with him. I wanted to be a good wife and mommy. I kept driving quietly. I wanted a family too.

Keith put his hand on mine and said, "I hope to get closer and closer to you, if that is okay."

I looked down at my knees, then up at all the traffic on the road. San Francisco was always so busy. What if I got too attached to him? What if we got married, then he got sick? What if he ran off with someone else?

"Hello? Keith Rashaad to Chantell."

"Sorry." I nodded my head and said, "I'd like that."

"Are you sure, Chantell? I'm not trying to pressure you, I just—"

"No, I'm sure. I'd like that."

And I think we became something of a couple.

## 44

# attitudinal

I pulled up to the office park in Los Gatos where Skyway Modems was located, in my extra shiny, freshly waxed black vehicle. I took the sidewalk past the freshly mowed green grass. The maintenance people were working to get it all cleaned up and into bags. My shoes clicked as I walked. The day had a bit of an overcast, so I removed my sunglasses. I was putting them in my purse when I looked up to meet Mina Everett's gaze. She was on her way out of the building, and as she eyed me, her walk turned into sort of a Cindy Crawford strut, and she made a face as though something stunk. I fought hard and resisted the urge to move like I was on the catwalk.

When I got up to the office door, I was proud of myself because I'd ignored her invitation for our energies to battle. I was facing my issues one at a time. Then I thought about the present that I'd sent her, and for the first time I realized that it wasn't cool.

The receptionist said Mr. Strautimeyer was ready to see me, so I walked into his office. He stood up from behind his desk to shake my hand, and we got right down to business. I pulled out a proof sheet.

"This is the ad, the way that it is set to run." He reviewed it and signed off. "Great," I said. "We are going to run the ad for two days, Friday and Sunday. Right?"

"That's correct, and I get 20 percent off on next Monday's run. Right?"

"Yep. That's the plan," I said.

"Great."

"Awesome. I'll see you next week."

He waved and went back to his papers on his desk. I wondered why Mr. Strautimeyer never said good-bye.

When I got back out to my Jeep, I noticed that it looked a little lopsided. I walked around the vehicle and found that, sure enough, the back rear tire was as flat as the pavement it sat on. I supposed that Mina had her suspicions about where the pooh-pooh gift came from.

I sighed and called Triple A.

# 45

## c'est la vie

I sat on the grass in the park, with Keith's head in my lap, and took in the simpler things in life. There were two squirrels running back and forth up a tree just six feet in front of us. We sat there squeezing each other's hands and rubbing each other's hair and shoulders while we relaxed and watched them work. They weren't afraid of us. They had seen far too many people to be afraid.

Since our first date Keith had said several times with a certainty that he'd always loved me. I'd tried not to fall for him. And even though we both decided that we were going to continue taking the celibacy route, somehow I still found that I was in over my head. How deep was I in over my head? That was the question that I wondered about. Now the three months had come and gone, and I was scared to death of being left.

A little squirrel kept looking in the grass, fiddling through the twigs on the ground. Then it would run up the tree's trunk with a couple of little sticks before reappearing and starting its search all over again.

"Selective little thing, huh?" he said.

"That it is," I said, massaging Keith's palms and fingers. He looked so relaxed. "Are things going according to plan down at the hospital?"

"Oh yeah," he said, and his eyes lit up. "In fact, we're ahead of schedule. Pretty soon hospitals across the country should start using the new Netzer laser skin-grafting equipment. Maybe in as early as six months."

"Really? Wow, you guys should really be proud of yourselves. I know I'm proud of you, Keith Talbit."

He took my finger from his temple and put it to his lips and kissed it. "Yeah, I think it's really going to help a lot of people." This man really loved his job.

"You should see it, Chawnee. We are seeing results where the healing process is sped up, occurring two to three times faster than with conventional burn treatments. It's like Neosporin in a vacuum!"

I laughed.

"By the way, Chantell, can you keep next Friday open? The hospital's planning a dinner; it's to mark the unveiling of the technology. You'll be there, won't you?" His eyes were wide open.

"Of course, babe. What time does it start?"

"It kicks off at six, right after work, I believe. I'll confirm all of the information and get it to you later today. But what I do know thus far is that it's going to be semi-formal, and there will be a special presentation to our group, to thank us for our participation."

He was so excited, but to be completely honest, my stomach turned. It marked the end of his time here, and I didn't know where we were going with us. My eyes watered up, but I willed it away, and no tears fell.

"The best part of all of this, Chantell, is that the machines are economical. So they'll be cost-effective and available for nearly all medical centers with burn units across the country." He smiled a smile that I remembered from long ago.

"So how much more time will you and your group be working on Project Netzer?" I asked.

He spoke with energy and passion. "Well, technically we're finishing up in the next two weeks."

Yep, he'd be leaving soon. Soul-mate-Colgate-patrol-mate, to heck with it. He was out of here. No matter what Tia said, I knew from my parents' lives and my own that there were far fewer tears when life was planned out. Things just worked out better that way.

". . . So I'm not sure how much longer the hospital will need me. But I will be here as long as I am asked to be."

"That's great, Keith Rashaad." I stretched. "Well, you know, I am getting a little tired."

"Okay, babe, it is getting a little late. Let's head out."

He got up and pulled me up by my hands to a standing position. I gathered the blanket and he gathered the water bottles.

"Maybe I can get to the hospital a little earlier than planned tomorrow morning."

We drove home, and Keith kept talking about all of the new technology's potential. He said that he was going to call the doctor in Boston who recommended him into the fellowship program and invite him to the dinner. I tried to smile.

"Things can only get better from here, Chantell, I'm telling you."

I looked straight ahead and listened as attentively as I could.

# the dinner party

It was the day of Keith's dinner, and my day hadn't gone so well. For starters, I was tired from the night before. Dad wasn't feeling well last night so I spent the night at his home in case Charlotte and I needed to rush him to the emergency room. My back was still hurting from sleeping on my childhood twin-size bed. Dad was feeling fine today, but work was a bit stressful. Buildyourownshoes.com, one of my accounts, had gone into collections, owing the newspaper over $50,000. Our accounting office informed me that the client's phone number was disconnected, so I went over to the building where their offices were located, and as we feared, the office was no more. The doors were locked and a "For Leasing Information" sign was displayed in the window.

My manager, Canun Ramsey, wanted to know why I hadn't kept a better watch on the account, like it was my job to monitor their bill-paying.

I told him, "Their credit limit was a hundred and five thousand, and they were barely at half of that." But Canun didn't care. He insisted that I should have prevented this. Whatever! He could really drain me.

Keith's award banquet was less than two hours away. I picked up my phone to dial his number, but Susan, the woman upstairs from accounting, was on my line. She was frantic. "Hello, Chantell, can you please come upstairs with your file on Marquis Jewelers, so that I can determine this accounts payment history?"

After a long, deep breath, I said, "Sure, but we have to make it fast."

The clock was ticking, and I already was more than tired. When Susan suggested that we go over the account's bill payment history for a third time, I put the brakes on.

"I'm sorry, Susan, I've gotta run. I have plans this evening."

I grabbed my keys and my purse and ran to the elevator. Keith's dinner marked a closing chapter in his life—in our life—and he needed me there to witness it. I rushed home as fast as traffic would allow. It was 5:05 when I walked into the living room. I had just enough time.

There was so much tension in my shoulders. I ran to my closet and took out a pink-and-black suit. I turned on the radio and went into the bathroom to run my bathwater. The bubbles filled the tub, and I thought of all the things that we'd done together. The walks in the park. Saturday bike rides. Church on Sunday mornings together. I inhaled the steam as the warm, misty fog covered the mirrors. The water felt warm and silky, and my head was heavy. I closed my eyes, laid my head back on the inflated pillow for just a moment, and listened to Wynton Marsalis blare from my bedroom.

After my bath, I felt so exhausted that I lay down on my bed, thinking that I would just rest my eyes for a moment. I didn't want to go to this "project end" dinner. Sometimes you get what you want . . .

It was 6:25 when I woke up and realized what had happened. The Convention Center was a few minutes away from where I lived and the folks there were probably already eating dinner!

"Augh! How could I have let this happen?"

I called Keith. His voice mail came on. "Keith, I am so sorry. I'm late," I said. "It's been a crazy day. But I am on my way. Okay? Bye."

I was racing around the house. Grab my purse, get my keys, get my cell phone, turn off the lights. I bumped my knee on the coffee table and ripped my nylons. Maybe I should have just given up.

I ran into a pharmacy, bought a new pair of pantyhose, put them on in the Jeep, and sped to the Convention Center. When I reached the Marietta Room, the clock on the wall said it was 7:06 p.m.

I pulled on the handle and opened the doors. People were seated at probably thirty round tables arranged about the room. The waiters and waitresses were taking plates away. There were still a few people eating what looked like mousse or cheesecake. I looked around for Keith Rashaad and spotted him at the table in the front center. I waved hello. He motioned for me to come up front.

"I was worried about you."

"Sorry," I whispered. "It has been a rough day."

"Is everything okay?" he whispered back with a genuine look of concern on his face.

"Yeah. Everything's fine," I tried to reassure him. "I just fell asleep."

"Oh. Okay," he said, and quickly looked away from me and back up at the speaker.

The speaker closed the evening out. Everyone got up, gathering their purses and coats. Keith introduced me to a few of his coworkers and the chief of staff but he just didn't seem like himself. I apologized to him again. He seemed to cheer up some by the time we left. Keith Talbit was always pleasant. He could never stay mad for very long. It just wasn't in his nature. Sure enough, by the time we left, Keith Rashaad was smiling again.

## 47

# pick me up

Though I was running late, I lay in my bed with one of my mother's books in hand. I had a lot on my mind. Keith hadn't left yet and that was a good thing. But we still hadn't worked out the logistics of our relationship. I'd brought up our future once to him, and he'd smiled and said that we'd work things out. I'd said of course we would, but I now wondered how much longer he'd stick around. I removed the scarf from my hair and thought about what I was going to do with all of my mom's paintings. There was one gallery suggesting I auction them, and another one suggesting displaying them in a museum. All of this was going on, not to mention my boss, Canun, and all of the drama he added to my life.

My phone rang. I smiled when I looked at my new caller ID and saw that it was Keith's home phone number.

"Hello," I answered in a sexy tone.

"How's my girl?"

"I'm good, Keith." I sat up in bed. "How are you this morning?"

"Not bad. I did twelve hours last night, and I just got in the door. I'm so glad to be home."

"You poor baby."

"I'll be alright. Hey, I thought you'd be at work already."

"I'm going in later this morning."

"I see. I had an idea, so I was going to leave you a message."

"What's up?"

"I was thinking," he said. "When was the last time you ran?"

"Oh, I don't know, it's been a while." I smiled. "What's on your mind?"

"I'm going to run the lake. Would you be down to run it with me?"

"Umm, yeah, sure," I said without batting an eye. "When?" I needed some exercise.

"Tomorrow's Saturday. How about in the morning?"

"Oh, I am so down!" I said. "I haven't run the lake in years. But Keith, I must warn you, I ran for distance all through school. So don't come up there half-steppin', okay? Bring your A game."

Keith laughed. "What are you trying to say?"

"Nothing. I'll go easy on you." I giggled.

He teased back, "Oh, I see, you got jokes this morning? Girl, you need to recognize. I'm a sprinter!"

"Baby, you ain't saying anything," I taunted.

"You know what? If you weren't my woman, I'd take you down to that lake and leave you in the wind. But I'm a gentleman, and I ain't gone do you like that."

I laughed. "Oh, okay! Whatever, dude. In the morning!"

"Yeah." He laughed. "In the morning."

That was Keith Talbit. Be it over the phone, or through my door, or via mail, he could come in and pick me right up. I got out of bed and sang Patti LaBelle's version of "Somewhere over the Rainbow" all the way to work.

## 48

# run for your life

I parked on the street by Fairyland, where the lake wasn't visible. It was a cool Saturday morning. I was in a good mood. Yesterday at work, I'd closed another $40,000 in business, which put me over my goal for the month again. Today Keith and I both had the entire day off. It would be a good day. I'd put my hair in a big clip and pinned it up. A strip of hair fell down my cheek. I didn't have any makeup on except for eyeliner, and Chap Stick. I wore blue shorts, a white shirt, a dark blue windbreaker that I tied around my waist in case the wind kicked up, and Reeboks. I looked around and I didn't see Keith's borrowed Lincoln anywhere yet. I moved over to the grass and stretched out.

"Chawnee!" Keith's voice called from across the street. He jogged in my direction. His great physical condition shone. He reminded me of Michael Jordan running across the street. He wore black nylon sweats, a white T-shirt with a Nike swoosh across the front, and white Avia running shoes. I tried not to stare at his lean, muscular frame. I knew that he ran a few times a week, but it looked like brotherman ran 24/7/365.

"Hi," I said and gave him a smack on his lips.

He stared at my unpolished lips for a moment. "Hi back," he said.

I looked him up and down and said, "How often did you say you ran?"

"Three or four times a week. Don't get scared now. Are we going to do this or what?"

"Yeah!" I said, remembering all of the trash I talked. "I ain't har'ly skuury. Let's do it."

We stretched a bit, and we were off. I hadn't run much in the last few years, and my body, though shapely, was getting pretty soft. We started slow, pacing ourselves, but I couldn't resist teasing a little. "Okay, c'mon. Whatchu' you waiting fo? What the problem is?"

"Hey, I'm just hanging with you," he said.

I picked up the pace a bit. I heard people behind us, a lot of them, huffing and puffing. I turned my head and looked back, and a group of senior citizens power-walked right by us. We laughed.

"Just for the record, I'm following your lead," I said.

He tisked. "And you have the gumption to be bragging about running in school." He shook his head as though I was pathetic.

"Oh, don't even try it . . . You know what? Forget it! I'll show you what I got," I mumbled. "I was trying to go easy on a brothah." I jogged faster, kicking up my heels like I was Marion Jones.

Keith just laughed. "Chantell, you're silly."

We ran around the bin and approached the Fairyland entrance sign. The signs always reminded me of the Hollywood letters sitting on the hills in Los Angeles, only this sign was a gazillion times smaller. Today there were ducks on the little grassy hill. Huge ducks quacking and waddling. A lady with a double stroller was sitting on the grass watching her two little ones play. The kids looked like they were maybe two and three years old, dressed in little blue nylon windbreakers. They were throwing bread crumbs over in the direction of the ducks, but the ducks kept their distance. A runner with a CD player on his hip passed us going in the opposite direction. We picked up the pace a little more. It felt good. I was determined to become active again. This was so good for me. We approached three ladies in all-black leotards. They were thin, and solid, like they had been running all of their lives. We passed them.

"You cool?" he asked me.

"Yeah. You?" I asked.

"You want to turn it up a little?"

"Bring it on, baby," I said, looking directly at him and licking my increasingly dry lips.

He smirked, intrigued, and looked at me.

The air was crispy. "Wait. Hold on a minute," I said and applied some Chap Stick to my lips and to his.

"Your lips look great natural."

"Thanks. Glad you noticed," I said.

"I notice everything about you." He rubbed his lips together. "Mmm. Thank you. Okay, let's do this!" he added, revived.

We jogged a little faster. I could feel my blood pumping and my heart beating, and I could hear Keith breathing shallow runner's breaths. We made the turn and approached a perfect view of the water.

Keith slowed up a bit.

"What's wrong?" I asked.

"Oh, nothing. I was just thinking. If I slow up and pace myself," he breathed, "maybe I can go around twice."

"See now, I was with you on the 'let's run once around the lake thing,' but I'm not even going to pretend that I'm going to go around with you twice!" That was over six miles.

He laughed. "You can do it."

"No thank you."

Keith slowed a bit more. I didn't.

It was much busier on this side of the lake. There were cars lined up along the lake and lots of runners going in both directions. People were coming and going. Cars were zooming by. There were women in braids, or ponytails, and many in sports bras. There were babies in wagons and strollers. And there were men in shorts and shirtless, in spandex and sweatpants. Some people walked, some jogged, some lounged with friends. There was a gold Lexus ahead parked at the curb. Its door was open, and strong bass lines bounced through the air in time. Three guys sat on the grass near the car laughing. I kept running. Keith and I were bonding more and more each time our sneakers hit the pavement. Maybe we could be that family that he spoke of having one day. I felt good, like I was in tip-top shape. I was in college again, in my own world. I encouraged myself like I was a track coach: "Go girl, work that body!" I recited a mantra: "I am as graceful as a cheetah." This was what it was all about. I was doing my thing. I could feel my stomach muscles firming up now. I kept going.

I got closer to the Lexus, and that was when I heard one of the guys laugh and say, "Oh, snap! Look at that shiznit!"

I was thinking of Keith's lips, and focusing on my breathing. "How are you doing, Keith?" I yelled back to him.

He didn't answer.

Then a football player's frame stepped out in front of me on the sidewalk. I bumped into him and stumbled back.

It was Eric "I wish I were Shemar Moore" Summit. He stood there boldly in front of me with his chest out, like he was the king of the lake.

"Hey, Eric," I said in a tone to let him know he wasn't intimidating anybody.

"Where you been, baby?"

"Handling my business, and I'm not your baby."

His friend Rob, who was not doing a great job of trying to hold a straight face, howled, "Aw man, it's over! Chantell is straight clownin' you, son!"

"Yeah, come away from the light, Eric! Come away from the light!" That was his friend Maynard, who was over at the car.

Eric laughed and spoke in a tone he used when he was caught in an uncomfortable predicament. "Man y'all tripping! Don't get it twisted. That's going to forever be my booty!"

Keith Rashaad approached us and said, "Hey, what's up?"

Eric looked at him and said, "Nothin', niggah, dang, you see I'm talkin'. Step!" And he motioned with his big football-playing hand like he was shooing a fly away.

I stood next to Keith and said to Eric, "You need to step!"

Then Eric looked over at his buddy Rob and said, "Oh. I see how it is." He turned to his friend at the car, and said, "Hey, I ain't even trippin'. I'ma let y'all do y'all thang, but before you go, I'ma sing you your theme song. I made it up just for you." Then he bobbed his head to an imaginary beat and pointed at me and sang, "*You ain't nothin but a fake a—— b——, please get to steppin' little fake a—— t——."*

He laughed. "Damn that was tight! Yo, I need to lay that on wax! I can go platinum with rhymes like that!"

I knew that he was not dogging me like that!

"Hey, Eric. Chill out man. Be cool," said Rob.

Eric was trying to embarrass me, and I didn't appreciate it one iota.

Keith shook his head and sighed like this was too ridiculous for words. "Yeah, alright man, whatever." He touched my shoulder. "Let's keep running."

But I was angry. "Oh no no no!" Who did he think he was clownin'?

If Eric thought that he could front me off like that, in front of everybody, he was sadly mistaken. He must have had me confused with someone else. I stretched my arm back and swung it to slap the taste out of his disrespectful mouth. I aimed for his jaw. My hand hit his neck. His eyes bugged open bigger than I'd ever seen, and he rushed me like I was a quarterback with the ball in my hand. I hit the ground and lay on my side. The impact made me dizzy, and dazed.

Keith Rashaad punched Eric. Eric punched Keith. It was all happening so fast.

"Hey! Hey! Y'all chill all that out!" said Rob. Both Rob and Eric's other friend Maynard jumped up. One grabbed Keith and the other grabbed Eric.

"This is crazy! Y'all some grown a—— men out here acting like children!" shouted Maynard. "All of y'all out here acting like some d**n fools!"

I slowly stood up and dusted myself off. People were standing around watching. A couple of people were on their cell phones calling the police.

Keith looked at me and said, "Come on!" in a tone I hadn't heard in a long long time. I walked alongside of him and was quiet.

"Who was that? Your other man?" he said.

"What? No! I used to . . ."

Keith looked so mad. "What's wrong with you? Chantell, you can't go around charging at people! Especially men! We could all have ended up in jail! We are not kids!"

"I know, but did you hear him trying to disrespect me?"

"Chantell, you should have let me handle it."

"I know, but he was—"

"I don't care what he was doing. You don't rush no grown man! Have you lost your mind?" Keith was furious with me.

I was quiet. Nobody got hurt. I didn't know what the big deal was. Keith Rashaad continued mumbling under his breath as we walked back toward our cars. Maybe he was jealous?

"Look," I said, "Eric is the one who got out of line with me."

I didn't know if Keith's jaw was twitching because he was angry or if he needed some ice. "You know what, Chantell? I don't know if this is some kind of game that you and your little boyfriend go around playing, but it's stupid and immature."

It was strange. Eric had called me all kinds of dirty names just twenty minutes ago, and I was all but ready to forget about that. Yet when Keith Rashaad said I was being "stupid and immature," I wanted to burst into tears and howl. But I contained myself. Then I figured out what the real problem was. Keith had been at Harvard too long, and he'd obviously forgotten what we in the neighborhood do when somebody has crossed the line. Eric had called me a b—— and worse. Yep, I thought, that's what this was. Apparently Keith had forgotten what was tolerable and what was not.

I tried again to explain it to him, so that he could understand things from my perspective. I said, "Keith, it's not about him being my little boyfriend, and he got out of line with *me*. So what was I supposed—"

"You were supposed to stop trying to control everything and let me handle it!"

I looked at the sidewalk, with my hands held together. Keith Rashaad wasn't getting it, so I tried a different approach. "Keith, you called me immature. But I don't see how you can say that. I pay my own mortgage, and my own car note, I buy my own clothes. I don't ask anybody for anything. So from what I can see, that makes me full-grown!"

He got this look of frustration and anger on his face. His eyes squinted and he got these two creases between his eyebrows, like he couldn't take it anymore. "No, that makes you immature. Just like I said. Chantell, you know what? You need to get your priorities in order." He said, "The things that you think are important need to be reexamined!"

Keith had yelled more in the last five minutes than he had in the entire time I'd known him.

"Clothes. Money, beauty, cars!" He flipped his arms like they were nothing. "What good is all that if you've never felt the beauty of a sunrise? Huh?"

Everything that Keith loved about me he'd told me over the last few months. Everything that he hated he laid on me right then right there.

"What good is ambition if all you know are anger and fear?" he continued. "Huh? What good is making sure everyone sees you with your hair done if you can't express your emotions? And owning a home means nothing if you don't own up to what is in your heart and soul. Do you get what I am trying to say?

"Happiness is not out there," Keith said, waving around his hand. "It's in here!" And he hit his chest.

Then he sighed and said, "I am in love with you, Chantell. I always have been. I probably always will be."

There it was. Cards on the table, only nobody had ever said anything that real to me before, and I didn't know what to say, or how to act, so I just stood there dumbfounded.

"See, that's exactly what I mean. You leave me hanging, Chantell. You pretty much no-showed at dinner the other day! Do you have any idea how silly I felt, bragging to everyone about how wonderful and how smart and how beautiful and perfect you are? How together you are, then for you to not even show up until the dinner was over! No, of course you don't understand that because you'd never put yourself on the line for anybody. But I did, and I do, and I felt like a d**n fool."

"Keith, I'm sorry. Everyone leaves. And I was afraid that because your project was ending—"

"Stop. Just save it! I'm done."

How had we gotten here? In the past he'd always read my eyes, but now he wasn't even looking at me. I stood there like an idiot.

"Please listen to me, Keith!"

He said, "No, you please listen to me. I cannot make you be something or someone who you don't want to be."

If he had looked in them, he would have seen that my eyes said, "I love you too." He would have seen that they said, "I love the air that you breathe. I loved you when I first kissed you in the balcony at church. And I loved you that day you had the asthma attack and I ran to get your inhaler. And I loved you at TGIF's in Jack London Square, when you told me why you never called me." My eyes said it all. But he wouldn't look at me.

His face was swollen now from where Eric had hit him. I reached to touch his jaw. He yanked his head away. I fought the urge to cry. If I had let myself cry then, I would have broken down into a thousand-million pieces, and I couldn't do that. I wouldn't have been able to think. So I just bit my lip and stood there being the coward I was. Afraid of emotion and feelings. He walked across the street and got in his car, and I held it all in. Until finally, the dam broke, and I cried big coward tears. The way big cowards do. Keith didn't even look at me. He just drove by.

--------

# piece of cake

Keith Talbit had said he was done with me, but he had also said
he was in love with me. I chose to hold on to the latter remark.
Six days had passed and I hadn't spoken to him. He'd always been
such a forgiving, loving person, I would never have imagined that he
could go this long without calling me.

I thought of all that had transpired, and I was in anguish—the
kind that takes your stomach and churns it like an old-time washing
machine. The kind that makes some people not eat for days, and others eat without hunger. It was just a little tussle that he and Eric had
at the lake; it wasn't serious, right? And the recognition dinner that
I missed shouldn't have been held against me. I'd had a lot of work
to do, I fell asleep, and my nylons ripped.

I'd tried to call him several times but never got to the seventh
digit. I remembered our dinner in Santa Cruz, at the Thai restaurant,
and wondered if Keith had been trying to tell me something when I'd
left him at the table to go to the ladies' room.

I got out of bed and into the shower. By the time I was done, I decided it had been a week too long. We needed to stop this game of
who could hold out the longest. I couldn't take it anymore. I loved
this man with everything in me, and I'd never been more serious
about anything in my life. I got to the seventh digit and pressed it
without hesitation. The answering machine picked up right away.

"Hi, Keith, it's me, Chantell. It's early, and I know you're probably sleeping, but I had to call you, because you're on my mind. I've been really worried about you, about us. I've been thinking about everything that transpired, and I really have to talk to you."

I was bordering on desperation, and I hoped it wasn't coming through in my voice, but I was determined not to blow it with him again. "If it's okay, I want to swing by and try to catch up with you tonight after work. I really miss you, Keith Rashaad. I really do. Okay, bye."

It was a good day at the office, and I was feeling good about all of the changes and discoveries I was finding in me. Like admiration for people, and respect, and love. I remembered the therapist who said that change takes time, and he was right. The dashboard clock said it was 7:53 p.m., and I was on the 880 freeway, headed to Keith's house. I stopped off at Starbucks to grab us an evening snack.

I walked through the doors of the dimly lit coffeehouse. Eight at night and it was packed. Bob Marley played, helping to set up atmosphere.

For the first time, I was going to put my true feelings out there into the universe; God did want good things for me. I just had to know what I wanted for myself and be open to it and believe that I could have it. I loved Keith, that was all there was to it, and I had no fear or second thoughts at all. I even sang a little with Bob as he talked about being in love and sharing what you have with that special person. Sing it, Bob Marley!

I was in love. I was popping the fingers of one hand and rubbing my fingers over the not-so-fresh coffee beans on display with the other. I played with the oatmeal-colored beans and bopped around.

Bob Marley always sang from his heart. That is what I was about to do, if I ever got through the coffee lovers' line and to my beau's house.

I knew everything that I wanted to say to him. I had it all rehearsed in my head. Actually, I had repeated it so much that I had it memorized, like I did when I gave a big presentation to a client. So I wasn't nervous. There were three people left in front of me. I was going to speak like I'd drunk from some truth serum. I'd say: "Keith, you said that you loved me and that you've always loved me, and the truth is, I've always loved you too. I simply didn't know how to show it. You are everything that I want and desire in a man."

After I'd told him everything, he'd hug me and we'd probably kiss and maybe even cry together. Because he was in touch with his sensitive side like that.

There were two people left in line ahead of me. A lady in a purple jogging suit and a man in all black with a San Francisco 49ers hat on.

"Hi. Can I have a venti, almond rocha, lowfat latte, with room for extra cream?"

"Sure thing," said the lady behind the counter. "And what will you have, sir?"

The man said, "I'll have a triple espresso."

"Coming up!" said the lady behind the counter. She wrote on two cups and passed them along. The customers went over to the other side of the bar and waited.

"Hi, may I help you?" she asked.

I didn't know what Keith drank, so I ordered what I usually got. "Yes, can I have two decaf, soy, grande caramel macchiatos, and two coffeecakes?"

"You got it!"

I looked at my watch. It was 8:33 when I drove away. Keith Rashaad should have been home by then. He was an amazing man. I was so glad that I'd matured enough to come to my senses. I loved him so much, and all he wanted me to do was to show it. And I just couldn't wait to get to his house!

My hands were full with the coffee, the pastries, and my clutch handbag, so I closed the door with my backside. I walked up to Keith's door and knocked lightly. There was no answer. I set my things down and knocked again. Louder this time, but there was no answer. I knocked even harder. A blond guy in jeans and a sweatshirt must have heard me knocking because he came out of the apartment from next door and said, "Can I help you?"

"Oh, no thank you, I'm just stopping by to see my friend."

"Who? You mean Talbit?"

"Uh-huh."

"He's gone. He left yesterday."

"No. He was supposed to stay around another week, I thought."

"He was, but he didn't. My name is David Peralta. I'm the complex manager here. Keith signed out last night."

I ignored him and went over to Keith's window by the door. David don't know nothing. The off-white tweed curtains were slightly open. Inside, the furniture was still there, but all of his personal things were gone. His board with the pictures. Gone.

He was gone. How could this be happening? I didn't even have his phone number. I wasn't able to tell him that I understood what he was saying. And he thought that I didn't love him.

David stood there with me.

"But I didn't get to say good-bye."

He shook his head and said, "That's tough. I'm sorry. But maybe it will still work out. Maybe he will call you."

His words really got to me. What was he talking about, "maybe it will still work out"? Didn't he just say so himself that the man was gone?

I left the coffeecakes and the coffee in the tray on the ground and ran to the Jeep. Inside, I put my arms around the steering wheel, hid my face, and cried. It startled me when David, the manager, knocked at my window. He had my stuff. I rolled down the window and he handed me the bags and my coffee.

"Here. Cheer up. Things happen, but you never know how they'll turn out."

"Thank you," I said and wiped my eyes. David was trying to be nice. I didn't turn and hide. I told myself that it was okay to be vulnerable, that there was nothing for me to be ashamed of. That's what that therapist said, anyway.

"Hey David?"

"Yes?"

"Want a coffeecake?"

He smiled. "Sure. Thanks."

On the way home, I tried to call Keith on his cell phone. The recording said the number was no longer in service. And I remembered Keith saying that it was the hospital's phone.

## 50

# a deer/dear

I arrived in Hayward and drove up the big hill that led to the college. I'd always thought it strange that someone would put a university up on a hill. The letters CSUH had been sculpted into the grass, and a red-and-black triangle sign directed you to the little road that led to the campus. Why did love have to be so difficult and so hard?

I was stopped at the light for a few moments, while students crossed the street and headed for the dorms. Then, from nowhere, something moved quickly in my peripheral vision. It was big. Although it was rare, mountain lions had been known to come down from deep in the hills of the Bay Area, to visit the humans. I was more than a little scared.

It was probably just a big dog. Then a big deer bolted across the semi-busy street right in front of my Jeep. With its huge antlers, it moved swiftly and gracefully as if it were a ballerina and the street were a stage. It happened so fast that I might have thought I was dreaming, except that cars had to slam on their brakes, and students froze in their tracks. I watched the galloping deer, front legs in the air almost ready to touch the ground and the back legs pushing off the street at a perfect slant.

Lovesick, I squeezed the steering wheel tightly. The deer was beautiful, and he made me cry. I shifted to overdrive and drove past a few well-kept neighborhoods with perfectly manicured lawns. A raccoon lay dead in the street, while a man walked a little brown-and-white beagle on the sidewalk with no leash. I hoped the dog wouldn't run out into harm's way. I passed them, and in my rearview mirror I saw the man pick up the little dog.

I finally reached Ron and Tia's house, and saw Tia's convertible Sebring in the driveway and Ron's green-and-white fishing truck next to it. I reached in the backseat and took out the bowl of ambrosia salad that I'd made for our dinner. I went in through the garage carrying the glass bowl. The walls were lined with supplies and cans of sprays and linoleum rolls. I knocked on the door that led to the kitchen and it opened slightly.

"Hello, anybody home?" I said.

"Come in. We're in here!" said Tia from a distance. I walked in through the kitchen and set the bowl on the table.

"Hey," I said.

"Hey," they greeted me.

Ron and Tia were on the couch together. She was sitting between his legs with her head back on his chest, reading a magazine. Those two could sit underneath each other all day.

"What are you guys up to?" I said, trying to sound cheerful.

"Oh, not much, just enjoying my husband's day off. He'd work eight days a week if he could."

"Hush, woman. If I stayed here every day, you'd be so sick of me," said Ron jokingly.

Tia put her magazine on the table in front of her and walked barefoot over to the bowl that I had brought. "Yumm, Chawnee, did you put lots of pineapples in the salad?" she said and looked at me. Then she saw the phony smile I wore.

"Uh-oh, what's wrong with you?"

"Nothing, I'm okay. I did. I put in a lot of pineapples because I knew that you'd be looking for them." I tried to giggle.

Over on the couch, Ron yelled, "Hey, Chawnee, where is this new guy Tia say you're seeing? I was hoping you'd bring him and we could play some tonk."

I was about to cry. Tia waved at Ron and said, "Hold on a minute, baby." She walked over to the couch and leaned down to him. "Baby, Chantell and I are going to talk in the back room. We'll be back."

By the time we got down the hall, I felt terrible because I was crying wholeheartedly and spoiling the dinner party. I sat down on her bed and began to recount the story. I told her everything, not just the good parts about eating fresh strawberry cake while he washed my car. I told her about the dinner that I missed, and how I kept feeling he was going to leave me and go back to Boston. I told her about how he'd said things like "I love you," and "I trust you," but I didn't know how to reciprocate. I told her about shoplifting Lemonheads, and the board he had at his apartment with a picture of us on Halloween. I even told her about the trip to Santa Cruz and the rented bikes and the kiss and little girl singing about the babies coming in the carriage, and how it scared me.

When I told her about the lake, and how Eric had sung his rap song where he called me a fake bi——, her eyes got big. And then I told her how I hit him, and he knocked me down, and how Keith Rashaad fought to protect me.

She stopped me. "Wait a minute, missy. I want to make sure I understand you right. Are you telling me that you hit the man? In front of the man's friends? And in front of your new man?" Even I had to laugh at the ridiculousness of it. She was dumbfounded. "Girl, you'd lost your mind!"

I kept talking, and it felt good to tell the whole truth. I thought about the therapist who told me to "feel your feelings." I told Tia the stories, but really I was speaking for me. The more I spoke, the clearer I felt. Renewed, washed in realness and truth.

"When all was said and done, he told me I didn't have my priorities in order. He asked me what good was money and clothes if I'd never even felt the beauty of a sun rising. He told me ambition was nothing if you really didn't know what happiness was."

Tia sat there quietly with her hands folded in her lap. "Keith Rashaad's a good guy."

"I know," I cried. "And I lost him. Tia, I mixed him up with mine and Eric's foolishness and I lost him! He just walked away from me, and I haven't heard from him since. What am I going to do, Tia?"

"Well, right now, you are going to calm down and you're going to get a hold of yourself, and we're going to go have some dinner." My friend put her arm around my shoulder, and we walked back down the hall. "Then you're going to listen, and trust. Isn't that what you're learning in church?"

I nodded. We went back into the kitchen. Ron stood at the stove stirring a big pot of jambalaya.

"I was getting worried. Everything okay?" he asked.

"Yes, we just needed to do some girl talking," said Tia.

"Yeah, Tia was lending me her ear, and listening to my problems. But I'm okay now."

"Well, I'm sure glad. Now let's eat," he said.

We sat down and ate dinner at their little farm table near the kitchen. There were fresh yellow flowers on the table, and I could smell their fragrance.

"So what are you going to do with the paintings?" Tia asked.

"I have been thinking about it. I don't know yet. I've put in calls to some of the art societies, and I am going to get their advice."

"Good idea."

Ron's food was delicious, as usual. He was a wonderful cook. I looked at him. There was something that I really wanted to know. "Ron," I said, "how did you know that Tia was the one for you?"

"Well, I knew something was up when I realized that I thought of her both as my friend, and yet romantically. I'd looked at her flaws and they didn't matter. When she and I were together nobody else existed. When she wasn't around, I could smell her. Then it dawned on me that there was nobody on earth more important to me than she was."

"You're so good to me," said Tia.

I looked at them. Seeing their love and trust made me smile. Then I looked up at the new painting that I had given her. She'd put it on the wall in the dining area. It was my mother's painting of a farmhouse.

"What do you think? Does it go good in here?" asked Tia.

"Yes, it looks perfect right there," I said.

# 51

## metamorphosis

I t was the middle of the night, and I'd tossed and turned, back and forth, till finally I got out of bed. I needed to get out of there. I needed to go see the sunrise.

In the dark, I walked over to the closet. I turned on the light and put on some gray sweats and a gray sweatshirt. My heart and my soul needed some attention.

The clock on the wall read 3:57 a.m. when I walked out my front door. I drove around with the window down so that the breeze hit my face. I approached the toll for the Bay Bridge to San Francisco. Out of my ashtray, I scraped together two dollars in change and rolled down the window a bit more. The toll collector was a very slow-moving woman. My arm was extended to hand her the money for what seemed like forever. She finally took the money and I drove through.

I drove around San Francisco. It was dark, and the water surrounding the city made the air really cold. I rolled up the window and turned on the heat. It blasted me like puffs of air shot in your eye during an eye examination. I drove around the city past the people. The wanderers of the night.

My clock read 4:22 when I came to a big paved hill. I drove up it as I had so many times in high school. It was a steep drive, and the lighted cathedral at the top illuminated the dark sky.

Tonight, there were other cars parked on the street at the top of the hill. There were people relaxing and enjoying the view, mostly couples and teenagers. Some folks sat in their cars and talked, others sat along the steep hillside. I got out, pulled up the hood of my sweatshirt, and drew the strings tight. I wasn't sure what I was doing out there. I had no plans. I walked up to the top of the hill, stood next to the cathedral, and looked out at the bay.

The view was incredible. I could see the bridges and expanses of water. I could see San Mateo, all the way down to Palo Alto, and beyond. I saw huge skyscrapers and cars and boats and trees. The trees at the top swayed uniformly, like maybe they were dancing. Dancing the dance of the earth, or bowing and praying to God.

Trees were just trees; nothing phony; they lived to serve their purpose. I recalled Keith's calling me on what I thought was important: "Cars, shoes, clothes, and money." Is that who I was? A material thing, is that what I'd been? I knew the answer.

Material things were indeed my cover. I'd showed the world that I was about possessions. But I needed to peel them off so I could find me. I sat down on a rock and thought. I'd been afraid to be vulnerable. I couldn't even tell Keith that I loved him too. He'd said he couldn't make me be someone or something that I didn't want to be.

If I had a pen and paper handy maybe I would have written down all of the things that I wanted to work on about me. Maybe I would have written down the pros and the cons of my behavior and analyzed them or something, but I couldn't. So I moved down to the grass and sat with my knees up to my chest. I picked up a little rock for each time I realized something about me that I needed to change. I took a breath and looked out into the dark sky. It was starting. The sky was starting to turn to a lighter blue.

I wanted to put the materialistic thinking behind me. I picked up a rock. I'd been afraid to be vulnerable. But you had to trust someone, at some point, or your life would be hollow. I picked up another little rock. I was obsessed with looks, mine and everyone else's, so I picked up two little rocks and put them in the growing pile. I'd been angry because I never got to know my mom. I picked up another rock. As a child, I felt like the rug had been pulled out from underneath me when Mom, Grandma, and Keith left. I was really afraid of being abandoned. I picked up a rock for each of them.

I looked out to the sky, and rays of orange and yellow poked out above a blue horizon. I had all of my little rocks in a pile. I put them in a circle like a gemstone necklace, or a tiara. Yes, a tiara for a princess. I looked up and the sun's round head peered above the earth. The sky was white and light blue. The trees stood still, as if to show respect for the rising ball of light. I'd felt the beauty of a sunrise, and it was breathtaking.

A tear rolled down my face and onto my sweatshirt. I looked at my hands, at the dirt under my fingernails, at my clear fingernail polish that had started to peel. I pushed my tiara of rocks into the moist ground so that they would stay there. It was time for the spoiled princess to become a queen. I was going to have to find a way to talk with Keith Talbit.

When I got back in the Jeep, the door light came on. I looked at my Bible still in the backseat from church. I started the engine, reached in the back, and grabbed it. It fell open to the bookmark at Jeremiah 29. I scanned the page and found the verse that Pastor Fields had told us to read, Jeremiah 29:11, and read aloud: *"For I know the thoughts that I think of toward you, saith the Lord, thoughts of peace and not of evil, to give you an expected end."*

I repeated it several times, and it was comforting. *"Thoughts of peace and not of evil, to give you an expected end."*

As I reflected deep within myself, I saw that this was exactly the way it had worked out for me. I'd expected to have a lot of material possessions. I had expected to meet my goals at work. I had expected to be in relationships that had no realness to them. I had expected to argue with Charlotte all my life. I had expected Keith Talbit to leave me sooner or later. Just like the scripture promised, God had given me what I believed. My expected end.

When I got home that morning, I filled up the tub and took a long bubble bath. I didn't know if it was God or not, but the idea of seeing Keith sounded better and better to me. Only I had no address, no telephone number, not even an e-mail address. Then I remembered David, the manager of the apartment complex where Keith used to live.

## 52

# seek and you shall find

As soon as I got off from work the next day, I drove over to the complex where Keith used to live. David the manager opened the door.

"Hi, David," I said, trying to hide my nervousness.

"Hi." He looked like he was trying to remember. ". . . Chantell, right?"

"Yes. I am sorry to bother you, but I had to ask you something."

"What's up?"

"Well, it's a long story, but, see, Keith and I have been friends since we were little kids, and well, he said that he loved me, and well, I was acting really dumb, and see . . ." I swallowed. David studied me with one eye peering down and the other wide open. "And he left upset. And I love him, and see, he doesn't know it. And I have to tell him." This wasn't coming out quite right, so I just looked at him and hoped that he understood.

David stared at me like he was waiting for me to get to the reason I was knocking on his door. Finally, with my eyes full of water, I said, "Can I have his address, please? I let him go because I was afraid. But I want to make it right."

He was quiet. I had no idea if I'd gotten through to him.

For all he knew, I could be a stalker. Then, with his lips pursed together, he said, "Wait right here."

I stood there for a moment. He came back with a contract in his hand and read aloud, ". . . All of the information provided in this said agreement is strictly confidential, and to be used as such herewith—"

"Okay. I get it!" I said. David could be rude. I turned to walk away.

Then he said, "Hold on for a moment. I didn't thank you for the coffeecake. My parents were here last weekend, and my mom makes the best raspberry tart you could ever eat. I grew up on the stuff. You have to try some."

David was probably a really cool dude and all, and I knew he wasn't trying to push up on me. But didn't he hear a word of what I'd just said? I was grieving! What was wrong with people? Plus, I didn't even eat no raspberries! I was going to say no thank you and excuse myself, but he grabbed me by my wrist and said, "Come in, I don't bite. I'll get you some."

I didn't know what his deal was. That is, until he did something that was so cool. He set Keith's contract down on the counter in front of me and flipped to the side where Keith's previous address was listed. Then he patted my arm and smiled broadly. "I'll just set this here and go get you some of that tart."

I was overjoyed. I knew it! Somehow, someway, I knew I was going to Boston. I took a pen out of my purse and wrote down the address in my phone book.

David returned after I had finished and handed me a Baggie with the dessert in it.

"Thank you," I said, "so much."

"Oh, it's no big deal really. Mom brings it all the time."

I hugged him and left.

# 53

## to boston

The address said that he was in Cambridge, which was not far from Boston. I wasn't going to tell anybody that I was going, but Tia knew something was up when I accidentally told her that I was dusting off my little suitcase. And so I had to confess.

I switched ears on the phone, and said, "Yes, I got a good price on a plane ticket on priceline.com and I gave them my credit card number already, so I can't back out. I leave tomorrow."

"How long are you staying?"

"Just the night. I arrive in Cambridge tomorrow afternoon, and I'll turn around and fly right back on Sunday."

"How do you feel?"

"Well, I'm a little nervous, but I have to tell him, Tia. I have to." I told her how I got the address.

"Well, I'm shocked, but I'm proud of you. Go get your man then, girlfriend. Do what you gotta do. You know I am rooting for you."

"Thanks, Tia."

I finished packing my overnight case and went to bed.

The next morning I was excited. I arrived at the airport half an hour early. I parked my car and checked in. The plane was only half full. And everyone seemed to still be half asleep. I had a window seat; the chair next to me was empty, and a man sat in the seat closest to the aisle. He was in his twenties and had a full head of salt-and-pepper hair and a pen in his shirt pocket. He read from the morning paper, stopping often to make notes in the margins. Across from us was a lady with stirrup pants that went down into short boots. She had on a red floral shirt that was shaped like a teepee. I hadn't had much sleep and asked the man, "I am going to close this windowshade, do you mind?"

"No, not at all," he said and turned on the little reading light above his head. I pulled closed the windowshade, wrapped myself in the little yellow blanket that the plane provided, and waited for takeoff.

I closed my eyes, but opened them again at the revving sound of a little motor coming from across our aisle. It made me wonder if the man two seats over had started shaving. I looked in his direction, across the aisle, and saw that it was the woman with the red floral shirt pumping her milk. She sat there quietly with her hands under her teepee shirt working like a bumblebee. I was tired, but who could get mad at that? Maybe one day Keith and I would have children and I'd do that too.

I lifted the cover to the window and looked out onto the runway. Two young attendants were putting luggage on the plane.

I was deep in thought when the plane took off. When I found Keith Rashaad, I would seal our love. I would tell him everything that I'd been holding in. I tried to remember the lines that I'd prepared for him on the evening that I brought coffee and cake over: "Keith, I really love you. I think we should be together. Because you're very special to me. As I hope I am to you. My eyes are open, and I know that you're the one, so let's give it another chance." Then I thought again, maybe I shouldn't rehearse anything. Maybe I should just speak from the heart. The plane's big engines revved, and with the force of ten elephants we took off.

It was cold in Boston, so cold that each time I took a breath it froze, or so it seemed. I took a taxi to what I hoped was the correct address. I stood before a beautiful old gray-and-white stucco building trimmed in black. I could hear a central heat and air unit humming. Maybe twenty years ago it had been one monstrous home. But now it was divided into four apartments.

I took my address book out of my purse and double-checked it one last time. This was it. I walked between the two white stone pillars and stepped onto the square red carpet just outside the double doors. I walked up the stairs holding on to the black fancy railing that wrapped around the house, and stood on the welcome mat that I hoped was Keith's.

I knocked on the door and heard footsteps approaching. There was a peephole, and my heart beat double time as I stood there wondering if he was looking through it.

"Who is it?" said my Keith Rashaad's wonderful voice from within. My heart was beating through my blouse. I'd come too far to turn back.

"Umm . . . Hi, Keith, it's me, Chantell." I waited for the door handle to turn. It didn't.

I said, "Keith, can we talk?"

No answer.

"Keith, are you there?"

The door handle turned, and the door opened. Keith's beautiful brown face looked at me.

Silence.

"Chantell. Why are you here?" He looked so serious. I looked straight in his eyes, but he didn't look at me in mine.

"Umm. Keith." What was I supposed to say? "I, um, I came here—" No, that wasn't a serious look, it was a sad one. "I, um, came here to tell you that I love you too. And that you were right. And that I've learned a lot from you, Keith."

He looked at the ground and said, "I'm glad . . . Chantell, a lot has transpired between us. But I've realized that my focus needs to be on my patients."

What was he saying? I said that I loved him too. And I really, really meant it.

Keith went on, while staring at the tree branches behind me: "So while I think it was very noble of you to come here and share with me, emotionally I am just not prepared for a relationship right now. I am sorry if I misled you."

I said nothing. I just listened outside his front door and gave a simple smile, and folded my gloved hands.

"Well, hey, I've got to get to work." He sighed. "It was nice seeing you again, Chantell, but I've got to get ready to leave."

"Oh, okay," I said like I was indifferent to how he really felt, and turned around. "Well, good-bye."

Keith closed the door. I took one step down the stairs, then another one. Then I realized that I'd come too far to turn back. I hadn't told him what I needed to tell him. I walked back to his front door.

I knocked. My voice cracked: "Keith? Keith," I said again. "My priorities were in all the wrong places. It's not about appearances. I know that. It's how you feel on the inside. It's how you feel about you. And how you feel about the world around you."

He didn't respond. He'd gone away from the door and was ignoring me.

"Keith, and it's how I feel about you!" I screamed. I put my hand against his door. "I just wanted you to know that." I cried. The cold air had worked its way right through my gloves. I hoped he was still at the door. "And Keith, Eric means nothing to me. I love you, Keith Rashaad, and I had to tell you that."

I didn't know what to do or say. My speech that I'd rehearsed had completely vanished. And the word "honesty" came to me. I had nothing to lose, so I just spoke from my heart. "I, I want to massage your back, and kiss your temples. I want take care of you after long stressful days. And I want you to hold me, Keith, like you did that day at the beach . . ."

Tears rolled down my cheeks and fell all over my dark green jacket. "Keith, are you listening to me?" My voice cracked. "I am not a princess, or prissy Chantell Meyers. I am just your girl, Keith. Always."

He didn't respond. Maybe I was talking to the door, but I was desperate, and this was my chance. "I am staying in town for the night, at the Park Place Inn. If you can hear me, I am in room 172." I turned and headed back to the cab that waited for me at the curb.

When I got back to the hotel room, the light was blinking on my phone. I had a message. I was excited. Keith had come to his senses. I had gotten through to him, and he was going to give us another chance. I darted to the phone like I was still on the track team in high school and pressed the message button.

"You have one message. . . . Mr. Davis, uh, this is Wilma Scott, I just wanted to see if you made it in okay. I got the registration form and I've mailed it back already. Please call me when you get this message. Thanks and talk to you soon." A wrong number!

I was so hurt. So angry and sad. I had done everything! I went to church. I was working on my issues. I was trying to be nice to everyone. I said aloud, "What am I supposed to do, God?"

Weary, I just wanted to go to bed. I slipped into some yellow flannel pajamas, got under the covers, and bawled.

My perception of the hotel that I was staying in had changed. What I first thought of as a beautiful, historic place now seemed cold, old, and drab. And in my room, it was dark, except for a tiny dim reading lamp on the nightstand. My window with the view out onto the street was covered by big, fancy golden drapes. As I lay on my back tears rolled out the corners of my eyes and to my earlobes. I could hear cars going by outside on the street. I got out of bed and went over to the thermostat and turned up the heat.

Keith didn't love me. That literally hurt to think about. I felt like I wanted to throw up.

The competitive side of me was telling me that I'd lost, yet I was desperate to win back again the love that he'd said he felt for me. I heard a car turn and pull into the hotel's driveway.

Keith! I thought. I knew he'd come around! I knew he wouldn't let me come this far and turn me away like that.

I ran over to my window and looked out. It was a Lincoln Town Car, like the one that Keith borrowed in Oakland. What's he doing with a car like that in Boston too? I smiled. I looked closely, and my smile quickly dissipated. A middle-aged white couple parked the car and got out.

Moments later, another car pulled into the parking lot. Again, I ran to the window. Again, only to be let down. I'd lost my mind. I didn't know why I was putting myself through that kind of torture. Every time another car pulled in I was hopeful, until I realized it was over. I had tried to fix it. I swear I tried. My opportunity to build a life with him had come and gone. I cried until I went to sleep.

# a sweet bye-bye

The plane ride home was awful. A father and child were reading from a Dr. Seuss book, so I couldn't hear the movie that was playing up above. I got little rest and was tired. The man of my dreams wanted nothing to do with me. The turbulence was almost unbearable. I just sat there in silence until we landed in Oakland.

At the office I sat in my little cubicle and tried to get some work done. "Chantell, you look peaky, are you okay?" said Cameron.

"Umph-humph," I said and kept filling out the ad space reservation form for the half-page ad that was to run next Tuesday.

"Well, you know that flu that is going around? It put my sister out of commission for two weeks, so if you start feeling sick, go home and get some rest. Okay?"

"Umph-humph. Thanks, Cam."

I felt terrible, nauseous, I had no appetite, and my hair was ugly. Keith didn't love me. Tears welled up, and I got up and went to the bathroom.

That was pretty much how my weeks went. My feelings fluctuated. There'd be tears, then I'd get angry about how everything had turned out. Then I'd think about losing Keith again. Then I'd cry some more. I blamed myself for not seeing what God had put before me.

When Sunday rolled around, I dragged myself into church.

"Faith and works go together!" said Pastor Fields as she took her place at the stand surrounded by flowers. "You can't have one and not the other. And that is what I am supposed to talk about today."

Everyone listened.

"You can't believe that you can sit on your rump and ask God to do things for you and He's just going to do it for you. When God puts something in your spirit, you have to be willing to 'step out on faith.' But you also need to know that you can't start working on plans and not 'believe' that they are going to work out.

"Faith and works go together. We need to get that in our souls," she said and pointed to her own chest.

"What is faith?" she asked.

All of the congregation all started talking at once. I sat there listening with my wall still up around me.

"Turn with me if you will," she said, "to Hebrews 11. And let's read it aloud together." And we read, *"Now faith is the substance of things hoped for, the evidence of things not seen."*

"We have to be able to see what we're hoping for. It's got to be real to us. Because the Bible is saying that it's our unseen belief that brings the things hoped for, to pass."

She put her elbow on the stand in front of her, set her chin in the palm of her hand, and said, "You have to let go at some point and believe that God will intervene on your behalf." She smiled. "That's heavy stuff, huh? But that's the ticket.

"So, do you have that kind of faith?" And some people stood up and waved their hands in the air.

She smiled. "Turn with me to Mark 11:24 and let's read what it says." The congregation read, *"Therefore, I say unto you, what things soever ye desire, when ye pray, believe that ye receive them, and ye shall have them."*

"Do you believe that God will handle your situation for you? Have you listened for Him to give you answers? Do you rely on Him to handle it?"

It was about that time that I started to cry, because though I loved God, I didn't listen for anything. And I didn't trust God or anyone on this earth to work anything out for me. Did I really believe that *He would* handle it? Naw! That's why I handled it. I'd been praying to God and telling Him what I wanted, minus the faith; then I'd go out and push for it. I would say, "God help me," and then I would just try to take the problem by the horns. And if it worked, it worked. If it didn't, it didn't.

She may as well have been talking directly to me, because I got what she was saying loud and clear. I did love God, yet I was hardly practicing faith. I got it, and apparently I wasn't the only one in the congregation who did.

"Thank you, Jesus!"

"Say it again, Pastor!"

"Amen!"

I thought back to my father's collapse, and I realized that you can't bargain or barter with God. God didn't need me to make deals with Him to heal my dad. Just my faith was good enough. I closed my eyes, cried, and talked to the Lord.

"Thank You, God, for increasing my level of understanding. I'm sorry. I get it!" I realized that I was talking aloud but it didn't matter who heard. "And I know I fall sometimes, but I am going to keep moving closer and closer toward You. I am dependent upon You, God, I am open, and I want to hear You speak through me to me. I cannot handle everything, because I am not in control, God. You are."

Pastor Fields finished the message, and even before the lady from the audience walked up to the microphone and sang like a hummingbird, *"I can feel Je-sus renewing my so-oul. Oh great comfort! He's ma-king me who-ole,"* I felt Him, and I was comforted.

At home, I walked over to my mother's bookshelf and pulled out her journal. She'd written out her thoughts often. And just weeks before she died, she'd started writing in the blue journal that I had in my hand. I turned forward a few pages and started a new chapter. I grabbed a pen and wrote:

I have so much to be thankful for that I cannot even begin to list it all. Mostly I am thankful that He died on the cross so that I could start anew. I am thankful that He loves me and is willing to walk through life with me.

Gone are the days that clothes, lipstick, and jewelry lead me. I have no reason for shallow thoughts. I'm learning to do things in a kinder, gentler, more peaceful way, I'm growing stronger in God every day.

# beep

The day was long. When I got home that evening, I walked through the door with a new supply of Frombradi incense in my hand. I looked toward the answering machine without that feeling of desperation that maybe today would be the day that Keith Rashaad Talbit would call.

In the few months that passed, I'd found myself in a different place. A better place. The kind of love that I felt for Keith was not angry or jealous. It was not resentful or manipulative, and it had nothing to do with love going in both directions. It just was. I'd learned that there were few things greater than that kind of love.

I pressed the answering machine button, went over to my bed, and lay back.

*Beep.*

"Hi, babygirl, it's your daddy." I smiled, I knew who it was. Daddy had finished up all of his chemo treatments and was doing well.

"Where you at? It's been two days. How come we haven't heard from you? You call me when you get this message. Okay? Bye."

Okay, Daddy.

*Beep.*

"Chantell, it's Tia. You have been on my mind. Call me. I'm at home."

I'd call them both back as soon as I grabbed a bite to eat.

*Beep.*

"Hey, Chantell. How are you doing? It's me, Eric. I just wanted . . . well, I just wanted to say that I was sorry about everything that happened at the lake. And I wanted to see how you were doing. And to tell you that I miss you, girl, and I'd like to see you. You know, just to talk. My new cellular number is 555-8054. Call me, okay?"

I guess you could say that I had a revelation, because God spoke to me, through me. I let go of my pillow and grabbed my mother's journal and wrote: "Every day I am learning. Every day I am getting stronger. There are some things that I have to do. I just have to hold on to what I know in my heart is right. I have to forgive my enemies. I have to tell Eric to stop calling me. I have to follow my spirit." Then I closed the book and went to the kitchen to fix myself some dinner.

# the conference room

On my way to the office, I thought of the things that I had to do. My watch said it was 8:17 a.m. I grabbed a bright green sticky pad from my desk and wrote: "Please go to conference room C at 8:30." I stuck it on Mina's monitor when no one else was around and went back to my desk. At 8:28, I went into the conference room, turned on the lights, closed the blinds, and waited.

When the clock on the wall read 8:31, the door opened. With a manila file in her arms, Mina peered at me. Then she abruptly did an about-face and was about to leave.

"Please, Mina, stay," I said. "I'd like to talk."

She took a seat at the other end of the table, holding her files close to her chest.

I looked at her, eye to eye, and said, "Mina, I just wanted to tell you that I am very sorry for any chaos I may have caused you."

She looked at me, and her stern expression smoothed out a bit. "What? You mean the Tiffany box of pooh?"

I looked at her and nodded. "Yes, and all of the battling and tension between us, I want it to stop."

Mina folded her arms and looked at me with a weird smile. "So you're going to stop trying to win all the time?"

"No, I am going to keep doing the best job that I can. I just don't want it to be taken like I am competing with you, and vice versa."

"I don't always want to feel like I am competing with you either, Chantell. I am competing with myself. Trying to do better than I did the last time."

I nodded. Even though the company encouraged competition, she and I were on the same page.

I was shocked when she smiled and said, "I have to tell you, though. That dog-pooh prank was an original." She laughed. "Where'd you get an idea like that from?"

Surprised that she had a sense of humor, I shrugged my shoulders. "I don't know. It was wrong, though, and I am sorry."

"Well, while you're apologizing, I am sorry too."

I looked at her and said with a forgiving smile, "For what? You mean for trying to take away my business, for setting your friend up with my boyfriend, or for letting the air out of my tire?"

She put her hand over her eyes and said, "Yes, yes, yes!"

We vowed to stop all the drama, and in the spirit of Rodney King, just all tried to get along.

Yeah, letting my spirit be my guide was definitely a good thing.

# thank you very much

It was Wednesday night, and poetry night at Dorsey's Locker, on the Oakland/Berkeley border. I arrived at 8:30 with my mother's blue journal in hand. I couldn't describe how good it felt to be praying, and listening, and letting God lead the way. I was there mainly because I wanted to hear people speaking from their hearts—their truths, whatever they'd found them to be. I was excited to be there. The place was dimly lit, and closed in, but my eyes and ears and heart were open for truth.

I walked over to the bar in the center of the little building and ordered a ginger ale. I was realizing more and more truths every day. Truths that I had known deep inside of me but had ignored for so long that I'd forgotten they existed. Things like: Everybody loves; everybody wants to be happy; everybody hurts sometimes; everyone wins; and everybody loses sometimes. These are things that you know, but you're taught to act like you don't know. Or at least that's the way it was for me.

Now I felt peaceful and full, 300 percent calmer than when I left Cambridge almost seven months ago. And 1,000 percent better than where I was at this time last year. I hadn't spoken to Keith Rashaad Talbit, but he was in my heart. I'd learned a few things about life from him, and that is what it was all about. Learning and loving. I reveled in my little truth and told myself that this peace I felt, right then and right there—now that I knew it existed—I wasn't going to let it go. I was going strive to hold on to it as best I could.

I sat back in a chair, watched the array of people, and remembered why I loved the Bay Area so much. An Asian guy and his black girl-friend sat right next to me, but the entire place was sprinkled with enough colors to make you wonder if MLK's "I have a dream" speech hadn't come to pass. I walked to the front, signed up to say a few words, and was placed fourth on the list.

A gentleman stood up and welcomed the small crowd. Then a heavy-set man with a bandanna around his head kicked off the evening with a poem. He talked about "going to Carolina but not the town." He said that he was "sneaking to see my lover no matter who'd frown."

Then a black woman with her hair wrapped up in a purple-and-yellow cloth walked up to the mike. She started out by saying she was half Jewish and half black, and, with a hint of sadness in her eyes, she called herself an oxymoron. Then she said with a very serious look that she was and always would be a revolutionary. She read a poem about her love for Will Smith, Lauryn Hill, and Tupac Shakur. She had a little gold stud in her nose. She read a beautiful poem that said race and color and creed didn't matter because we were all one. And that all we needed was good love and Jah. "Amen!" I wanted to shout out. Then she read another poem. She said that everyone should meditate. And that whether we recognized it or not, God was in each of us. "That's right!" I blurted out. I didn't mean to, but I couldn't help it. This conscious sis-tah was on a roll! Then she said that we should all light up a fat one and share our sex. And I laughed and thought, Umm . . . no, girlfriend went a little too far for me!

Next up was a middle-aged, silver-haired Caucasian man with salt-and-pepper whiskers. He wore a bright red Hawaiian print shirt pulled tight across a round stomach and beige polyester slacks that were a little bit too short. He also wore a yellow plastic lei around his neck, and looked like he'd just flown in from Waikiki. He walked up through the center of our little group with blue-and-white Gilligan tennis shoes on and headed up to the microphone. He read a short essay that said he loved black women for their uniqueness and their candor. He said that he loved black culture, and that he loved freshly manicured long black fingers, and skin. I couldn't help but smile, cuz dude was a trip.

It was my turn next. The mood had been everywhere, so I figured I should focus on my own thoughts. I went up to the microphone and said, "Hi, I am not a poet by any means. But I was inspired to write a couple of poems and I wanted to share them. This is called 'Au Naturel,' and I wrote it at a time when I was down and was searching for something or someone to pick me up. I looked within and this is what I came up with:"

> *I am Au Naturel.*
> *Of the Earth and like the Sun.*
> *My brown skin darkens with each outside excursion.*
> *I am the essence of dirt, the grass, and the trees.*
> *I reflect the light's rays and beam so bright.*
> *My possibilities are endless.*
> *And I can do all things through Christ that strengthens me.*

I took a long deep breath and looked at the crowd. And they clapped and snapped their fingers.

"Thank you very much. I don't know if this next one is a poem or not, but I call it 'Maybe.'"

Then I closed my eyes and said:

*Nobody knew how much I needed to be loved.*
*Because I didn't know how to show it.*
*Maybe God sent you to show me the possibilities.*
*To show me how nice it feels to see goodness in someone you find so sexy.*
*To hear positivity come from someone's mouth who makes you dizzy.*
*And to talk to someone you find so intelligent and attractive and strong*
*. . . Maybe.*

I opened my eyes and dabbed the corner where a tiny tear threatened. I smiled and looked at all the smiling faces staring at me. They nodded. Maybe they got some truth out of it too. As I walked back to my seat, Mr. Hawaii raised his eyebrows and gave me a thumbs-up.

# you make the call

When I got in the door, my answering machine was blinking, so I pressed the button.

*Beep.* "Hi, uh, Chantell, it's me, Eric, again. Hey, you didn't call me back, and so I was trying to catch you at home. Look, Chantell, I still love you, and I'm not seeing anybody right now, and I wanted us to talk . . . I was thinking maybe we could do some of those things that we always talked about. You know, like rent a limo and ride to Napa Valley. Anyways, I miss you. Call me back."

I looked at the phone for a moment, then picked up the receiver and dialed the number that showed on the caller ID.

"Hello?"

"Hello, Eric."

"Hi, Chantell. How are you?"

"I'm good. What about you?"

"Oh, I'm fine. You know me, I am just chillin'." He laughed nervously.

"That's good."

I thought about the day that I struck him in my bed when he told me we weren't getting married, and then again at the lake.

"Hey, Eric, I just—"

"Chantell, I—"

We laughed.

"You first," I said.

"Nope, ladies first."

"Okay, I wanted to apologize for the day at the lake. And for any other times that I put my hands on you or was rude. I was way out of line."

"It's okay. I was out of line too. You think maybe we could get together and talk later on? You know, about us?"

"Eric, that's not a good idea," I said while I twisted my fingers up in the curly cord of the phone.

"Why, you got a man?"

I stopped twisting. "No. I don't—"

"Then what's the problem?"

"Eric." I sat back in the dining room chair and said, "In my heart, I know that our time has passed."

"Oh, I see, it's a God thing. Okay. I'll wait for you."

"No sense in waiting, Eric. We had some fun times together, but you're right. It is a God thing. He's working on me. I will always hold a special place in my heart for you, but I want to let our past stay in the past."

"Whaaaat?" he said with a sudden attitude. "Like that? Dude at the lake must have really put it—"

"Stop it, Eric. You don't know what you're talking about," I said, my voice getting louder. "Look, I will always care about you. Take care of yourself, okay?"

"Chantell—"

"Bye, Eric."

He sighed. "Yeah, whatever."

# sealing the circle

W hen I opened my eyes that Sunday morning, the sun, which had been warming my face, seemed to wink at me. Good morning, Lord.

I got out of bed and made myself a cup of chamomile tea, a bowl of that new cereal with the strawberries in it, and two pieces of chicken apple sausage, a treat I'd found in the grocery store the day before. More at peace with my decision and myself, I was five pounds lighter, and my green pajama bottoms hung off my hips.

I took a bite of sausage, then I grabbed the phone and dialed Tia's number. Ron was away on a business trip and wouldn't be back until Wednesday. Their phone rang.

"Hello," said a groggy voice.

I set down my tea and said, "Good morning, heifer."

"Mornin'."

"Are you still going to church with me?"

"Oh, I was sleeping good. What time is it?"

"It's after nine. C'mon, get your butt up and let's go. You promised!"

"I am, I am." She yawned.

"Okay. I'll pick you up at ten-thirty."

"I'll be ready," she grumbled.

When I arrived at Tia's house not only was she dressed and ready to go, but she was chipper.

"Good morning!" she said.

"Good morning."

She got in the car and we headed down the big hill.

"So, did you get an opportunity to speak to that man from the museum?" she asked, inquiring about my plans for my mother's paintings.

"I did. In fact, I've decided that I'm going to have my mom's work shown there until I can get Zarina's Gallery opened."

"What! Your own gallery?"

"Yep." I smiled proudly.

"Look at you, Miss Entrepreneur! Do your thing, girlfriend! Are you looking at locations yet?"

"No, it's still a bit too early, but I'm in the process of doing the business plan now, and I've already found a company to reproduce my mother's work."

Tia looked impressed. "Sounds a little costly, are you okay?"

"Yeah, I should be. It's costing me all of my 401(k), plus I had to cash out all of my online investments, but I should be okay."

"Well, it'll be worth it. And you could always talk to Ron if you needed more cash."

"Thanks, I appreciate that, Tia. Hey, I'm also thinking of starting a Web site and selling Zarina's art online in a virtual gallery around the world."

"Good idea," Tia said. "I can see it now, ZestyZarinaArt.com."

I looked at her corny butt and laughed. "Or how about just, 'ChantellsGallery.com'?"

"Umph-umph. There's no twang to that."

"What? That's catchy! And what is a twang? You speaking Ron-speak again?"

We laughed as I pulled into the church grounds.

Inside the church, the podium had its usual fresh floral arrangements all around. Tia and I sat with Molina, my friend from long ago in my early churchgoing days. We glanced back at the doors excitedly every now and then, anticipating the choir that would burst through the doors in a moment, singing as though their lives depended on it. In my mind, we were a big circle. The choir and the congregation. They sang and praised God, and it reached over and blessed us, and we in turn prayed to God for them and with them every Sunday, and I believed our prayers reached over and touched them. It was a circle that kept going and going like the bunny in the battery commercial.

I looked over to my right, and Pastor Fields was sitting in her usual oak chair. The pews were already filled to the brim. The young gentleman usher who led us to our seat had walked back to his place at the door. I looked in Pastor Fields' direction again, and when I caught her attention I gave her a big smile, and she smiled back.

An announcer asked the congregation to rise to receive the choir. Everyone stood, and on cue the choir marched in clapping their hands in celebration. They sang about lifting their hands to God and dancing like David danced. They sang all the way up to the choir stand.

A lady two people down from me sat fanning her face with the schedule of the day's program. She rocked from side to side in her checkered two-piece suit. Her matching black-and-white hat was tilted to the side like she was Foxy Brown. I knew she had just gotten married to a man who had recently joined the church. He was a bit shorter than she was, and always wore a suede jacket, no matter what the occasion. They were in their late forties and looked very happy together.

The church's "Mothers' Row" was filled to the brim with wisdom. They sat there looking like debutantes of the past, complete in hat and gloves, waiting for the service to begin. All the mothers wore their hair in various shades of silver. Most wore curls—either their own hair or wigs. That is, except for my favorite, Mother Sarah, who bleached her entire head platinum blond; she also wore a striking blue eye shadow.

The Sunday prior, Pastor Fields had said that we were going to partner with an organization that was building homes on donated land for the homeless. Now she asked us to put on some old clothes and roll up our sleeves and go with her to help them to build.

With my head straight and my eyes rolled over toward Tia, I whispered, "I'm going to do that."

She murmured through clenched teeth, "I think Ron and I will too."

I smiled. Tia hadn't been to church in I don't know how long. I looked around at all of the flesh tones that ranged from chalk to chocolate. It was a sea of richness, and if you really allowed your soul to settle down and absorb the physical aspect of the church, you could smell it. It was like a combination of light perfumes, cologne, and fresh flowers from the altar, sprinkled with baby powder, spit-up, and the beginning of heat and perspiration as more and more bodies nestled into the church. It smelled like life.

The church was filled, including the balcony. There was definitely a spiritual revolution going on, and I was still in awe of it. God was speaking and folks were listening. I was glad I had accepted God into my life. I looked over at my best friend and new Bible study partner and gave her a quirky smile. She shook her head and looked straight ahead. God definitely had a way of doing things on His own watch, and in His own way.

The speaker said, "Please be aware that we are sponsoring the Bone Marrow Drive on November twelfth at the Community Center Park in conjunction with the Oakland Raiders organization. This is a time to bring out your families, and your friends. Brochures and informational flyers will be out front for you to take with you. Please remember that though you agree to donate marrow, it is only if you are a match for someone in need. It doesn't mean that you'll actually be called to donate. And the chances of actually being called to donate are slim. But it's great to be a blessing to someone! Amen?"

"Amen," agreed the people.

"Our goal is to register a thousand people. So let's show up on the twelfth. We could save someone's life. Amen?"

"Amen," went the congregation.

The choir did a selection. It wasn't a lot of stanzas, just a few, but I really enjoyed the song. They sang, *"God will not forsake you. Never ever, no! Not ever!"* Simple and to the point. Then they looked at one another and asked, *"Don't you know?"* They peered into the crowd and sang their answer: *"God will not forsake you. Never ever, no! Not ever!"*

When Pastor Fields came up to speak, she said, "I love that song, because the words ring so true. God may not do everything that you want, the way that you want Him to do it, but He will not forsake you." An attendant walked up to the side of the podium and set a glass of water next to where the preacher stood speaking.

"In the book of Hebrews, chapter thirteen verse five, God says He will never leave you. God will make provisions for you. Psalm 58:11 says that He will reward you."

I nodded, because with Eric's and my being over, and Mina's and my actually speaking to each other, I knew that I'd definitely made some changes and I believed that God was pleased. I felt I was striving toward righteousness. This diva of the past had no regrets. I prayed every day that I might continue to have no desire to fight or to claw to hold on to things because I thought they looked good; and that I might resist immediately going into combat mode with every other woman I saw.

Pastor Fields went on, "First Corinthians three and eight says every man shall receive his own rewards. So understand that we each have our own life path. What God has for you is for you! I can't receive what He has for you, and you can't receive what He has for me." I nodded—indeed.

Moments after Pastor Fields finished her message, a lady wearing a white-and-yellow-flowered dress and a big white flower in her hair went up to the microphone and smiled. She said, "At this time, we would ask our first-time visitors to please stand."

Tia stood up with about twelve other people. The announcer then told them that they were welcome and that "we at the Faith Center hope that you will enjoy your visit and will come and visit with us again." She then asked if anyone would like to say a few words.

A tall figure stood up in the balcony where we used to sit as children and walked down the stairway that led to the main floor. I was looking straight ahead, and Tia noticed him first. She leaned down and spoke out the side of her mouth: "Pssst, KT at six o'clock."

"What are you whispering about?" I whispered.

She nodded at the long, lean figure walking down the steps of the balcony. He wore a black wool petticoat jacket, a gray, ribbed turtleneck sweater, and charcoal-colored trousers. I was trying to be calm, but the rapid pace of my heart kept reminding me that I was nervous. Pastor Fields nodded as he made his way to the front to speak.

The announcer smiled and said, "Brothers and sisters, this is our very own Dr. Keith Rashaad Talbit."

"Hello everyone," he said, "I'm Keith Talbit. A lot of you know me as Keith Rashaad. I'll just be up here for a moment. I promise I won't take up a lot of your time." I looked up at him.

"I'm so happy to be in God's house today, and to see so many familiar faces. I love all of you. You are my spiritual family, and although I am not here every Sunday, know that I walk in faith with you. I have something that I want to do and I wanted all of you to share in this moment with me."

What in the world was going on?

He looked directly at me.

"Chantell, I want to tell you that I love you too. I love the laugh in your voice. Your hair. Your scent. Your hands. Your mind."

He closed his eyes for a long second, then opened them again.

"Chantell, I heard every word that you said to me that day in Boston at my door. Every word. I was trying to focus on my job and move on with my life, but I can't. At least, not without you. And I love you just as much today as I did last month, if not more. Always have, always will. You are my girl for life."

Breathe, Chantell, breathe, I thought.

I swallowed hard, and saw beads of sweat forming on his head.

Then he looked at me and smiled.

"Chantell, in spite of all the names you used to called me when we were children . . ." He held out his fingers and counted as he spoke: "Let's see, Frog Face, Big Head, Ashy Boy . . ." The congregation laughed. "You've always had the key to my heart."

I could feel lines of tears flowing down my face.

"We met right here in this church, and I've been in love with you for almost as long as I've been alive." His voice cracked, and a tear fell. "Will you marry me?"

I stood up and nodded yes. I ran up to him and wrapped my arms around him tightly.

Thank you, God.

With my arms still around him, I looked out at the church, and tears were falling and hands were clutched everywhere.

Keith whispered in my ear, "I love you, Chantell, and with God, we can do this. No walls, no mask. Using our hearts and our minds and our spirits we will be okay."

"I love you, Keith Rashaad," I said.

We took a seat in the second row, hand in hand, and I thought about that scripture again. Jeremiah 29:11. God had shown me time and time again that He did think good thoughts of us, thoughts of peace and not of evil. All you had to do was to try, then trust and believe Him. He'd give you your expected end.

# six months later

Once upon a time there was a young woman who was spoiled and materialistic and superficial . . . All right, I guess I'll stop talking in the third person, cuz I know I'm not foolin' anybody.

Not too long ago, I looked happy. Obviously, however, that wasn't the truth. My mom was gone, my father had almost died, and Charlotte and I were not communicating. I was desperate for love from Eric because we looked good together in other people's eyes.

It may sound like a cliché, but I didn't love myself. How could I? I didn't even know myself. I felt alone. And to compensate for that seemingly ever-present feeling inside of me, I put on a new Donna Karan dress and held on to my Chanel handbag for dear life.

So much has taken place since that fateful day in the church. I'll do my best to fill you in.

Two months after Keith Rashaad proposed, Daddy had improved enough to get a doctor's release, and he returned to the shop to work. Charlotte and I continued to grow closer than we'd ever been before. We went to the movies together, we cooked together, and we even went to church together.

God had stretched me. And He is still teaching me valuable life lessons. Things like: Life is not perfect, for if it were, then what would we have to strive for? And: God wants us dependent upon Him. Perfect balance and moderation are achieved through Him. We can have it all, if we just remember one thing, "And He is before all things, and by Him all things consist." Colossians 1:17.

Okay, so I was going to bring you up to date—Keith and I are still committed to each other. But for now he lives in Boston. We haven't set a date yet, but we use our frequent-flyer miles and manage to see each other two or three times a month. Keith is planning to move out to California, but this time apart has allowed me to strengthen myself. We are happily taking things slowly and really working on ourselves. And I can do this in the meantime with peace, because God is married to the world, and Isaiah 54:5 teaches me that He is your husband.

Just about the time that Daddy went back to work, Tia found out she was pregnant. She and Ron are having a baby girl. My goddaughter's name will be Natalie Ariel.

I recently opened the doors to Studio Z, and at first it was a scary decision. If you'll recall, I thought that perhaps I'd open an art gallery and send my mom's paintings all over the world. I'd never owned my own business before, so I was afraid and dragging my feet. I wondered if I could handle it all. I tried to let the whole idea go and focus my attention on myself and my upcoming marriage to Keith. But in my soul, I kept hearing, "Just try."

Still afraid, with little belief that I could pull off something like this, I remembered Hebrews 11. That night, I read verse six aloud; it said, "But without faith it is impossible to please Him: for He that cometh to God must believe that He is, and that He is a rewarder of them that diligently seek Him."

The very next morning, I got up and said my prayers. I prayed for the wisdom to make good choices and for the courage to stand and see them through. Then I pulled out the business plan I'd placed on my mother's bookshelf. I called Keith Rashaad in Boston. He and I prayed together again. Then I got dressed, went down to the Realtor's office, and signed a three-year lease on a small building in downtown San Francisco.

Zarina's gallery, officially named "Studio Z," is growing and doing well.

Keith's wise grandmother used to say, "Life is not a big bed of roses, and if it is, then you can bet that there'll be some stickers in there somewhere." Grandma Edna had a way with words, and how right she was! Things happen, people change. We grow.

I myself had made plenty of mistakes, and I was still learning. And I thank God for a sound mind, a good spirit, and a heart that tells me when to let go. You see, with Eric I was concerned about how the public perceived us. With Keith Talbit, I was hoping that because he and I were together, I could finally be happy. But you can't depend on your relationship to make you happy. Real happiness, real peace, real love—that comes from God.

Relationships take work. They require communication, compromise, understanding, commitment, honesty, trust, and forgiveness. Mine and Keith's time apart was so good for me because I was still getting to know me. It was important that I didn't base my existence on Keith or on the gallery. I realized that if I got caught up doing that, then I hadn't learned anything. Although being Keith's fiancée and the owner of Studio Z were important to me, they were *not* what made me important!

I didn't have all the answers, but I knew this: getting closer to God is what allowed me to be able to look in the mirror and be happy with me. I didn't ever want to lose that sense of who I was again. I understood very clearly that I was the daughter of the King of Kings!

Life is not always easy, and God did not promise that it would be, but the Bible says that if you believe in Him, He will give you an expected end, so I believe that good things are in store. And after I've basked in His greatness a while longer, and I've gotten to know myself a bit better, Keith and I will stand before God and the world and vow to be together until the end.

I know that God's word cannot come back void! I say my prayers often, and I keep my faith fed by studying His words. I trust and believe God, and I lay my burdens at His feet.

Well, that's it. That's my story. I'll keep going. I hope you'll do the same.

## About the Author

DENISE MICHELLE HARRIS is an advertising sales executive for a major corporation. A member of Alpha Kappa Alpha sorority, she has a master's degree in creative writing from New College of California and is listed in *Who's Who in America*. A former Christian preschool teacher, Denise lives in northern California with her son. *Sweet Bye-Bye* is her writing debut.